Brennan leaped out of bed

The French door leading to the bedroom's private deck stood open. Moonlight poured into the room, providing a backdrop that was no longer romantic. At the end of the bed stood an intruder who pointed a rifle directly at Catherine.

"Who are you?" she whispered, fear pounding inside her.

The intruder's accent changed. "I'm the ghost of Christmas past, honey."

At that moment, Brennan hurled himself forward. The gun's hammer exploded as the barrel spewed fire and smoke. "Catherine, get away!" Brennan hollered.

She pulled herself to her feet and ran. The gun went off again. Just as she turned, it fired a third and final time.

ABOUT THE AUTHOR

California native M.L. Gamble thought her old neighborhood in Pasadena provided an ideal setting for her fourth Intrigue. A believer in the philosophy "write what you know," this Bayville, New York, resident is hard at work on her fifth Intrigue. An avid fan of mystery and romantic suspense, she conducts creative-writing workshops and is busy raising her two children, Olivia and Allen.

Books by M.L. Gamble

HARLEQUIN INTRIGUE
110–STRANGER THAN FICTION
146–DIAMOND OF DECEIT
153–WHEN MURDER CALLS

If Looks Could Kill

M.L. Gamble

Harlequin Books

TORONTO • NEW YORK • LONDON
AMSTERDAM • PARIS • SYDNEY • HAMBURG
STOCKHOLM • ATHENS • TOKYO • MILAN

For Allen Patrick Nuccio,
the prince of my heart

Harlequin Intrigue edition published October 1991

ISBN 0-373-22172-X

IF LOOKS COULD KILL

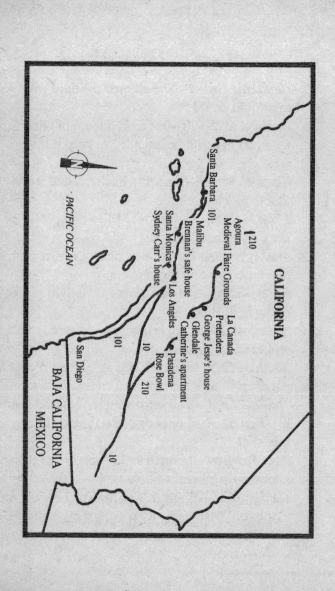

CAST OF CHARACTERS

Catherine Grand—She learned the hard way that looks could kill.

Brennan Richards—He retired from public life ten years ago and he intended to keep it that way.

Ellen Richards—She lost a husband and stood to lose much more.

Liam McKinney—He loved Ellen and protected her past secrets.

Mickey Stolie—Catherine's photographer took great pictures and big chances.

Karen Keller—She was never in the right place at the right time.

Sydney Carr—A big grudge was all that remained of his past.

Siobhan Carr—She took things into her own hands.

Johnnie Lord—The actor who looked and sang like Brennan had only one goal . . . and it got him shot.

Jane Scarlett—Brennan's old backup singer had a loose grip on reality.

George Jesse—Brennan's ex-manager owned the nightclub Pretenders, a very appropriate name.

Chapter One

Catherine Grand reached across her cluttered desk and snapped down the first blinking button on the phone. All five lights had come on within seconds of each other. Each represented an interruption she could ill afford. "Grand Illusions, may I help you?"

"I need to speak to Miss Grand. It's urgent."

"One moment, please." Catherine put the caller on hold, then hit the second button, toppling a pile of file folders onto the floor. "Grand Illusions."

"Cath? This is Cheryl. Mom wants to know who she's supposed to ask for at the Hilton."

"Hang on, sis." Catherine smacked the hold button, then the third. If Karen Keller, her dippy redheaded secretary, ever got back from her audition, Catherine decided, she was going to fire her. Or kill her. She perused the mess on the floor. "Grand Illusions."

"This is *People* magazine calling. Is Miss Grand available?"

"Hold on, please." Catherine rolled her eyes. Publicity was necessary in her line of work, but she should have never agreed to have a writer and photographer follow her around for three days. At least not this month. *The price of fame...*

She broke her nail on the fourth button. "Grand Illu—"

"Catherine Grand," the voice interrupted curtly. "This is Burbank Studios call—"

"Hang on." Catherine cut in, feeling a fleeting satisfaction at her reciprocal use of bad manners. Going tit for tat when people acted rudely was her worst attribute, she thought, but today she was just incapable of rising above herself.

The fifth line continued to ring, the tone now more grating than a minute ago. Catherine glanced at her watch. It was one-thirty. Silently she vowed to hire a part-timer so she would never be left at the mercy of Karen's extended lunchhour auditions again. She pressed the last button. "Grand Illusions. May I help you?"

Silence, save for the faint crackle of long distance static, filled her ear. Then a voice, fractured and fuzzy, whispered garbled sounds.

"I'm sorry, you'll have to speak up."

"Catherine Grand, please. I'm calling long distance from Ireland." The voice was male and full of authority despite the faint volume.

"Hang on a minute, sir." She zapped down the hold button, then gamely returned to the first caller. "Thanks for holding. May I take a message, please? Miss Grand will call you back at four."

She wrote furiously then pushed the second. "Cheryl, tell Mom to see Liz Thornton. You guys need to be there before four. Bye." The third caller dropped off just as she picked up. "So much for fame," she said to the dial tone.

Catherine took a number from the woman at Burbank Studios. She wanted a laser show and fireworks for a party celebrating the success of a new sitcom.

Catherine punched the last button. "Sir, sorry to keep you. This is Catherine Grand. How can I help you?"

Lines one and two began to ring again simultaneously. Much to Catherine's relief, Karen appeared through the door and picked up the calls. Catherine kicked her office door closed and stuck her finger in her left ear, trying to boost the volume of hearing in her right.

"...letting you know that he won't stand for this gross invasion of privacy."

Catherine shook her head. She'd missed the beginning of the man's complaint, but his brusque tone was clear enough. "Who is this, please?"

"Liam McKinney..." The line garbled, bleeped and cracked. "...for Brennan Richards. I'm sending the papers tomorrow."

Brennan Richards? Catherine thought. What about Brennan Richards? "This is a bad connection, sir. Could you start from the beginning, please."

There was a flat click, followed by humming. Then a loud, clear dial tone signaled the end of the call.

Karen knocked, then opened the door. "Why are you still here? Mickey needed you in Agoura five minutes ago."

Catherine hung up the receiver and frowned. "What are you talking about?"

Karen walked on top of the spilled file folders and bent down. She pushed several of the files aside, retrieving a scrawled note. "I left this before you got in this morning. Mickey's doing publicity stills for the Medieval Days Faire and he wants you to okay the stage set before the carpenters leave."

Catherine took the note. Her last caller's words echoed in her skull. It was a weird coincidence that she'd get an angry call about Brennan Richards. She'd just hired a singer to do an impersonation of the retired rock star, and her gut wrenched as she considered the implications. If the guy who phoned was a lawyer, it was bound to mean bad news.

Two more lines began to ring as she followed Karen to the reception desk and fished in her purse for her car keys.

"What's going on today? I've never seen it so busy." Karen pouted.

"Don't knock it, kiddo. It's paying the rent." Catherine grabbed an unlined cotton blazer from the closet and slipped on her sunglasses, deciding to let a lecture to Karen about tardiness wait. Her secretary was obviously upset.

"Please call Mickey and tell him I'll be there in forty-five minutes. Then call Sue Willis and tell her she needs to lose five more pounds before the fifth. The auto show people don't want a size-ten Cher. Also, see if you can break it to that pain in the rear Tommy Lyle that, despite the success of *Look Who's Talking,* no one's hiring John Travolta look-alikes right now. Tommy's called ten days in a row."

"Tommy's not so bad." Karen sniffed. "He's got problems, like everybody, that's all."

Catherine turned and stared. Karen was putting on another layer of purple lipstick and peering into a tiny mirror while the unanswered phone lines continued their shriek.

Catherine silently counted to ten. "How'd your audition go?"

Karen made a face, then snapped the case closed. "Dirt bags. Said I looked too old. But I'm only twenty-nine."

Thirty-six, Catherine corrected silently. In L.A. everyone she knew wanted to be in show biz at some point in their lives. Even her ex-husband was still chasing that dream. All he had to show for it was a résumé full of walk-ons and a two-week stint as a gangster on *One Life to Live.*

It was a good thing she had never had the hots for fame, Catherine thought. If she had, she could have been the aging starlet sitting at the tiny desk in front of her. "I'm sorry, Karen. Hang in there."

"Humph."

Catherine turned the doorknob, craning her neck to deliver a last instruction. "One more thing. If a long distance call comes through from someone mentioning Brennan Richards, be sure and get a number."

"Richards? What's up?"

Before Catherine could answer, the door opened. She stepped back to avoid it then watched as a richly dressed blond woman stomped into the room. "I need to speak to Catherine Grand!" the woman announced to Karen.

"You—you don't have an appointment," Karen stuttered, openly appraising the woman.

The blonde crossed her arms over her Armani silk jacket and tilted her head. "Where's your boss?"

"Here. I'm right here," Catherine replied, moving away from the open door and into the woman's direct field of vision. "But I'm on my way out. If you'd like to make an appointment, tomorrow afternoon is good."

"I told you to call and make an appointment the last time you were here," Karen interjected.

Catherine removed her sunglasses and met Karen's hostile glance. "Last time?"

"This woman came to see you last week. Since she wouldn't leave her name, I didn't mention it."

The blonde frowned at Karen and dismissed her with a toss of her head. She extended an expensively manicured hand. "Miss Grand. I have a matter of the utmost urgency to discuss with you. It really can't wait until tomorrow."

"I see. Well, then won't you please come into my office? Miss..." Catherine's voice trailed off but the woman offered no name. She merely turned on her Italian leather shoes and walked into the private office. Catherine raised her shoulders to Karen in puzzlement and followed.

Catherine closed her office door and went around to her chair, embarrassed by the unusual clutter. Through the glass office wall, Catherine could see that Karen was busy with the phone. Catherine pushed a clump of hair off her neck and suddenly noticed that she had chipped the polish on her right thumbnail. Irritated, she sat up straight and put on her most in-charge tone. "Now, what can I do for you?"

The woman's long lashes flickered against her tinted sunglass frames. "I have something for you." Her red nails disappeared into a Chanel bag. "Here."

Catherine took the envelope and opened the flap. Inside was a cashier's check made out to her. It was drawn on the Beverly Hills branch of the Bank of America and dated with that day's date.

The sum payable was ten thousand dollars.

"I don't understand." Catherine's reply sounded idiotic to her own ears, but she felt baffled. Within two minutes this mystery woman had reduced her usual professional demeanor to cream of wheat. She cleared her throat and attempted to return the check. "There's some mistake here."

The blonde glanced at the proffered envelope then sat back and crossed her arms. "The money is for you. To help defray the cost of lost business."

"Lost business?" Catherine echoed the words, feeling like Alice down the rabbit hole. The envelope dangled, feeling heavier by the moment.

The blonde removed her sunglasses. Her green eyes were as hard as ice. "I want you to cancel your contract with Sydney Carr and not stage the Brennan Richards look-alike concert."

Catherine's first reaction was to laugh. Maybe this woman was an actress, trying out for a job. She kind of looked like a young Lana Turner. But playing what? A Mafia princess? Catherine dropped the envelope with a plop and folded her hands together. Her voice made her sound more patient than she felt. "I have no idea what's going on here. Why don't you start at the top and give me your name?"

"That's not an important factor in our discussion."

"I think it is. Because I don't have discussions with people who try to bribe me."

"Don't think of it as a bribe. Think of it as a fee."

"I don't have discussions with unidentified people about fees."

The blonde's voice was steady. Her lip curled over her top teeth, which were surprisingly crooked. "There's going to be a lot of trouble if you let that look-alike perform."

"How do you know that?" Catherine demanded.

"I know. Take the money. It'll be easier on everyone."

Several seconds passed. Finally Catherine stood and picked up her purse. She fully expected the woman to lean forward and introduce herself, but she didn't. The blonde only looked at her closely. Then she also stood, slipped her shades on again, picked up the envelope and walked out.

Catherine felt totally mystified. The door slammed and Karen came scurrying in. "Who was she? Did you get a load of those shoes?" Karen asked.

"I have no idea who she was." Catherine shook her head. "I'll be back in a couple of hours. Try to straighten up in here. You know I can't think when everything's a mess." Catherine almost felt that she'd hallucinated the whole incident. The blank look Karen gave her did nothing to alleviate the weird feeling.

OUTSIDE IN THE parking lot Catherine cranked down the window of her ancient Mercedes and started the engine. The September afternoon was like a furnace. It was overcast and bleary even though the temperature was in the upper nineties. The day was typical of L.A.; it looked one way but felt quite another.

"Miss Grand!"

Catherine turned and tried to hide her dismay. The tall, rangy, dark-haired actor Tommy Lyle, who was currently on her rolls as a John Travolta look-alike, was walking across the lot toward her. "Hi, Tommy."

"Hi. I'm glad I caught you. I need to discuss a really important job."

"Look, Tommy, I'm in a hurry. Can this wait?"

The young man adjusted his omnipresent sunglasses and shook his head. "I hate to sit on this, Miss Grand. I just heard about a big gig at MGM, a retro of their movies. Sounds like you could do a lot of business with them."

Catherine doubted it, but didn't have the heart to dismiss Tommy. "I'm going out to Agoura. Want to ride along and tell me about it?"

"Sure. I wanted to apply for a job out there anyway." Tommy folded his frame into the passenger seat of the Mercedes and hummed happily to himself.

Catherine muttered under her breath about actors being children and grouchily backed out of the lot. She waited for the traffic to let her in, and wondered about the blond woman. Then she wondered about the tall, black-haired Irishman with the sky-blue eyes and the ponytail who was the likely reason for the blonde's visit. Brennan Richards. He had been a legend in his own time who had chucked the public life when tragedy struck. Not a cult hero like Elvis or Janis Joplin, Richards had been immensely popular with both young and old fans.

"You're working on the Brennan Richards concert in Agoura?" Tommy offered as though he were reading her mind.

"Yeah. How'd you know?"

"I saw your ad for actors a few weeks back. Then Karen told me when I called that you had to go to Agoura. How's it going?"

"Fine. No more than the usual screwups."

"Did you ever see the real guy perform?" Tommy asked quietly.

"No. Almost did. But he quit before I got the chance."

"His music was dreamy," Tommy said softly. "Did you like it?"

"I was impressed by his serious, poignant lyrics, but he wasn't my favorite. You couldn't dance to Brennan Richards, and when I was young, disco was king."

"I loved the way he dressed. That medieval-style tunic with blue jeans was really cool," Tommy said.

"Yeah, but what about the eye patch?" Catherine said jokingly. "Don't you think that was overly theatrical?"

Tommy's rhinestone-encrusted sunglasses reflected light toward her. Catherine felt herself color. Overly theatrical was a good way to describe the actor next to her, and they both knew it.

Taking no offense, Tommy giggled and put a hand on each side of his face to pretend shock. "Yeah, I do. But overtheatrical is always dreamy."

His pose triggered a cloudy memory in Catherine's mind, and she realized that Tommy was much older than she had been led to believe. In the light of the summer day, she saw the crow's-feet and his slightly dimpled chin line. Lyle was about fifteen years older than he'd told her, she would bet. More forty than twenty-five.

"I read that the patch somehow symbolized the underground political thrust of his music," Catherine offered. "But I think he must have liked the touch of mystery that helped sell tickets." She smiled at her jaded opinion. It wasn't that she doubted Brennan Richards's sincerity, but she knew that the public more readily accepted politics in music if the entertainer was dramatic, handsome and sexy. "It's always the show-biz touch that gets and keeps the world's attention."

"You're right there, Miss Grand."

While she speculated on what Richards was doing now, Catherine slid the Mercedes into second and merged with the cars flowing toward the Pasadena freeway. The demands of her present life pushed the rock star from her mind for a moment, then the bizarre visit from the blond woman crowded her thoughts again.

While Tommy Lyle chatted about the cattle call audition he had gone to today, Catherine silently organized the list of calls she'd make once she was through with Mickey. As owner of Grand Illusions, a company that staged special events for a corporate clientele, Catherine wore many hats. Not only was her company responsible for providing whatever personnel and models the client's gala theme demanded, she also arranged to have stages built, audiovisual equipment rented and publicity done.

Her current largest account was Knight Records. The owner, Sydney Carr, had contracted her three months ago about staging his twentieth anniversary party at the Medieval Days Faire. The Faire was a popular southern California event. People dressed in Renaissance garb and watched jugglers, jousters and Shakespeare in the park.

Carr had asked her to get a Richards look-alike, and she'd found a kid who looked and sounded like the real thing. She wasn't crazy about using look-alikes when the real celebrities had tragic connections to their public images, but Carr had been insistent that a Richards impersonator would provide the right touch. So far things had gone smoothly, but the big day was two weeks away and Catherine knew a few things were still bound to go wrong. They always did.

She wondered again about the blonde and her motives for trying to buy her off. Was she a Carr competitor out to cause trouble for the record mogul? He was legendary for making enemies. Just then she remembered the long distance phone call, also about Richards. The twin problems made her squint with worry, but then Catherine sighed and banished the thoughts.

Aside from Carr's show, she had several other potential clients. Grand Illusions was fast becoming *the* special-events company in L.A. Movie and record studios, corporate party planners, and ad agencies were eager to have her handle the details for their promotional events. Her reputation was growing.

Carr had been referred to her by Stan Firestone after she had pulled off a private party celebrating his wife's thirtieth birthday. Firestone's wife, a *Gone With the Wind* fan, had been delighted with the look-alikes Catherine had sent, and the miniature burning of Atlanta in the Firestone backyard had made the eleven o'clock news. Which proved, Catherine thought, that one thing about Hollywood was true. You were only as good as your last deal.

Struggling out of her jacket, she nosed the German car into the fast lane of the narrow freeway. "Is that right?" she said responding to Tommy. He was excited that he had seen Donna Mills at the studio lot.

As Tommy talked, Catherine roared by several stopped vehicles, more and more ticked off with herself that she had invited Tommy to come. She needed quiet. But at least Tommy kept up a steady stream of talk. All she really had to do was make the right noises. The man had always struck her as more fragile than most of the actors she'd met, and letting him ride along wasn't going to ruin her day.

"You think we'll have any brushfires?" Tommy finally asked, forty minutes and thirty miles later.

"Probably." Catherine glanced at the parched, brown hillsides of the western San Fernando Valley. Every year they burned black in the summer, but the next spring, with just an inch or two of rain, the hills redeemed themselves with rolling grasslands and wild poppies of riotous colors. "You know California. It loves its own drama."

"That's what made it such a natural place for the birth of the movies," Tommy said, then fell silent.

Catherine nodded, then took the Agoura turnoff. "You're right there. California is the land of instant history, where everyone and everything adopts a new look and a new image, pretending the past never happened. A place where people got rich selling the sizzle, not the steak."

"I agree, Miss Grand. My agent says that is *the* lesson to learn." Tommy affected a thick British accent and raised his thin brows above his sunglasses.

"That's a very good accent. So when did you get an agent?"

"I just signed. But don't worry, it won't interfere with our contract, Miss Grand."

"I wasn't worried about that, Tommy." Catherine pulled into a parking lot. Up ahead, the Faire buildings sat hunched on an open, dusty field. "Do you want to come in?"

"No. I'll just walk over to the employment trailer. Like I said, I wanted to apply for a job. And now that I'm out here, I'm going to call a friend who has been bugging me to come see him in Westlake Village. So you don't need to wait."

"I don't mind if you want to check with that friend first," Catherine said, parking the car.

"No, I'm fine." Lyle's glasses sparkled in the sunshine. "Thanks for taking me along, Miss Grand."

"Suit yourself." Catherine watched the actor walk away, more than a little confused as to what Tommy's real purpose was for riding with her. For the first time since she had hired him, he hadn't badgered her about gigs. "Oh, well," she said aloud. The reason he'd come would surface sooner or later. Catherine got out of the car quickly and headed for the Faire offices, mentally toughing up for Mickey.

Mickey Stolie, ex-hippie, Vietnam vet and all around neurotic creative type, had worked for her for two years. He was a brilliant still photographer and set designer who wanted to be a rock video producer. And he was a royal pain in the neck.

Catherine slipped through a side door and stood a minute to let her body adjust to the frigid air-conditioning. She heard a murmur of voices in the back room Mickey used as a studio and walked quietly down the hall. Peering through an open door, she spotted Mickey at work.

His thin back was to her. He focused his Leica on a model who sat on the dramatically backlit couch in the center of the working area. The red lips of America's favorite fifties sex symbol smiled at the lens, the platinum hair perfect, the beauty mark and long lashes darkened for the photos.

"Pout a little, Marilyn. Wet your lips for me, baby," the shaggy-haired cameraman cajoled. His shutter snapped with machine-gun rapidity while the blonde tilted back on the crimson couch to offer a fuller view of her body. Her breasts spilled out of the top of the Merry Widow bra, white skin glimmering against black lace.

"Good, baby. Really, really good. Tighten your shoulder a bit. Let's see the cleavage. Hold it, Marilyn."

While the model flexed, Mickey's camera clicked, and the clicks sounded like smacking lips. Catherine watched, uncomfortable with the faintly lurid posture of the model. She was also aware of the girl's own fleeting sense of embarrassment. "Mickey, I'm here whenever you're ready."

The Leica continued to snap and Mickey's voice was dreamy. "Hang on, boss lady. I'm almost done." He clicked off the last eight frames then winked at the model. "Take ten, Marilyn. But don't forget to rub a little oil on your lips." He turned to Catherine. "What do you think?"

Catherine's face stiffened but she maintained her smile. "She's beautiful. Is her name really Marilyn?"

"It is today."

"Part of the mood, right? But why are you doing this shoot out here?"

"Hey, my time is very valuable. When Karen called and said you got held up, I went ahead and moved up my schedule. The Faire people don't care. They said the studio's mine until Monday."

"Efficient of you." She rolled her eyes at the model. "Who's she modeling for?"

"Oto Cameras. I'm doing Farrah Fawcett and Cheryl Tiegs look-alikes tomorrow. Sam Oto wants a seventies retrospective for his 1992 calendar. He's delighted I found girls who look so much like the real thing."

"Should be hot," Catherine said. "Can we check out the Brennan Richards set now?"

"Sure. Let's go out the back. I told the carpenters to wait. You owe them time and a half, by the way." Mickey hurried to the exit, seeming pleased at the news.

He almost swerved into a wall with his shoulder rather than brush against her, Catherine noticed. Typical Mickey. In all the time she'd known him, Mickey had never instigated any physical contact. He had actually winced the one time she'd tried to shake hands with him.

Catherine followed Mickey out into the blinding heat. It was over a hundred degrees in the open. Elsewhere, the sun had parched the grass, but on the fifty acres the Faire had leased the grasses swept off in golden arcs in all directions. The landscape was marred only by skeletal construction efforts. Tommy Lyle was nowhere in sight.

Several hundred feet from the offices, four shirtless men in hard hats sat in the shade of two trucks, drinking from soda cans. They watched silently as Catherine and Mickey walked over.

Time and a half for sitting, Catherine complained to herself. Sydney Carr was in for a big bill. "Hi, guys. Everything nearly done?"

"Yeah. Except we can't do the turrets until the electrician shows up. He's got to wire the inside light. And he's not due out until Monday." The lead man smiled, confrontation written all over his face.

Shading her eyes, Catherine looked at the set they had erected to Mickey's specifications. The plywood backdrop was styled like a castle. On the stage's platform, the crew had built a bridge. The plan was to run water under it to simulate a moat. In this heat, the water bill was going to be a small fortune, Catherine realized. The Brennan Richards look-alike was going to perform songs here during the opening-night champagne reception.

Two huge turrets, made from two-by-fours and other lumber, were suspended above the stage. Once the support pilings they were to be fitted onto were wired for the amplifiers and lights, the crew could nail them into place.

"Monday?" Catherine turned to Mickey. "We can't get him out here any sooner?"

"No. Unless you want to pay triple time on Sunday." Mickey grinned. "I thought I'd let you authorize that yourself when I heard the news."

Catherine suddenly wondered if turning down the blonde's check had been the dumbest thing she had ever done. "Monday will be fine." Catherine nodded toward the construction crew. Carr would have a fit over triple time. "Everything looks great. I'll see you guys back out here Monday, okay?"

Energized by her words, the crew was in the trucks and heading down the dusty road within a minute of her dismissal. Catherine turned to find Mickey boosting himself onto the platform.

"Come on up and see this."

She pulled herself up the side, then watched as he pointed out the various light and sound positions he'd choreographed for the show. "Now wait here a minute. I'll get one of the cutouts and you can see how effective this is going to be."

He jumped down and hurried into the studio. He returned with a life-size picture of the Richards impersonator tacked to a piece of plywood.

"Looks just like the real thing, doesn't he?" Mickey asked.

"Yes. And sounds even more like him than he looks." Catherine glanced at the photographer. "How was Johnnie Lord to work with?" Lord, the twenty-six-year-old studio musician she'd hired to portray Brennan Richards, had struck her as a little jumpy when she had last talked to him.

"He was great last night. I had him meet me out here to do some stills, just to get a feel for how he'd look in costume. He was eager. Dedicated." Mickey grinned. "To say nothing of freaky."

"Why freaky?" Catherine was surprised at Mickey's comment. He rarely passed judgment on people. She looked into her photographer's eyes. "Tell me what you mean."

"He's always singing Richards's songs. Always."

Catherine laughed and paced the length of the stage. It was big enough for the backup musicians, but she made a mental note that Lord would have to have plenty of rehearsal time or he'd find himself in the moat. "He's being paid a lot of money to look and sound like Brennan Richards. He's practicing, Mickey."

"Practicing? If you say so." Mickey set the cutout down, under the shadow of one of the hanging turrets, then stepped back and looked dreamily at his set. "Why didn't Knight Records get the real thing to come out of retirement? Everyone else is these days. The Who, Jagger, even McCartney."

"I asked Sydney Carr that. According to him, Richards meant it when he said he'd never perform again. Besides, Richards didn't record but one album for Knight Records. I get the feeling there's some bad blood there."

"Big egos. Big feuds." Mickey smirked. "And big bucks. Wait here a minute. I'm going to get another cutout and we can shoot some for scale."

Wiping a trickle of sweat from her forehead, Catherine nodded. The seconds ticked by and Mickey didn't reappear. Catherine moved into the shade of the turret, beside the cutout figure. Studying the picture up close, she was struck again by the similarity between Richards and his impersonator.

"Catherine."

She glanced behind her and found Mickey motioning to her from the door to the offices. Had Tommy Lyle showed up looking for her? she wondered.

"Carr wants you on the telephone!" Mickey waved the receiver in the air.

Taking one step, Catherine heard a snap. Was it her imagination? Or, in the breezeless sunshine, was the wood above her swaying? Adreneline-driven instinct made her run. She leaped from the stage and stared at the turret. Another snap sounded ominously.

"Geez," Catherine whispered. The turret was definitely moving now, rocking in slow motion. She opened her mouth to call for Mickey, but before she could make a sound the turret crashed down. It landed on the spot where she had stood seconds before, and pulverized the picture of Brennan Richards's look-alike into a splintered heap of trash.

Chapter Two

Catherine got to her office before five, a stack of mail and a bagful of office supplies balanced precariously on top of a pizza box. She stood outside the door, knocking with her foot. Karen didn't answer, so Catherine put the things down and fished in her bag for her keys again.

The door stuck at the bottom, and Catherine cursed the humidity. If there was even a drop of it in the Los Angeles air, she needed an Arnold Schwarzenegger type to help deal with the door. Inside, the office was empty. Lights off, answering machine on, Karen nowhere in sight. Exasperated, Catherine hauled her things in and shut the door with a bang. She promised herself that she would confront Karen the first thing tomorrow about her propensity to work twenty-five-hour weeks while collecting pay for forty hours.

A note was addressed to her, folded in half and stuck to the phone. Catherine ignored it. She was not up to reading her secretary's latest excuse for leaving early. She put the mail on her desk, opened the pizza box and grabbed a piece. She tried to sort through the worries that stormed around in her brain.

While she and Mickey had sat staring at each other in amazement over her close call, the construction foreman she'd called out arrived on the scene. He'd inspected the crane and pronounced the event an accident. Mickey had suggested they call the police, but Catherine deferred to the hard hat's assessment. He thought a cable had expanded in the heat of the previous day, then contracted during the cooler night. The cable had then slipped, unbracing the turret for today's near hit.

They were going to have to file a report since it was a union job, but the foreman didn't think the federal safety organization would hold up production. Catherine hoped he was right. She took another bite of pizza and worried about the possibility of being closed down during a lengthy inspection.

After she finished eating, she sorted through bank statements and a few interesting-looking pieces of correspondence that she hoped contained requests for Grand Illusions bids. She listened with half an ear as the answering machine clicked on and off collecting messages; her concentration was suddenly absorbed by the envelope in her hand.

It was addressed to her personally, her name spelled out with printed letters of varying sizes that appeared to be cut from a magazine. The envelope had been postmarked several days before in Minneapolis. Catherine slid her paper knife under the flap and pulled out a single sheet of heavy white bond to which more letters had been glued. They read:

Dear Cath.
Ever hear of Chicken Little? The sky's not the only thing set to fall. I'm going to shoot the stars and be free.

Catherine's heartbeat began a slow increase as she read the message over and over. It made no sense to her, but the presence of danger, of malice even, seeped off the page and into the air around her. With trembling fingers, she folded the letter and stuck it in its envelope. What did people do who got junk like this in the mail? she wondered. Call the police?

"And say what?" she asked aloud. It was easy to imagine a cop's sarcasm over her possible phone call. She could hardly complain about an anonymous letter writer menacing her with Chicken Little.

Shaking her head, Catherine glanced at the ornate frame on her desk. Her father, Leonard, and mother, Dot, stood behind her in the old picture. She sat in a chair. On the floor at her feet were her smiling brother, Patrick, and the baby of the family, Cheryl. It was a good picture of the Grand family, who'd always called their oldest daughter by the nickname Cath. Her ex-husband had shortened her name to Cat during their brief marriage primarily because it annoyed her. But no one else had ever used a similar tag. In school she'd been called Catherine.

The fact that someone who'd seen too many episodes of television cop shows had chosen to address her as Cath for this bizarre hate-mail gag shouldn't upset her, Catherine decided. She thought suddenly of the blonde. L.A. was full of kooks. And so, it appeared, was Minneapolis.

But it did upset her, she realized. She pulled the offensive page out of its envelope again and scanned it. It was perverse, the way it foreshadowed the accident today. And it had been an accident, she told herself firmly.

At that moment, bare knuckles rapped loudly on the office door. Catherine started, for a second too startled to think clearly. A second knock made her pull herself together. She straightened her hair.

"Just a second," she hollered, struggling with the door. Finally she managed to pull it open. A man was standing on the other side. Beyond him Catherine saw that a huge motorcycle was parked by the steps. A helmet hung from the handlebars, gleaming in the fading light like some jumbo polished black skull.

She turned her eyes to the man, taking in the details. He was tall and graceful, hard muscles showing under a faded black T-shirt. His jeans were snug and well-worn, his heavy leather boots polished. She looked at his unsmiling face. A single gold earring dangled from his right ear. Dark hair curled around his neck and forehead.

He wore opaque sunglasses, which he removed to reveal eyes as dark and blue as a winter sea, and just as cold. "Miss Grand?" the man asked, with neither doubt nor friendliness in his voice.

Catherine nodded slowly. The shock of recognition coursed through her with a physical force, nearly making her stagger. She kept her voice calm, though her body and mind felt anything but.

"Yes. Hello."

She continued to stare, knowing it was rude, knowing it was obvious. She prayed that her earlier brush with disaster was not bringing on hallucinations. "Hello," she babbled a second time. "Won't you come in?"

The man stared. His lilting accent did nothing to soften the unmistakable anger in his voice. "I need to talk with you, Miss Grand. It's rather important."

Catherine nodded again and stood aside. In a day of strange occurrences, finding Brennan Richards on her doorstep was the strangest yet.

BRENNAN RICHARDS SAT and stared at the woman across from him. She'd overcome her obvious shock of fifteen minutes ago and now seemed quite in control of herself. She was a fine-looking American girl, curvy and fresh, with shining brown hair and sparkling hazel eyes.

They all looked so healthy and vibrant here, he found himself thinking. *It's too bloody bad their morals have all been addled by the sun.*

"So you see, I understand your feelings, Mr. Richards," the Grand woman was saying. "But you have to understand my position. Your image is in the public domain. You haven't any right to demand that an actor not portray you, particularly in a performance that is clearly advertised as an impersonation."

"I have every right, miss. It's my life, my voice, my face, even! How can I have no rights in this matter?"

Catherine stared at the man leaning on her desk. Though he was furious, she felt no threat or menace from him. She was glad that she'd finally been able to stop grinning at him like a fool. She folded her hands together and kept her voice calm. "You do have rights, of course. But as a public figure—"

"I'm no longer a public figure, Miss Grand. I retired from public life more than ten years ago!"

Meeting his gaze, Catherine took a deep breath. "I've always been careful about how I use models and impersonators, Mr. Richards. There is never any attempt to fool the public or to make concert appearances that misrepresent the authenticity of the performers. The publicity my look-alike impersonator is beginning to attract is really a compliment to you."

"How's that?"

"He's good. You were good."

"I *am* good."

"Of course you are."

"Don't patronize me, Miss Grand."

Catherine colored slightly and leaned toward him. "That wasn't my intention, Mr. Richards. But instead of us arguing about this, why don't you come see for yourself. Johnnie Lord is going to perform Thursday night, the twenty-first, at a nightclub near here called Pretenders. Why don't you come and see for yourself?"

"Thanks. I'd rather not."

"I assure you the performer portraying you will use good taste and not attempt to malign your image or music in any way."

"So what you're telling me is that my wishes will not change your plans to stage this concert?" Brennan glared at Catherine, his blue eyes stormy.

"I signed a contract to do this job, Mr. Richards. Even if I wanted to back out, I couldn't now." To her own ears she sounded like a schoolmarm giving a lecture, so she softened her tone. "You see, Mr. Richards, I think there's a right way and a wrong way to do things."

"How clever of you."

Catherine's eyes narrowed. "Thank you. Now, if you'll excuse me, I have a lot of work to do."

Brennan didn't budge. "So it's money, then. What if I pay you? Pay your man? Will that do?" He ran through some figures in his mind. He seldom thought about money. He had no idea how much it would take to make this woman cooperate.

Catherine bit her lip to suppress the anger she was beginning to feel. His persistence was understandable, but his attitude was an unappealing one she'd grown familiar with in her years of working with performers and their people. She wondered suddenly if he had sent the blond woman. He must have. The idea made Catherine give in to her anger. "Decide to come in person this time to discuss a bribe?"

"What are you talking about?" he shot back.

Not wanting to prolong the game, Catherine stood. "Thanks for coming by to see me, Mr. Richards. I'm sorry you're displeased with our project, but I have no intention of reneging on a valid business deal."

He ignored her outstretched hand. Silently he debated how much he could tell her. She seemed to be a sensible girl, one with integrity. Though her type of business was less than honorable in his opinion, she appeared on the up-and-up. "If you go ahead with this, I'll be hounded. All the rags and glossy dirt magazines in the world will be looking up old Brennan Richards to see what he's been doing."

"First money, now pity?" Catherine inhaled and told herself to keep her patience. "I understand that's part of the price of fame."

Suddenly he reached out and took her hand in his, squeezing it to make his point. "Don't you see, miss? I don't want the press hounds back in my life. I'm a private man now, and I want to stay that way."

Catherine felt a jolt move up her arm at his touch. His hand was warm and calloused, and his rich voice seemed to fill her. It was as if his words were air she'd inhaled. She dropped her hand. "I'm sorry, but..."

Brennan grabbed the picture from her desk and held it close to her face. "This is your family, then? Is your family important to you, Miss Grand?"

Snatching the photo away from him, Catherine retorted coldly, "There's no need to bring my personal life into this, Mr. Richards. Please don't let your temper get the better of you."

"My temper is the better of me, miss," Brennan replied. "And you've only seen a tiny edge of it."

"Don't threaten me."

"That's just the point, my girl." His face was close to hers, and he saw her eyes widen at the intimate proximity. "I'm not threatening you. Someone's threatening me. And I'm wondering if a certain businesswoman who stands to profit by a rash of cheap publicity is behind some very nasty business.''

''What are you talking about?''

Brennan saw that his comment had touched a nerve. The urge to tell her more was suddenly strong. ''Let's just say I've been getting the raw end of what smells like a publicity-stunt setup. And I'm thinking you're the perfect person to be behind it.''

''I'd never do anything like that, Mr. Richards.'' The bizarre letter she'd received came into her mind, but she pushed it out and concentrated on Brennan. She felt the blood rush to her face as her voice rose to match Brennan's. ''Look, if you have anything further to add in this matter, maybe you better do it through an attorney.''

Her words dashed his impulse to be honest. ''Hiding behind the law? Fine. You'll be hearing from Liam McKinney, if you haven't already. He'll bloody well file a restraining order against your company if he must. And against that sod at Knight Records, too.''

Before Catherine could reply, another knock rang out at her front door. She hurried past a glaring Brennan Richards and flung the door wide, surprised that this time it didn't stick at all.

''Hello, Miss Grand. Are you busy?''

Of all people. And in costume no less! ''Johnnie,'' she mumbled to her tunic-clad visitor. At least he's not wearing the damn eye patch, she thought. ''Come in.''

As the Brennan Richards look-alike entered, the real thing sauntered out of her private office. The introduction stuck in her throat. Johnnie gasped and Brennan Richards jerked to a standstill.

''You,'' Brennan whispered, making the single word sound like an epitaph.

"Miss Grand." Johnnie turned on Catherine with his hands on his hips. "You haven't hired another impersonator, have you? I thought I had an exclusive. Besides, this guy is years too old!"

Brennan took three steps and grabbed the actor's arm. "I'm no pasty-faced counterfeit, you little rodent." With a glare at Catherine, he slapped on his shades and went out with a slam of the door.

The roar of his motorcycle filled Catherine's tiny office, but before she could go after him, the noise subsided. Brennan Richards was already headed down the street.

"Oh, my gosh. Was that really—" Johnnie asked, shock edging his voice.

"Yes. That was really." Catherine sighed. "Come in and sit down, Johnnie. Something's come up that we need to discuss."

Chapter Three

Catherine drove the Mercedes up the steep hill to her apartment and parked. She sat for a moment while the sounds of the engine echoed away. She was lost in thought about the two Brennan Richardses. She'd never seen an impersonator and his subject stand side by side before. It was a revelation. As much as Johnnie Lord's facial structure and body type were reminiscent of a young Brennan, the two men were as different as good Scotch and cherry soda.

Could some people simply not be emulated with any degree of accuracy? she asked herself. Brennan Richards had a richness to him. There was depth in his eyes, character in the shadows and crevices of his voice, passion and humor in his movements. He was a man on whom maturity had stamped itself with palpable, though not serene, results.

Next to him, Johnnie Lord was merely a good-looking boy. Catherine rested her head on the steering wheel and sighed. Was hiring someone to impersonate a star as unique as Brennan Richards going to stunt her firm's growing reputation? Would Johnnie's performance make them a laughingstock in the industry?

"Cath?"

Catherine jerked her head up and looked outside the car. Her sister, Cheryl, stared at her. Catherine spoke through one of the open car windows. "Cheryl, what are you doing here? Didn't you and Mom go to the job at the Hilton?"

"Didn't you hear, Cath?" The younger woman opened the car door. "I told Karen all about it when I called at four. The woman at the Hilton, Liz Thornton, canceled our appearance. She said that because of your new prices, she no longer wanted us to do the trade show."

"Hold on. What new prices? What's going on here?" Catherine got out of the car and the two walked down a cobblestone path to Catherine's two-story condo.

"Liz said she got an invoice for three thousand dollars. She said it was more than double what you'd agreed on."

"I never sent any invoice." Catherine's head started to pound.

Cheryl shrugged. She was dressed in her Madonna costume. She sported black lips, finger-waved blond hair and a purple spandex mini dress that poured over her supple body. The outfit was completed by a Lucite crucifix and bangle earrings. "Someone did."

"Well, it wasn't me! Did you see the other models?"

"Yeah. We caught Queen Elizabeth and Princess Diana coming across the parking lot. That Diana had on some great rhinestones!"

"I can't believe this." Catherine opened the front door and bent over to grab her orange tabby, Sally. "I'm sorry you guys went through the trouble of dressing for nothing."

"Oh, it was fun. Mom was in her Liza Minnelli Halston dress and wore three pairs of false eyelashes. I was dressed like this. We got a lot of stares when we stopped for dinner." Cheryl giggled.

Closing the door behind them, Catherine frowned. She put down her purse and keys. "I'll deal with this screwup tomorrow. And don't worry, I'll still pay you for tonight."

"Don't be dumb. Keep your money. I know you'll get us other bookings."

Catherine hugged her sister and dropped the cat onto the couch, unable to ignore the incredibly bad coincidences that had befallen Grand Illusions today. "How long have you been waiting for me?"

"Only about fifteen minutes. I let myself in, then saw you sitting in the car. Did you eat dinner? There's nothing in your refrig."

"I had pizza." Catherine crossed to the old-fashioned louvered windows and cranked them open. With a whoosh, the sheers blew in her face, and the Pacific breezes from thirty miles away greeted her as they passed by on their evening sojourn to the foothills behind her home. She checked the refrigerator herself. "You're right. There's nothing in here."

Joining her sister on the couch, she popped open a diet soda. "Madonna and Liza stopping for dinner. I'll bet you guys made everyone's day."

"Yeah." Cheryl giggled. "But what's up with you? You look like yours was rotten."

Catherine let Sally settle in her lap and began to fill Cheryl in on her encounter with the blonde, the wayward stage set and her meeting with Brennan Richards.

"Mom's going to be scared sick when you tell her about that close call," Cheryl said, her eyes wide.

"So let's don't tell her."

"She'll kill me. And you. She'd find out someday."

"Okay. I'll tell her. In a couple of weeks, when it's ancient history."

Cheryl nodded. "This Brennan jerk sounds like a real bozo to me, Cath. Who does he think he is? He can't make you lose the Medieval Days contract, can he?"

"I don't really know." Catherine leaned back and closed her eyes for a moment. Her sister's reaction, or rather lack of reaction, to the fact that she had met Brennan Richards in person made her feel as if more than twelve years separated them. Nineteen-year-old Cheryl was as impressed as if Catherine had told her she had met Perry Como.

She looked at Cheryl and took another sip of soda. In the soft light, her sister really did look like Madonna. Cheryl and her mother had been her first models and were still among the most popular with clients.

"Well?"

Catherine blinked and realized Cheryl was waiting for her to say more. "Well, what?"

"What are you going to do about Richards? Daddy's a lawyer. Why don't you hire him to defend the company? He'd be great."

"Dad's a tax attorney." This unquestioning faith in their father's abilities again reminded Catherine of her own age. Cheryl was still a teenager. "Don't worry about this. And don't mention it to the folks. There's no sense in getting them upset for no reason. I think Richards may be bluffing."

Cheryl watched Catherine intently. "I wish you'd patch up your quarrel with Mom and Dad. It's eating you up."

"Don't be foolish," Catherine shot back.

"I'm sorry. I know you don't want to talk about it, but—"

"You're right, Cheryl. I don't." Catherine hated the anxiety on her sister's face, but the younger woman was right. Catherine didn't want to talk about the ten-month-old rift between her and her parents. Not now. Maybe not ever. "Besides, it's not a quarrel. After all, Mom's still my favorite model, right?"

"If you want to change the subject, do. But don't try to lie to me. I may not know the particulars, but I know you guys are having some kind of problem."

Catherine blinked. Her sister suddenly seemed as mature as she looked. She felt her stomach rumble and decided to take Cheryl's earlier advice. "Do you want to go get something more to eat? Frozen yogurt? A taco?"

"No, thanks." Cheryl got up slowly. "I'm heading to Fandango's. Wanna come?"

"As what? Your chaperone?"

Cheryl pretended shock. "Did you take your Geritol today, Cath? I can go get you some."

Catherine laughed, the tension between them gone. She stood and squeezed her sister's shoulder. "Get going. And don't worry about me. I'm just out of sorts. You've heard of that happening to women of a certain age, right?"

"Yeah. Our gym teacher told us. Mostly with older ladies, like in their thirties. Maybe you should go see Dr. Lowry."

Catherine pushed her sibling toward the door. "Go. But if you're heading for a rock club, you'll probably get mobbed."

Cheryl struck a *Vogue* pose, then smiled. "Nah. Madonna's gone dark these days. She's wearing white silk. No one will look twice unless I have someone famous on my arm." She kissed Catherine on the cheek and waved, then disappeared into the night.

Shutting the door behind her sister, Catherine doubted that. No matter who Cheryl dressed like, the child always attracted attention. She was beautiful, with her mother's big eyes and generous mouth and their dad's wide brow and nice nose.

A pain she didn't want to deal with pulsed through her. In her bedroom, Catherine allowed a searching look at her own reflection in the mirror as she sat and unlaced her high tops. For the first time in several days, she allowed herself to wonder what her natural mother and father looked like. From whom had she inherited the dimple in her chin? The half-moons at the base of her fingernails?

Leaving her clothes in a heap, Catherine padded into the bathroom. It seemed obscene to have an identity crisis at her age, yet that's what the psychologist she'd kept four appointments with had said she was suffering from. Finding out a few months ago that she was adopted had shaken her to her toes. Her foundation, who she was, was now an illusion.

Her parents had good reasons for their deception. But the damage had been done nonetheless. The hardest thing to take was the feeling that she had been incredibly stupid. She should have guessed, Catherine realized. She looked so different from the other members of her family.

She turned on the shower, slipped off her underwear, then stood beneath the warm spray. Tonight wasn't the night to deal with bruised feelings. The day had thrown too many problems her way, and they needed to be addressed.

Who could have sent Liz Thornton a phony bill? she wondered. Why would anyone do such a thing? Faint chimes signaled that someone was at the door. Now what? Catherine wrapped herself in her robe and hurried to the door, hoping it wasn't Cheryl with car problems.

"Coming," she yelled, then stopped and pressed her eye to the peephole. Pulling the belt tighter on her wrap, she opened the door a crack. "Hello."

Brennan Richards was scowling again, but his voice had returned to the normal ranges of civility. "Miss Grand, I'm sorry for not calling first. I'm staying at the Huntington Sheraton down the street and thought I'd chance another meeting with you. Should I come back later?'' He eyed a sliver of her bare leg, then met her glance.

"How did you know where I live?''

"My lawyer found out. I hope you don't mind our research into *your* private life.''

So he was still ready for a fight, she thought. "Come on in and wait while I change. We can have a glass of wine or something.''

Catherine opened the door and gestured toward the sofa, then marched into her bedroom and closed the door. Her heart was pounding as if she'd jogged four miles, and the silly grin was sneaking back to her lips. I bet celebrities get tired of this nervous reaction from the public, she thought.

For a moment, she stared at the solid wall of clothes in her closet in panic. "What should I wear?'' But at that muttered question, common sense wrested control from her and her pulse slowed to normal. The man isn't here for a date, she told herself. He's come to sue you!

Struggling into a black sleeveless suit, she clumsily snapped the belt then slipped on red heels. If red was a power color, maybe it would help her maintain some control. She raked her hand through her thick, shoulder-length hair and walked to the living room.

Brennan was sitting cross-legged on the floor in front of her record collection. He was holding Carol King's *Tapestry* album in one hand and Joni Mitchell's *Blue* in the other. His gaze met hers. "I like your taste in musicians. Both these woman are wonderful writers. But where's the current stuff?''

"Hey, they're current. They're from the seventies.''

"Caught in a time warp, are you?''

Sitting down near him, Catherine pulled two more records from the collection. She grinned, then realized what she was doing and forced less of a smile onto her face. "Well, I guess I've been too busy to keep up these last few years. I love Aretha Franklin and Janis Joplin, the Stones, the Beatles. And I didn't crush my Cat Stevens albums when he freaked out with the ayatollah. But I have all Dylan's new stuff." She handed him a stack of newer recordings.

"Dylan."

His tone sounded respectful to her ears. "Here's Annie Lennox and Sting and Def Leppard. And Madonna and Janet Jackson. Sinead O'Connor. Even Fresh Prince. Is that new enough?"

Brennan shook his head and stuck the albums into the spot she'd taken them from. "Interesting cross section of taste. But I'd have thought you were a Robert Palmer type."

Unsure of whether this was a compliment or a criticism, Catherine smiled. "Sorry, no. I've seen all Palmer's commercials, though. Does that count?"

Brennan scowled. "Rock and roll to sell cola. As bad as the Beatles pushing credit cards."

Catherine raised her brows. The man sure took rock and roll seriously, she thought. "Well, how about you? Who does a late seventies rock star listen to?"

"You mean an *oldie* like me?"

She blushed. That was twice today Brennan Richards had been told he was outdated. She got to her feet and took a step away. "I'm sorry. I didn't mean to imply—"

"Forget it." He waved his hand and smiled at her now, a sincere look that quickly became guarded. "It's not your fault I'm getting older. Time marches. I don't mind nearing the big four-oh."

For good reason, she thought as she inventoried his features again. He looked fine for his age. Fine for any age. His image stayed in her mind as she moved toward the kitchen. "Can I get you some wine?"

"Sure. Can I put on some music?"

"Please."

"I'll play my favorite."

"Great."

He watched her walk out of the room and took a breath. Despite their business conflict, he found Catherine Grand easy to be with. She didn't act snooty or cold; instead, she was bright and spunky.

She was also fabulous looking. Not pretty in a girl-next-door way, as he'd first judged, but in a more mature, womanly way. She had long legs and a disarming stare. Her eyelashes were soft and thick. They followed the slightly turned-down angle of her eyes like a brush stroke.

But it wasn't the time to think about things like her looks, he reminded himself. He had to get her to listen to reason about that damn imposter. Brennan touched the needle to the LP and turned around to find Catherine watching him.

The soft strains of "Chances Are" swelled from the speaker as Catherine handed Brennan a crystal wineglass. "Johnny Mathis? Very interesting." She almost added that it was her mother's album, but caught herself in time.

"Once a balladeer, always one," Brennan murmured. They sat across from one another on the overstuffed chintz-covered chairs, sipping the wine, each waiting for the other to open the conversation.

Brennan felt her nervousness but put off talking. He took another sip and let himself enjoy a few moments of evening shadows and cool breeze, the song and the presence of the woman across from him.

"After you left I found a note from my secretary. Your attorney, Mr. McKinney, called. Has he really filed an injunction against my firm?" Catherine finally asked, her voice gentle.

The anxiety began to coil in Brennan's stomach. "No. And we don't want to go that far. I'm sorry I lost my temper with your employee today, Miss Grand. But it's very important to me that you see my side in this matter."

Catherine blinked. His tone had been almost aristocratic when he'd said "employee." The fact that he had not bothered to introduce himself to her this afternoon came to her mind. Once a star, always a star, she thought. "Call me Catherine, please."

He nodded. "Right. And it's Brennan for me."

"Well, first let me say that I do see your side in this, Brennan. But you don't see mine." She took a deep breath. "I'm new in this business, and I have to fight incredible competition in order to make a buck. If I bow out of a contract with someone with as high a profile as Knight Records, I may as well close up shop."

Several seconds passed. Brennan stared at his glass. "If your man performs as me, it could be very dangerous," he finally said. "For both of us."

It was such a melodramatic statement that her first impulse was to laugh. But then she looked at his face. His eyes held anger and something else that sobered her immediately. Fear.

"Did you send a woman to my office today to bribe me to call off the concert?" She watched him closely and was surprised to see what looked like one hundred percent shock.

"No. Someone tried to bribe you on my behalf?"

"I'm not sure who she was working for." That was certainly true, but the fact that the woman and Richards both wanted the same thing struck her as too coincidental. "Look, why don't you explain this to me. Are you saying it's dangerous because of the publicity stunt you mentioned? What's it all about?"

Brennan wondered how he could have referred to the vile threats he'd received as a stunt. There was nothing lighthearted about the anonymous letters that haunted his life. The fact that they were done in the same style as those he had received ten years ago convinced him that they were truly dangerous. Before, he had not heeded the twisted enemy who'd sent them. Now he had to.

Could this woman have done it? He looked into her clear eyes. Heartened by the absence of guile, he plunged in. "Recently I got a copy of the ad you ran in *Variety,* the 'Be Brennan Richards' audition announcement. It was accompanied by a letter stating that if I thought I could sneak back into the public's good graces, I was mistaken and would be punished."

The blood in Catherine's veins seemed to roll into a hard, cold ball in her stomach. "Punished?"

"Five days later I got a second letter threatening some of my relatives." The image of his sister's children swam into his mind, accompanied, as always, by intense guilt. "This one demanded I stop the Knight Records concert at the Faire before the September fourth opening or I'd pay the 'ultimate price of fame.'"

Catherine inhaled sharply, and he saw how pale her knuckles were around the wineglass. He was telling her too much, but suddenly he wanted to tell her all of it. "I need your help to stop the concert."

"I couldn't if I wanted to, Brennan. Even if I did pull out, Knight Records will hire someone else and sue me. There's little I can do. Why don't you go right to Sydney Carr—"

"Fine." He stood, the scowl back. "Thanks for the wine."

Catherine watched him head for the door as Mathis went into his soulful rendition of "Misty." She stood, wondering if she should follow him. Suddenly a connection slammed into her consciousness. "Brennan! Wait a second."

"What?" He turned to face her.

Catherine put her wine down. The energy radiating from him was thick enough to touch. A compulsion to make him stay until she could understand more about his extraordinary request beat like a pulse in her brain.

"This is none of my business, but is part of the reason you retired after the—" Her voice caught. Should she ask him about the accident? she wondered. All she could remember was that it had occurred at an opening-night concert ten years before. Several fans had been seriously injured, and someone had died, but beyond that, she could remember no specifics.

Clenching his hand, Brennan looked directly into her eyes. "You've made your position clear, Catherine. Business comes first in the U.S. of A. I'm sure nothing I could say would convince you otherwise."

"Now wait just a minute." Catherine's temper snapped. "I've been very civil. I've listened to your side both here and in my office. You, on the other hand, have acted arrogant and rude. Yes, my business is important to me. Very, very important." She stopped a foot away from him and crossed her arms. "But I'd never act so irresponsibly as to put my job before another human being's safety. Level with me about why you believe the concert will be dangerous, and I'll go to the police with you, and to Sydney Carr."

For a moment he considered telling her everything. Several seconds passed. But it was too late. He just could not take the risk. "Thanks for your concern, Miss Grand. My solicitor will be in touch."

The door closed with a bang.

Catherine slapped her hand against it and swore, then turned to the empty room. The swelling melancholy of Mathis's voice made it feel even emptier. She crossed and snapped off the record, wishing she could silence the voice in her mind with the same ease.

Chapter Four

The next Wednesday and Thursday passed without a word from the Irish rock star or his attorney, and Catherine was jumpy. As she dressed Thursday night to go out with her sister, she thought over the week. It had been full of setbacks.

Every time the phone rang she waited for Karen to announce the worst. This afternoon she made a rare second trip to the post office to see if a summons had been sent. But the silence continued. Did this mean Brennan Richards had accepted the fact that Johnnie Lord was going to impersonate him? Something told her that wasn't the case, and it made the waiting worse.

And that was not her only worry. After calling Liz at the Hilton and explaining the mix-up in billing, Catherine discovered that two other clients had received phony invoices and had canceled Grand Illusions appearances.

She and Karen had gone through all the accounts payable and verified that no mistake had been made on their part. Now Catherine had to admit that the worst-case scenario was probably true. Someone was trying to ruin her business.

In addition to the billing screwup, the "About Town" columnist in *Variety* had run an article that said, "Grand

Illusions has signed to handle Disney Productions employee party." But that wasn't true. She had spent the whole of Wednesday running down the source of the rumor, only to be told by a terse young man in the columnist's office that he had a press release printed on Grand Illusions letterhead announcing the deal.

Maybe it was time to engage a lawyer, Catherine thought glumly as she laced her hair around hot rollers. Rumors and back stabbing were part of the entertainment industry, but false press releases shot this mess into the realm of fraud.

Maybe she should go to her dad, tell him the tale and see if he could give her any advice. Instantly, she dismissed that idea, and she nervously kept her eyes from meeting their reflection in the mirror. She was withdrawing from her parents, distancing herself from them. Why? a tiny voice in her head asked. To punish them?

"No!" Catherine whispered. Still, the possible truth of that made her uncomfortable as she rushed through the rest of her beauty routine.

Sitting next to Cheryl in her sister's tiny car later, Catherine realized she was really uptight. Her swirling thoughts only allowed her to half listen. Cheryl chattered about registration at the junior college she was to attend and a new boy she'd met. By the time they pulled into the Pretenders parking lot, Catherine wished the evening would end soon.

"Are you okay, Cath? Maybe you should take a vacation. Go to a health spa or something. You look like hell."

"I'm fine." Shooting Cheryl a daunting look, Catherine silently vowed to work out more, eat no fried foods and buy some iron tablets.

Pretenders was located in a converted auto showroom in La Canada, a bedroom suburb fifteen miles northeast of Los Angeles that was made up of rolling hills and $400,000 tract houses on quarter-acre parcels. The club attracted a good crowd of well-financed thirtyish fans and a smatter-ing of college kids from the San Fernando Valley and Glen-dale. As the two women pushed their way toward empty chairs, Catherine was startled to spot Mickey Stolie at a front table.

As if she had called out to him, the photographer turned and nodded, then swiveled toward the empty stage. He was alone and made no effort to socialize with the three strang-ers who were hunched around the other side of the table.

"Weird Mickey's here," Cheryl whispered.

Catherine nodded and fell into her chair as the house lights dimmed. Tonight, Johnnie Lord was going to try out his Brennan Richards impersonation, and Catherine forced her personal worries from her mind. *People* magazine was going to use Johnnie as part of their story on her company, and she was glad for this chance to watch him in front of an audience.

As the polite applause began, Catherine felt a flutter of anxiety. The owner of Pretenders, chubby, fiftyish George Jesse, came to the microphone wearing a moth-eaten tap-estry dinner jacket. He smiled and waved. Behind him the black curtains swayed and bobbed as the stage crew set up for the act.

"Hey, guys and gals. Thanks for coming to spend your Thursday night with me, Bad George, at the best oldies club in the world...Pretenders." To lukewarm applause and assorted catcalls from the younger kids in the crowd, he closed, "So give a big Pretenders welcome to that Irish rock idol, the rebel with a heartful of love. Brennan Richards!"

Cheryl whistled and Catherine clapped as Johnnie strode on stage. Catherine was struck now, as she had been when she first interviewed him, by how much more male and forceful Johnnie seemed when he was impersonating Brennan than when he was himself. The sign of a born actor, she thought as the spotlight dimmed.

The first number, a soulful tune from Brennan's first album, seemed a little rusty. The crowd was restless. But by the third song, he had them. Those in the audience who didn't know Brennan firsthand responded to Johnnie's renditions as if they were his own.

But Catherine and the fans her age plugged into the memories unleashed by those turbulent sounds from their teen years. With a rush, Catherine found herself in full flashback, lying on a nubby chenille bedspread in her mom's house, wishing sweet Henry from geometry class would call her for a date.

The applause swelled and the lights dimmed. Johnnie reached for the microphone and tossed his head. "This is for a special girl in my life," he breathed.

Listening to the soft strumming on the guitar strings, Catherine felt goose bumps rise on her arm. Johnnie had never been better than he was now. He was singing the title song from Brennan's first album, Silent Love. The song told the story of Brennan's parents' deaths in a Christmas explosion that had been linked to Irish terrorism, and Catherine was touched as never before by the bittersweet lyrics.

She closed her eyes for a moment and separated Johnnie Lord from Brennan. Her actor had the tempo and the sound right, but the emotion was off, Catherine decided. It should have been remorseful instead of apprehensive. She opened her eyes and stared at Johnnie. The patch blocked her view of his eyes, but his mouth was tense, with an edge. Of what? Fear? Nervousness?

Catherine looked at the crowd. Most of the people seemed engrossed, though Johnnie had lost Mickey. The photographer's chair was empty. Focusing on the stage, Catherine relaxed.

Then the night erupted into horror. From behind and above, the terrifying sound of a shot rang out, followed by a second. Johnnie screamed and grabbed his left shoulder, falling to the ground. For a tenth of a second it was deadly quiet, then a cacophonic chorus of fear and confusion broke out. The hanging spotlight crashed onto the stage floor, and the sound system began an ear-piercing shriek.

All around Catherine people were panicking. They screamed and cried as they overturned tables and crashed into each other in the dark. Amid the furor, glasses shattered on the tile floor and her sister called out her name.

"It's okay, Cheryl. Hang on to my hand." Catherine reached across and grabbed her sister. They both flattened against the back wall. Catherine smelled smoke and prayed it was only from hastily discarded cigarettes.

"What happened, Cath? I'm so scared!" her sister yelled.

"I don't know. But don't worry, honey, we're okay." Catherine was determined to get to the stage to see how Johnnie was, but the crush of running people made it too dangerous to move.

Suddenly George Jesse's voice came through the din as the houselights came on. "Calm down, everyone. Slow down. It's okay."

Catherine pulled Cheryl with her toward the stage. Several people were standing there in a circle, while George Jesse shouted out directions. The wail of sirens could be heard over the nervous chatter of the thinning crowd. Johnnie Lord was moaning. A pool of red spread like a halo around his head.

"Johnnie, it's going to be okay." Catherine knelt beside him, while Cheryl began to cry in earnest.

"We've called the police. I think the ambulance is here now," Jesse said, kneeling beside Catherine. He was trembling and white and seemed on the verge of collapsing beside the downed singer. "I can't believe it's happening again," he mumbled.

Catherine squeezed Johnnie's wrist for a pulse. Her eyes darted around the nightclub, noting the dark and vacant lighting box from which the shot had come. "Did anyone see who did this, George?"

"I don't know. I can't believe this!" He rose and bolted from the room, nearly colliding with Cheryl. She was carrying a blanket and heavy coat. Catherine took them, wondering for an instant what Jesse had meant about it happening again.

"What can I do? Should I call someone else?" Cheryl asked, interrupting her sister's thoughts.

"No, Cheryl. Stay put," Catherine replied. Gently she slipped the eye patch off and felt Johnnie's forehead. Just then he opened his eyes and raised his hand. Catherine leaned close to him and grasped his cold fingers. "Don't try to talk. Help's coming."

He wet his lips and tried to speak, but fell back unconscious as the paramedics rushed in with the cool night air.

CATHERINE DROPPED Cheryl off at two o'clock. She was relieved that their parents were asleep. She told Cheryl to schedule a family powwow for the next morning, when she would return her sister's car. It was clear to Catherine that she was going to need some legal advice, and her dad was the obvious choice for an attorney. The tension between her parents and herself was something she was going to have to stop avoiding.

As Catherine walked up the steps to her apartment, the nightmare of Johnnie's shooting replayed itself in her mind. The paramedics said he would be okay. The bullet seemed to have missed the bone. Still she could not push aside the fear that she could have kept the incident from happening at all. The words in the letter she'd received glowed inside her brain as though they were branded there.

What had happened tonight was her fault. She should have called the police and told them about the threat. She closed the door behind her, and tears stung her eyes for a moment before she blinked them away. *If Johnnie doesn't recover fully, I'll never forgive myself.*

Anger, acrid and trembling, mixed with frustration. Why did trying to do the right thing so often result in making huge mistakes? Catherine asked herself. She had judged the letter a prank, and thought that it was sent because of her company's newfound success. There was no way she should have taken some kook's threat to shoot the stars literally, was there?

Questioning her decision did nothing to make her feel less guilty. Opening the closet door in her bedroom, she hung up her jacket then stripped down. First thing tomorrow she would take the whole thing to the police. They could have a go at the crazy who'd sent the cutout correspondence. And it wouldn't hurt to get them looking for whoever it was that was sending out invoices on phony Grand Illusions stationery.

"We're going to call in the calvary," she murmured to Sally, who was wide awake and sitting in a condescending pose on a corner chair.

The cat looked at her and made no reply.

"What are you doing awake at this hour, baby?" Catherine asked. Sally seldom woke when her owner came in late. The feline was like a well-fed infant. Once asleep for the night, she remained asleep until she showed up, purring in Catherine's face at six on the dot. Maybe she sensed the events of the night, Catherine thought. She gave the cat a stroke, chilled by that possibility, then walked into the dark bathroom.

The first wave of warning struck when her hand touched the light switch. It felt greasy, and a knot of fear twisted in her stomach. The chill bumps raised across her skin as she flipped on the light. Illumination poured down the walls of the small room, and the night's terror took a personal turn.

Everywhere she looked—the mirror, the tile inside the shower—was covered in lipsticked messages. The scarlet words were printed in a bold hand. Their content made her dizzy with fear.

If the shower curtain had been closed, she'd have probably died of Anthony Perkins-induced heart failure. But it gaped open, and the message dripped down the white wall like a soundless scream. Catherine understood Sally's wakefulness. Someone had been in her home.

The mirror reflected the threats. "Stop. No Irishmen allowed." And the most frightening words sprawled across the mirror's center. "That's two warnings Cath. IS THE THIRD TIME THE CHARM?"

Fighting the nausea that scalded her throat, Catherine ran into her bedroom and pulled on some clothes. With shaking hands she reached for the phone, then froze in terror. The noise that she'd heard echoing from the living room registered. It was a second knock. Someone was at the door.

Did I lock it? she wondered frantically. Her fingers felt frozen as she put down the receiver and walked slowly to the center of her living room. The door was bolted, the lock horizontal, in its engaged position. Catherine crept closer, sure the stranger on the other side of the much too flimsy partition could hear her labored breathing or the pounding of her heart.

Catherine stopped a couple of feet away. Her knees turned to gelatin.

The knock sounded a third time, sharper and more demanding. "Catherine? Are you in there?"

Recognizing Brennan Richards's voice did nothing to calm her shattered nerves. "Go away. I'll talk to you in the morning!" she yelled.

"I'll not be going, Catherine. I need to see you. I heard about the shooting."

So it was already on the news. She should have thought of that, Catherine realized. Show business stories rated big newsbreaks in L.A. Her fears began to dissolve as anger over Johnnie's injuries resurfaced. It was damnable that a person couldn't be safe anywhere in this world. "Hang on." She opened the door.

"Can I come in?" he asked.

She nodded and he hurried by her. Catherine eyed the lock, aware suddenly of the gouges around the knob. Whoever had paid her a visit hadn't been very professional at lock picking, but he'd managed to get in. She turned the lock but suddenly felt it was ridiculous to trust it. After all, the maniac had gotten through it earlier without any problem at all. "Where did you hear about this?" Catherine demanded.

"All-night news station. How's your man? Hurt bad?"

"Bad enough." Catherine noted Brennan's flinch and felt a tingle of fear. She had told him Johnnie was going to perform tonight at Pretenders. But surely he wouldn't have resorted to violence, would he? "Did it surprise you?"

"What are you talking about?" Brennan paled, his dark brows knotting. "Surely you don't think I'd—"

"I don't know what to think, Brennan," she answered, suddenly trembling. "Were you at Pretenders tonight?"

"No. I was on the damned freeway for hours, picking up my solicitor at the airport."

Their glances locked. Catherine spoke in a firm voice. "Well, I'm sure the police will find out who did it. They interviewed everyone there. Someone had to see something."

"How is he?"

"Johnnie's going to be all right. The bullet missed all the important stuff, according to the paramedics."

Brennan paced, refusing Catherine's offer of coffee. She sat down and waited.

"It's my fault, you know," he announced suddenly.

For a moment she didn't comprehend his words, then when she did, her fear returned in a cold wave. "What do you mean?" she whispered, clenching her fingers together. Was this a confession? Had she just made the fatal mistake of inviting Johnnie's attacker inside? Catherine tensed, ready to spring from the couch and through the door. She thought again of the messages printed on the walls of her bathroom.

Brennan stared at Catherine, seeing the stark terror and fatigue on her face. She thinks I'm a brute, he realized. He had barreled into her home in the middle of the night and obviously scared her to death. He took a step toward her. "Catherine, don't let me scare you. I'm sorry for everything that happened tonight. Let me explain what I meant."

He eased onto the chair across from her, wanting suddenly to sit closer, though to comfort who he wasn't sure. Instead he slowly took out the letter that had been waiting for him tonight at the Sheraton. The cutout letters pasted on the front of the envelope tilted backward in a way that somehow seemed mocking. "I told you I had a problem. The problem just got bigger." Brennan tossed the envelope on the coffee table.

"What is it?" Catherine knew, but resisted the truth.

"It's a letter of the poison-pen variety."

Her lungs felt as if they'd burst. She studied the envelope. It was addressed to him, but the cutout shapes and sizes were identical to those on the letter she had received. "What does it say?"

Brennan swallowed and picked up the envelope, sensing her fear. "Before I read this, I need to ask your help. I'm not taking this to the police. I can't. Not yet, anyway. Can you keep this confidential?"

She stared at him in shock. It was clear that Grand Illusions was under attack and that Johnnie Lord was the first casualty. The possibility that the murder attempt was somehow connected to Brennan Richards was one she was eager to explore, but not at the cost of breaking the law. "I can't promise that, Brennan. A man's been shot. We have to do what we can to catch whoever's responsible."

"I can't force you not to speak out, of course. But give me a chance to explain why."

She crossed her arms. "I'm listening." And she was, with every cell of her body.

Chapter Five

"Ten years back I was on top of the rock scene," Brennan began. "I was proud of my success and proud of how I'd achieved it. I was fair with my people and tried not to use my considerable clout against blokes who'd done me wrong in the past." Brennan paused. His lip trembled, but he continued on, his blue eyes showing the turmoil he felt.

"But maybe I was arrogant. Certainly cocky. The week before an L.A. concert, I fired my manager and one of my singers who'd started the backup band with my sister. The girl was taking drugs. I discovered her supplier was my manager."

Catherine raised her brows. "Couldn't you have gotten them some treatment?"

"I had already paid for two drug clinic stays for the girl. I guess I took the easy way out with my manager." Brennan looked at his boots. "But it was the last straw with that bloke. You see, I had some evidence that linked him to a record-pirating scam the recording company had uncovered. While I couldn't prove George was involved, I took the opportunity to get rid of him."

"And?"

"Two days later I got a letter like this." He waved the paper. "And I ignored it."

The events surrounding Brennan's last concert pounded up from her memory, drowning out his words. Halfway into his opening number, a scaffold had collapsed on top of the crowd. The people had panicked and stampeded. Several had been hospitalized. Catherine recalled a follow-up article, stating that two teenagers would be quadraplegics for life.

But the most horrible thing she recalled was that someone in the crowd had started shooting, and a member of Brennan's entourage was killed in the melee. "I remember what happened, Brennan. Are you saying the letter threatened to sabotage your L.A. show?"

His jaw locked as he blinked back emotion. Brennan leaned toward Catherine. "Yes. The letter said I'd gotten too big for my britches and the sender was going to 'rain down vengeance.'" He covered his eyes for a moment then looked up. "The man who was killed, Mitch Chapin, was my brother-in-law. My sister was left alone with their children." Brennan slammed his hand against the table, trying to hold his voice steady. "And it was all my bloody fault!"

Catherine jumped at the noise. It was eerily reminiscent of the sound Johnnie Lord made when he hit the floor. "Did you tell the police all this? Didn't they investigate?"

"Yes. A cop named Gutierrez investigated for two years. Couldn't prove a thing. Said the scaffolding pin underneath the stage had been removed. They never located the gun or the shooter, but they cleared all the cops who were present for concert security. We had nothing to go on except the bullet, which was the kind you can buy in the states at any mall."

"What about the letter? Couldn't they trace it?"

"Bloody fool that I was, I had destroyed the letter. I had no proof."

Catherine pointed to the one he now held crumpled in his fist. "But you have this one. Give it to them. After what happened to Johnnie tonight, surely they'll take it seriously."

He shrugged, suddenly looking older than his years. His sigh was ragged. "I tried to run my own investigation back then. I looked up a few boys I'd been at odds with, checked into my ex-partners' whereabouts, and confronted my manager. George Jesse swore he had nothing to do—"

"George Jesse?" Catherine interrupted. Coincidences were one thing, but this connection raised a huge red flag in her mind. "George Jesse was your manager? The man you fired?"

"Yeah. What is it, Catherine?"

He sat stony-faced as she related Jesse's tie-in with Johnnie Lord's shooting. She stopped her story before telling him of Jesse's strange comment to her about "it happening again." To her mind, it sounded too much like a confession. "I know this isn't any of my business, Brennan. But I think you owe it to Johnnie Lord to take this information to the police."

Brennan's accent suddenly became stronger. "Look at this, lass. You'll see why I can't." He unfolded the letter. As he read, he moved his eyes from the page to meet hers often.

"Brennan . . . Stop the concert or Ellen's kids are dead. If you call the police, I'll be forced to act. Remember, there's only one price to pay for this show . . . and the kids are it."

Catherine's skin turned to goose flesh as Brennan read the words of the hateful message with his soft, lilting voice.

"Is Johnnie Lord hurt so badly that he won't be able to perform in three weeks?" Brennan said when he'd finished reading. His look was fierce. "I know it's a hell of a question to be asking, but I've got to know his plans."

"If he has any sense, he'll be too scared to perform," Catherine replied. "I'm certainly going to warn him off."

"What about Sydney Carr? He'll just want you to hire someone else, won't he?"

Catherine's stomach clenched at that question. She had told Brennan that Carr's contract was binding. Carr probably would do just that. "I don't know how Mr. Carr is going to react to any of this, Brennan. Why don't you go to him and tell him about the letter? Surely he'll change his plans."

"Carr would like nothing better than for me to ask him a favor. I'd burn in hell before I'd give him the satisfaction."

Catherine felt her entire body stiffen. "Brennan, we're not talking about your pride here. We're talking about the safety of an innocent performer and your sister's kids! Whatever ax you have to grind with Sydney Carr can't compare with the safety of the children."

"You don't understand. Sydney couldn't care less about my personal problems. In fact, he'd probably be delighted to add to them. Besides, even if Carr agreed to cancel the concert, your Johnnie Lord might well take his act elsewhere anyway."

That she was personally responsible for Johnnie Lord's new career made her feel ill. "Don't get ahead of yourself, Brennan. Johnnie may give this whole thing up now. Go to the police. Go to Sydney Carr. You've got to stop this maniac."

Brennan's face tightened into a stubborn scowl. "The police will need and take more time than I've got. I can take shortcuts."

Catherine returned the letter to its envelope and handed it to him. Was this the time to tell him about the letter she'd received? It now seemed less and less likely that her close call at the Faire site was an accident. Her eyes glanced nervously toward the bathroom. There was the mess in there, too. And that made one thing more than obvious. She and Brennan had somehow become connected in the mind of a psycho. They were twin targets of the same hunter.

"I got a letter, too."

"What?" His head jerked up, his blue eyes piercing through her.

She described the letter, then pointed at the bathroom. "Anyway, I didn't put any store in it until tonight when I got home and found—" Catherine stopped for a moment and took a deep breath. "Someone broke in here tonight and left another message. In the bathroom."

The skin around his nostrils tightened. Slowly he stood and marched into the room. She heard him curse.

He returned to the living room and sat down, resting his forehead against his hands. "I'm sorry you've gotten involved in this. I'll hire some protection for you. Here and at work, until this mess is over."

"Hold on. Why not just go to the police together? Tell them about everything?"

He started to shake his head, but stopped when he saw her look of fear. He didn't have any right to ask her to not report all this, he realized. "What do you mean by everything?"

His tone surprised her. The rich softness of a few minutes ago had vanished. "The letters, the bathroom... everything."

"It wouldn't do any good."

"Of course it would! They'll probably be able to get fingerprints and trace the letter delivery to your hotel. The police can do lots of things."

By the set of his mouth she saw his disbelief, and to her own ears she sounded like her sister, naively having faith in the overloaded police system's effectiveness. She folded her arms defensively. "Without the police, how can we find this crackpot? You said yourself you couldn't ten years ago."

Eagerly he leaned forward. "I gave up too easily ten years ago. I realize that now. I have several leads I can check out, especially if you cooperate."

Her mouth went dry. "Cooperate?"

"If the authorities get involved, the culprit may go to ground for ten years, like the last time. But if you and I do the sleuthing, we may smoke him out."

"I don't see how I can help getting the police involved. Johnnie Lord has a bullet in him, and they're very interested in it."

"That's true. But I know how the police think. First they're going to look for someone in *his* past with a personal vendetta. While they're working their way to the obvious, we can be doing some real legwork."

"Brennan, this is nuts. The police—"

"The police are going to be all over your office and all over your actors if you let them, Catherine," Brennan interrupted. "Especially when you show them your letter. Do you want this kind of publicity? They could close you down while they try to determine if it's you the psycho's after. Your employees will be screened, interviewed and scared off. Do you want them to comb through your past looking for a suspect?"

"Well, no. But—" She clamped her mouth shut. He might be right. If the police did look into the phony invoices, her business life could be ruined. Once the story hit the papers, no one would want to hire her because of the possibility of hassles. Maybe she should throw in with him, for a few days at least. If the two of them could find out who was behind this, they could keep the publicity to a minimum.

"Look, who do you suspect? I need for you to be honest with me, Brennan. Is it George Jesse?"

"He could be involved. Or the singer I fired, Jane Scarlett. She dropped out of sight after the accident, but I'm sure someone knows where she is. Unless she's dead. And there's always Sydney Carr."

"What's between you and Carr?" Catherine challenged.

He blinked, knowing the story wouldn't do much to raise her opinion of him. "Can't you just take it on faith that Sydney and I had differences?"

"Sorry. But no." She lifted her chin defensively. "I'm one of those people who needs proof."

"Money. I costed him several million."

Catherine swallowed, irate that her cheeks felt warm. She felt at a loss to ask the next question. All the possibilities seemed so personal.

"Sydney was my agent. I challenged a contract George Jesse had signed with Carr. And I won. Big."

The chimes from her Westminster clock struck the half hour, and Catherine felt a chill of foreboding. What had she expected? That Brennan was a knight in shining armor, untouched by the dirt of big business and real life? She smiled ruefully. The troubles in many people's lives could be reduced to the most basic battles, money and sex. Hers had been, although not so dramatically. "I see."

Brennan flushed. "You probably don't, but let's leave it at that, shall we?" It ate at him that Catherine Grand did not have a clear picture of the facts, but only the brief details. But neither of them had the time or the stamina to set the whole story straight now. "What do you say, Catherine? Can we be partners for a bit?"

It was ludicrous, Catherine told herself. The two of them ferreting out old enemies to explain this current mess. But if she didn't go along, she could lose Grand Illusions and who knew what else. "Are your suspects in California?"

"We can find out, probably quicker than the coppers. In the meantime, I'm going to hire several more security people for Ellen and the kids. We all live on a farm in Mancato. The isolation is nice, and no one knows I live there. But I want to take no chances."

A spark of warning struck in Catherine's brain, the tiny flame of fear igniting into paralyzing doubt. "Where's Mancato?"

"Minnesota. Land of ten thousand lakes. We moved there after the accident and tried to leave the past behind. Until now we've been pretty successful," Brennan added.

Catherine swallowed. "My letter was sent from Minnesota, Brennan. Your family may be in more urgent trouble than you realized."

"My God." His voice went flat and his eyes went blank for a moment, but then his hand shot out and grasped her arm. "Will you help me, Cath?"

His use of the nickname startled her. Doubts of his innocence in the night's bizarre series of events once again crossed her mind. "I will help you, Brennan. But I go by Catherine," she whispered.

Her words brought a grim smile to his face. "I wrote a song once about a girl named Catherine. It was my mom's name, too, but my dad called her Cath." A change seemed to come over Brennan, and he rose, all signs of anxiety gone. "Come on, then. I'll help you clean up that mess and then I'll be off. We can meet tomorrow and decide how to approach Carr. How'd that be?"

"Okay." She agreed, much to her own surprise. "But promise me you won't destroy any of the evidence. We're going to have to go to the police eventually."

He handed the letter to her. His hand was strong and warm, and Catherine felt the shock of physical awareness on her icy skin. "Fine. You keep this one with yours, and it will stay safe. Now where do you keep your cleanser?"

THE PHONE in the cheap hotel room rang once before the occupant grabbed it.

"Yeah?"

"Good shot, friend. And good work with the spotlight. George's going to have to buy a new one."

"Now what do I do?" the listener demanded.

The caller ignored the slightly dopey tone in the listener's voice. "Did you leave the message for Catherine Grand?"

"Yes. I bought gasoline, dynamite and two tubes of lipstick with the money you gave me, just like you said." That was a lie. Some of the money was spent on the recreational pharmaceuticals in the next room, but the caller didn't need to know that.

"And you delivered the letter to Richards?"

"Yes. I've done everything you asked. When do I get my money?"

The caller chuckled. "Hang on to your nerve, old friend. You'll get paid. Now remember. Go on as is. Don't draw suspicion to yourself. Act normal." The caller chuckled again. "Well, as normal as you can."

"Very funny," the listener retorted, glancing at the man's white silk suit that hung next to the bed. With one hand, the listener brushed nonexistent lint from the wide lapels. "When am I going to hear from you again?"

"Soon. Hang loose, friend. It's all going to happen."

The listener flinched as the dial tone buzzed. Slowly the receiver was replaced and the occupant of the room lay on the bed, motionless. After a while, slim fingers rolled down the silk hose that covered long feet. The conspirator stood and retrieved the rifle from under the bed then slowly cleaned and polished it, readying the gun for its next starring role.

Only then was the bulky cassette recorder turned on. The wailing laments of "Big Girls Don't Cry" filled the desolate motel room.

Chapter Six

"Sydney Carr is on three, Catherine."

Catherine closed the door and hurried past Karen's desk into her office. She dumped her purse on the floor and reached for the phone. "Good morning, Mr. Carr."

"Not much good about it, is there, Miss Grand?" a nasal voice snapped. "How's the singer?"

"Good. I just came from the hospital. They're going to release him Sunday." Catherine sat down, nearly pulling the phone off the desk and into her lap. She realized that the cord was wrapped around a large cardboard box. She glanced quickly at the package that sat in the midst of her papers. There was no return address, and the delivery slip showed no city of origin.

"How's Johnnie's voice?"

Catherine focused her attention on Carr and grimaced at his question. "He sounds fine. Seems remarkably cheery."

"Can he sing?"

"I didn't ask him to sing. As you can imagine, he's been through a bit much for that."

"Hell of thing to have happen. I couldn't have paid for better publicity." Carr laughed dryly. From the sucking sounds, Catherine knew he was drawing on one of his huge cigars. "Guess we'll have to spring for another costume or two. Though maybe wearing the bloodstained one would—"

"Mr. Carr!" Catherine interrupted. "I haven't inquired if Johnnie *can* perform in two weeks, much less if he *will*. Someone took a shot at him that very nearly killed him!"

"Yeah. Some audiences are really tough, aren't they?" Carr's laugh was fuller now. "Tell the kid I'll kick in another five hundred for the Faire performance if he shows signs of chickening out. I also want to talk to him about doing a video. I've got a concept in mind."

Concept. Catherine shivered. Carr was famous in a town of gimmicks for his poor-taste concepts. "A video? Not of the shooting?"

"Of course not. Even I'm not that crude, Miss Grand. But I want to have him star in a retro of Richards's last album. It may be an opportunity for a whole group of your look-alikes. Elvis, Jimi Hendrix, Janis Joplin, the dead Beach Boy. Think of it, Jim Morrison, Del Shannon, Otis Redding. We could do a whole series! Fox would probably bite to air it."

"I don't think I would be interested in this project, Mr. Carr," Catherine replied. "And if I may go on record here, it sounds in terrible taste."

"Don't be a prude, Miss Grand. It's bucks. Didn't you ever see *Wall Street?* Greed's what runs American business."

Catherine felt the urge to lecture him on the virtues of not giving in to base instincts but was wise enough to hold her tongue. "What do you want me to do about the press? Is your PR agency handling all the inquiries?"

"No. I want you to handle this. Let me know when Lord can be ready for some publicity shots. I'd like a network guy to cover his departure from the hospital, too. Can you do that?"

"Yes." Arranging for media coverage was part of her service. Still, the thought of requesting someone to cover a victim leaving a hospital bed sickened her. Catherine gritted her teeth. How had she gotten involved with someone so tawdry?

Suddenly she imagined the adjectives Brennan Richards would use to describe Carr's request. The list would begin with "exploitive." "I really think we should play down this whole event, Mr. Carr. From a public relations standpoint, to say nothing of Johnnie Lord's safety—"

"Gotta run, kiddo. I'll be in Santa Monica tomorrow morning if you need to come by. Remember, I want the networks at the hospital."

Catherine frowned at the dial tone. Last night she had promised Brennan Richards that they would meet today and plan some strategy for approaching Carr. At this moment, Sydney Carr was the last person she wanted to approach about anything. Grimly she punched the intercom button. It had begun to flash as soon as Carr disconnected. "Who is it, Karen?"

"Mickey. He says there's an emergency out at the Faire site."

"Damn it. What line?"

"One. But wait a minute. We have another invoice problem."

Catherine looked through the glass office wall and met Karen's glance. "What kind of a problem?"

Karen waved a piece of paper. "I just opened this. It's a note from Burbank Studios asking for clarification on your costs for their sitcom promotion. They sent a copy of an invoice charging $6,600 for one night's work for eight actors."

Catherine's breath caught in her throat. "What?" she croaked. "I quoted her $3,400! Did you send that invoice?"

Karen tapped her fingernail against the phone and shrugged her shoulders. "No," she mouthed and shook her head.

"I'll deal with that in a second." Catherine clicked off the intercom and picked up the blinking line, her senses reeling. One screwy invoice was a prank. Any more than that meant real trouble. Her business would be jeopardized if news of this got out. "What now, Mickey?"

"Can you come over to the studio this morning?"

"I thought Karen said the problem was out at the site."

"Oh, that. Yes, it is. The chief electrician called me a few minutes ago and said someone had tampered with the wiring under the set. He's going to have to replace a lot of it. We're talking mega moola."

"Tampered?" Last night's events marched in formation through her mind, the shooting, the break-in, the anonymous letters. And now there was more trouble at the Faire. "Did he give you an estimate?"

"He said about four."

"Hundred?"

"Thousand. The transformer was smashed, and the lead lines had a corrosive poured over them. It's a mess."

"Did they call the police?" she snapped.

"Yeah. The cops will be out later."

"Why are they waiting?"

"Malicious mischief doesn't rate a fast response."

The intercom began to beep again, and Catherine felt her patience slip. "Why do you need me to come by the studio?"

Mickey sighed. "Not enough to just ask, huh?"

"Mickey—"

"Okay, okay. I want you to look over some prints I took last night."

"Last night? You took pictures of Johnnie at Pretenders?"

"Him, too. I think you need to see them. Something's kind of strange."

Catherine bit her tongue to keep from asking what Mickey meant by strange. She didn't have the time to find out now. "I'll have to come tonight. Late. Are you going to be there?"

"As long as it's after eight. Okay?"

"Fine. See you then."

He rang off and she pressed the intercom, eyeing the box on her desk skeptically. "Now what, Karen?"

"A policeman is on line four, and Brennan Richards is on line two."

Muttering, Catherine pressed the second button. "Brennan?"

"Catherine. Have you talked with the police yet?"

He didn't even say "hello, how are you?" she thought. "I have an officer on the other line now. What's going on?"

"Are you okay? You sound like something's happened."

Catherine was tempted to recount the list of all that had happened in the past three days, but knew she would lose control if she indulged. She threw a question at him. "Have *you* talked to the police yet?"

"No. I thought we settled that last night."

"We did. What I mean is, did they call you?"

"Why would they?"

She inhaled, her attention diverted by a strange noise somewhere in the office. Catherine shifted and tucked the phone between her chin and shoulder and clutched the box in front of her. It was surprisingly light. She quickly set it on the floor. "I don't know why. I was hoping maybe one of them would connect Johnnie's shooting to what happened ten years ago."

Brennan's voice sounded tight. "I doubt if there is a connection. I'm this guy's target, not some kid."

"Okay, okay. When I talk to the cops I'm going to tell them what I saw at Pretenders. And answer anything else they ask."

There was a moment's silence. "We need to talk about seeing Sydney Carr. Can I come by for you after lunch?"

She leaned over the mess on her desk and flipped the calendar pages. She didn't want to tell him of Carr's glee over Johnnie Lord's shooting, not now, anyway. "I'm tied up until five."

"I'll be there at five, then. Catherine, there's one more thing."

"Yes?" Her brain finally computed the sound. It was faint and rhythmic. Ticking. She stared at the clock on the small table across the room. It read seven-fifteen, exactly as it had for the past year.

"Be careful, Catherine. This guy's no one to fool with."

Catherine smiled grimly at Brennan's tone. "I will be. See you at five."

She hung up then sighed, staring at the flickering buttons on the phone. Despite her agreement last night to help Brennan, she was unwilling to lie to a cop. She gave herself a second to get her voice under control. She stared at the cardboard box. Tentatively she pushed it with her foot. The ticking was coming from inside. Catherine frowned, had an absurd thought about mail bombs, then recalled her own instructions to Karen to buy a new clock for the reception area.

Catherine snapped down line four, irritated that Karen left it to her to unpack supplies. As depressing as the thought was, it was clear she was going to have to let her secretary go if things didn't change. "This is Catherine Grand."

"Hello, Miss Grand," a husky female voice answered. "This is Detective Susan Nelson. I'm looking into the Johnnie Lord case, and I'd like to come by today so we could talk."

"Today's pretty hectic. How about in the morning?"

The cop hesitated. "I'd don't usually work on Saturday morning. How about later, after five? I live in San Dimas, so I could swing by your office about five-thirty."

"Okay." Catherine agreed, forgetting for a moment about Brennan. Then she asked a question she knew she probably shouldn't. "Any suspects yet?"

"Do you have any nominations?" the voice replied.

"No." Catherine knew she didn't sound convincing. "Okay, I'll see you later."

"Five-thirty, Miss Grand," the officer replied.

"You have the address?"

"I do. Goodbye."

Catherine hung up the phone. That call had not gone well, her guilty conscience whispered. She should have told the officer to call Brennan Richards and ask about suspects who wrote threatening letters. With a sigh, Catherine crossed to the door and opened it.

"Let me have that note from Burbank Studios."

Karen handed it to her without a word. Catherine studied it. "Do you have the original invoice?"

Karen leaned down and yanked open her file drawer. She pulled out a red-tagged manila folder and gave it to her boss.

Catherine flipped it open. The invoice inside was for $3,400. She compared the forms. They were identical, except for the date. The forged one was sent two days after Karen's and bore the words "corrected invoice" in red. "Where do you keep the blank invoices?"

Karen pointed to a box on the bottom shelf of the credenza across from her desk. It was in plain sight and accessible to anyone who came in. "Is that where you always keep them?"

Karen nodded, her eyes glistening.

It suddenly hit Catherine that something was very wrong with her secretary. "What is it, Karen? Are you okay?"

A sob escaped the redhead. She crumpled into a heap in the chair beside her desk and burst into tears. "No. I'm not! I'm too old. Too old, according to that little geek at Ellis Casting. You should have heard how he talked to me."

Catherine gently patted Karen's shoulder. These scenes were becoming more common and were increasingly disruptive to the smooth running of an office. "I'm sorry, kiddo. You know how casting agents are, though. Don't let him get to you."

Karen continued to cry. Catherine was struck by how uncomforting her words sounded. Maybe she should level with Karen. Maybe she should express her sincere opinion that she was too old to be chasing stardom. But that was out of the question, Catherine realized. Besides, who was she to judge another person's dream?

She turned to go into her office. "Please hold my calls for an hour, Karen." Ignoring her secretary's look of defeat, Catherine closed the door and surveyed the chaos in her office again. She needed to get the billing files in order and make another call to the Hilton to request a copy of their false invoice. Then she needed to set up a time next week for *People* magazine.

And call an attorney, she thought. Catherine slipped a business card her father had given her that morning out of her wallet and taped it to her phone. The conversation with her parents earlier had been strained. She'd been prickly.

They were worried sick, but not about the forged billing or Johnnie Lord's shooting.

Her mother's eyes and the tone of her father's voice communicated clearly their anxiety about Catherine and the emotional distance she was keeping from them. For a moment, Catherine let herself feel the pain that welled up inside her, but then she quickly pushed the feeling aside.

"Get to work," she muttered. Karen's problems, Brennan's problems, even the problems with her parents would have to wait. She had her own difficulties. And a dream of her own to protect, too. She'd keep her business safely in the black if it killed her. The decision instantly filled Catherine with relief, though she was savvy enough to know it was of the temporary brand that came with postponed confrontations.

BRENNAN RICHARDS STARED at Catherine, wondering when she was going to stop avoiding his eyes and talk to him. She was working her way through an impressive stack of pink telephone messages that her secretary had apparently left.

He glanced at his watch, then crossed his leg and inspected the scuffed leather boot. Liam McKinney, his lawyer, had remarked a couple of hours ago that Brennan looked a bit like a thug on his motorcycle. Brennan smiled. Liam then immediately asked about Brennan's sister, Ellen, and her children.

If those two weren't so selfless and dense when it came to their own needs, Brennan thought for the hundredth time, maybe one of them would see how much in love they were.

"Brennan? Did you hear me?"

He looked up, pushing the thoughts of his sister from his mind. Catherine Grand was staring at him, and he was struck again by how attractive she was, despite the fatigue lines that rimmed her eyes. "Sorry. What did you say?"

"I asked if you wanted to try a surprise visit to Sydney Carr. I am going to take some invoices by his home tomorrow morning, and I thought that would be an opportune time for you to approach him about dropping Johnnie Lord."

"Carr was never one for surprises." Brennan grinned. "Let's do it."

Catherine made a neat pile out of the message slips and folded her hands. Still, she had a strange feeling that she'd forgotten something. She found herself inordinately irritated with Brennan's chipper attitude. "Owning your own business is a big responsibility, and I take it very seriously, Brennan. I don't make a habit of aggravating my customers."

"So don't aggravate him. I'll go by myself." His black eyebrows rose in challenge.

"No. I'll go, too. I agreed to help you get to the bottom of this and I will. I just don't want you to lose sight of how much my reputation is at stake here." She looked quickly at the pile of messages again, chiding herself for lecturing him. She picked up the top note. "By the way, is this your man?"

He glanced at the pink sheet. Liam McKinney's name and hotel number, and the words "re: B. Richards" were scrawled there. Liam had called two hours ago. "Yes," said Brennan.

Their eyes met. Catherine frowned. "I assumed after our conversation last night that you were going to call off your dogs."

"Liam's his own man."

"Which means what? You're asking me to help you but you're still suing me?"

Brennan grinned, baring even white teeth. "I never was suing you, Miss Grand. But Liam wants to chat with you and make sure you understand our official position on Johnnie Lord."

"Official position?" His cool response stung like a slap. Catherine sat back in her chair as the color rose in her cheeks. "Forgive me, Brennan, but I assumed that your official position was to support me in trying to find out what's going on."

"I'll certainly do that, Cath. But that doesn't mean I intend to allow Johnnie Lord to go on ripping me off!"

His response lit her already short fuse. The day had been a disaster, and this bantering was the last straw. Catherine glared at him and punched in McKinney's phone number with a vengeance, fully intending to blast the solicitor in full hearing of his smug client.

"Huntington Sheraton," an elegant voice answered.

Catherine switched to the speaker phone and barked her response. "Liam McKinney. Room 216."

There was a short pause, then the woman gave a gasp. "Ma'am, could you please hold?"

Brennan and Catherine exchanged hostile looks. A moment later a man's voice filled the air. "This is Justin Saint-Neau. To whom am I speaking, please?"

"I asked for Mr. McKinney," Catherine announced, ready to disconnect the phone."

"Saint-Neau?" Brennan cut in suddenly. "Aren't you the manager? This is Brennan Richards."

"Ah, Mr. Richards. Yes, I am the manager of the Sheraton. Are you a friend or relative of Mr. McKinney's, sir?"

"What's happened?" Brennan demanded, standing and staring at the small telephone box. "I'm a friend of his."

"Mr. McKinney was involved in an, ah, accident, Mr. Richards. We've taken him to the hospital. If you could come right over—"

"What the hell happened?" Brennan shouted.

Catherine swallowed the nervousness and anger of a few minutes before and stared at Brennan's face. His blue eyes were wild with worry, his face pale. The earring glittered coldly. She averted her eyes and stared at the phone. Finally the hotel manager's words seeped from the speaker. "There was a parcel delivered to your room, Mr. Richards. Mr. McKinney was there and signed for it. And it—evidently it contained an explosive device of some kind."

"A bomb?" Brennan gasped.

"I don't think we want to use that particular word, sir." The man replied as if he were calming a disgruntled guest who'd received a poor-quality bottle of wine. "Perhaps you could come to the hotel? The police are still here."

Brennan whirled from the phone and stomped toward the door. "I'm going," he announced, then turned with a fierce look. "Where's the hospital?"

"I'll take you," Catherine replied. "Thank you," she said stupidly to the phone. Then she disconnected the line and grabbed her purse. She ran after Brennan, slamming the office door behind her. Outside the August heat wafted up in scorching waves from the asphalt, making Catherine catch her breath.

"Come with me in the car," she gasped as Brennan slid onto the black leather motorcycle seat.

"This is faster," he replied. "Get on."

She glanced at her short denim skirt and frowned. "Look, I can't ride on that thing wearing this outfit." As she spoke she heard a car pull into the tiny lot. A green Honda Civic crunched on the gravel as Brennan's voice rose.

"For God's sake, Catherine. Tell me how to get to the hospital and I'll meet you there!"

She glanced at the car. A black woman, dressed in an efficient blue suit, was getting out. It must be the police officer, she realized. She knew she'd forgotten something.

Quickly, Catherine gave Brennan directions. He took off with a roar and belch of exhaust.

The woman was standing by her car, arms folded. Catherine walked toward her, unnerved at the sight of her own dual reflection in the woman's mirrored sunglasses. She held out her hand. "Hi. I'm Catherine Grand."

"Susan Nelson, L.A.P.D." The woman extended her hand with the requisite firm shake. "Who was that hunk?"

Catherine smiled, instantly nervous. Revealing Brennan Richards's identity to a woman investigating the attempted murder of the actor who was impersonating him seemed sure to cause problems. She was glad the woman hadn't recognized him. "A friend. Come on in out of this heat, Susan, so we can talk." Catherine walked toward the door. It stuck as she pushed it.

"The humidity," Catherine offered, putting her shoulder against the door, which still refused to budge.

"Can I help?" the policewoman responded.

"No, thanks. I think I've got—" But at that exact moment the door blasted open, knocking Catherine and the policewoman off their feet and onto the sharp, unwelcome bed of gravel in the parking lot. The explosion filled the air and blew debris from the small office, raining ash, plaster and wood chips on top of them.

Catherine lay stunned for a few seconds, aware of the pain in a thousand points of her body. She thought for an instant of Brennan and her parents, was aware of feelings of longing and guilt, then succumbed to a thick, black hole of unconsciousness that sucked away all reality.

Chapter Seven

Brennan watched idly from the window in Liam Mc-Kinney's hospital room, waiting for his lawyer and best friend to stop arguing with the woman on the phone. An ambulance, followed by a green-and-white Pasadena police car, rushed into the parking lot next to the emergency room.

Faintly he could hear the blare of the siren. For an instant Brennan was transported back in time. He was a boy in Ireland, full of fear and speculation over whose brother, father or mother was the latest victim of a war that was fought in the shadows.

He turned away quickly, unwilling to let the pain he'd experienced so long ago touch him. Whatever tragedy was being visited on the emergency room doctors three floors below had nothing to do with him, Brennan told himself. But the bald-headed man with the bandaged hands certainly did. Liam looked older by ten than his fifty years.

"Let me talk to Ellen," Brennan offered, walking closer to the bed.

Liam rolled his eyes and covered the phone receiver with a gauze-wrapped palm. "Damn her stubborn hide. She says she's flying in. Leaving the kids with Marta. Should I tell her it's not safe?"

The two men's glances locked, neither willing to admit that possibility aloud. "Let me talk to her," Brennan repeated softly. He took the phone from Liam and put a smile into his voice. "Hello, sister dear. How is my favorite girl?"

Across the many miles from Minnesota his sister's voice came clear and brogue-tinged. "Don't you be pulling that sweet and innocent act with me, Brennan Sean Richards. I'll be having none of it." Her no-nonsense tone changed quickly. "Tell me how he is, honestly."

He heard her fear, and her anger seemed like the impotent rage of ten years before. A madman had widowed her then, and orphaned her children only to melt away like a shadow at midnight. "Liam is fine, darlin'. He could use some of your cabbage and leek soup, and a slab of cobbler, but he's fine. His hands were burned, but he has no concussion or broken bones."

"Was it a mistake, then? Nothing really to do with us?"

Brennan opened his mouth to assuage her worries, but closed it again. He'd never been able to lie to Ellen. She'd been his mom, father and whole family since he was a boy. Truth was the glue that kept their small family together. "It looks like it was meant for me. It was a package bomb, sophisticated according to the coppers. But not one meant to kill. Only to warn."

"What kind of person would do such a thing," Ellen wailed. "I thought we'd left this behind us, Brennan, back in Ireland, where there's no reasoning with the hoodlums. But this, in America? How can this be happening here?" His sister's accent got thicker as her anguish increased.

"Calm yourself, Ellen. It's going to be okay. The police are looking into it. I'm sure they'll find out what's going on."

"You've got more faith in them than I do, then." Ellen startled them both with her bitterness. "I'm hanging up now. I've lots to do for the children. Pick me up at the airport at four-thirty tomorrow afternoon. Flight 918. And tell Liam McKinney to do nothing but what the doctors will be ordering. That stubborn mule."

Before he could argue any more, the phone went dead. Brennan smiled and shook his head at Liam. "You're in for it now, mate. She'll be here tomorrow."

Liam closed his eyes and seemed to relax. "But what about the children? What if—"

"I'll call the security people who patrol the farm. Make them aware. The kids will be fine." Even though his words sounded sincere, he felt a sick tug of fear in his stomach.

Liam's eyelids opened tiredly. "Snipers! A bomb! More letters! What's going on here, Brennan?"

"I don't know." He sat heavily in the chair, wondering why Catherine Grand had not shown up yet. It was thirty minutes after six, and he thought she would be right behind him. "The Grand woman thinks there's some connection to the anonymous letters and the shooting of that actor last night."

"You're convinced she's not involved?"

"As convinced as I can reasonably be. She was truly scared that someone broke into her house. And her letter was the same as mine. She'd be a fool to try to pull it off for publicity's sake."

"The police should be told. Everything," Liam said faintly, struggling against shock-induced fatigue.

"No! You know what the press will do with the news that an ex-rock star is getting letters from some crazy. There'll be no peace. The kids will be exposed to those vultures, and we'll have to fight all over again to lead a normal life."

Liam's eyes closed. "Don't be fooling yourself on how normal it is now, Brennan. Hired guards, an uncle who lives under an assumed name and works under an alias, and now this."

Swallowing an argument, Brennan took stock of his feelings. He was stung that Liam felt his niece and nephew didn't have an ideal life, though he knew his attorney spoke the truth. Brennan had moved heaven and earth to provide a safe, normal childhood for fourteen-year-old Neal and twelve-year-old Rose, but things were obviously lacking. He was a loving, doting elder, but still only a surrogate for their dead father. "Get some rest, Liam. I'll go down to the emergency room and complete some of your paperwork. Where are your health cards?"

Liam waved at the table beside the bed, and Brennan collected his friend's wallet. Suddenly the man's hand was on his arm. "Who do you think's behind this, Brennan?"

"I don't know. I thought ten years ago it might be Jane Scarlett."

"That foolish little addict? But why? You mean she'd kill because you fired her ten years ago?"

"I don't know. If not her, then maybe George Jesse? After all, it was a man who shot—" Brennan stopped before he'd said his brother-in-law's name, not wanting to feel the pain again and not wanting to remind Liam of Ellen's pain.

"It *was* a young man who shot Mitch, my boy. That policeman was sure of the description. Young, dark-haired, wild-eyed. That description never fit George Jesse. I think you may be looking for connections where there are none."

"But the letters, Liam. They prove a connection."

"They prove nothing. Every person who has ever seen a show about the cops and the kidnappers, or read about sending anonymous threats, would know how to send one, Brennan. Like I said, the letters prove nothing. You got the latest one because there's some publicity reminding the public of your existence. The only thing it proves is how sick some fans can be."

And sick fans can murder people, as John Lennon's case proved, Brennan thought morbidly. "Rest, Liam. I'm going to take care of some things."

Brennan made a silent journey downward in a huge steel elevator, struggling with a turmoil of thoughts and dim memories. Ten years of his life, a jumble of impressions and feelings, his small triumphs and his tentative start toward new goals, now seemed unreal. He *had* fooled himself, Brennan realized with a shock. He had thought the past was behind him, that with his money and the power it brought he could make his family safe.

But the past was not gone. The specter of it now haunted his future and the futures of those he held most dear. The truth taunted him.

The mechanical groan of the elevator doors opening brought Brennan back to the present. He stepped out to find the emergency room crowded with uniformed police. Two stood with a disheveled young black woman, her left cheek bleeding and her blouse torn, while three others surrounded a bed in the hallway.

Clenching his teeth, he unconsciously squared his shoulders. Perhaps it was time to take on the law-enforcement bureaucracy. If he was forceful, they surely could be convinced there was a madman on the prowl. "Officer, I would like a word with you," Brennan barked at the blue-clad backs of the two policemen nearest the emergency desk.

Both men turned, and Brennan heard the injured woman gasp. The older officer, a beefy-faced veteran with jangling keys and a scuffed gun holster, answered curtly. "Hang on, buddy. We're busy."

"That man was there!" the woman said, her black eyes wide with alarm. "He left right before the bomb exploded."

Confusion spread through Brennan's mind. He looked at the woman without recognition. "Who are you?"

"Hold it right there, buddy," the burly cop suddenly ordered. A hand clamped around Brennan's arm. His younger associate had his nightstick out, and they quickly flanked Brennan.

Brennan glared at the older officer. "What's going on here?"

"Come on with us."

"Wait a bloody minute," Brennan replied. He wanted to shake the man off, but the police officer stood his ground. "Were you at the hotel when the bomb went off?" Brennan asked the black woman.

She looked confused. "Hotel? I saw you leaving Grand Illusions on a motorcycle. Right?"

His anger died as a new dread flooded through him. Before Brennan could reply, a nightstick was wedged in the small of his back. A third officer barked into his ear. "We got a problem here?"

"No problem," the older, beefy man responded. "How's the Grand woman?" He motioned toward a gurney that was parked a few feet away.

"She's still out."

Brennan wrenched away from one officer and spun on his heel. "Catherine Grand? What has happened?"

"You know Miss Grand, buddy?" the older officer asked, squeezing Brennan's arm tighter.

"I do. What's happened to her?"

"You saw this guy at the bomb site?" someone asked the black woman.

"Yes. He left right before it went off."

With a tremendous shove, Brennan pushed away from the men and started toward the figure lying on the stretcher. The mass of dark hair was now frighteningly familiar. Before he took two steps he was knocked to the floor from behind and handcuffed. He felt someone's hot breath on his neck and knew that these officers were in no mood to talk.

One man began reciting his rights. Brennan watched numbly as two green-clad interns pushed Catherine Grand through some double doors and out of sight.

CATHERINE FLINCHED as her sister grabbed for the ringing phone beside the hospital bed. "Hello?" Cheryl raised her eyebrows as she listened, then mouthed the word "Karen" at Catherine.

"Let me talk to her," Catherine replied. She took the phone, careful not to hit the metal splint on her left hand. A few minutes before, she had clumsily bashed her injured pinky against the sink while brushing her teeth. It still throbbed. "Hi, Karen. Get a pencil. I need you to do several things."

"Catherine? Are you okay? I couldn't believe it when I saw our office on the news this morning. Then two policemen showed up at my house this morning at eight. What's going on?"

"I don't know, Karen. The damage looks worse than it is, according to the landlord, but we won't be able to get back in there for at least two weeks.

"Who sent the bomb?"

Catherine sighed. Her secretary's attention span was shorter than usual. "No one knows. UPS had no record of delivering the box so—"

"I told the police that the UPS guy didn't bring it," Karen interrupted, her annoyed voice rising. "It was on the steps first thing yesterday morning."

"Well, don't worry about it now. What I want you to do is call Mr. Palmieri, the printer, and have him run off fifty copies of all our business forms, as well as our letterhead and envelopes. My dad had the phone company transfer the main business line to my home phone, and Monday they're coming out to put in two more extensions. Can you be at my place by nine o'clock?"

"We're going to run Grand Illusions from your apartment?"

"Yes."

"But I thought you would never..."

Catherine frowned. Karen's voice had disappeared into a muffled mumble on the other end of the phone. "You thought I would never what, Karen?"

"Nothing." A false brightness lit Karen's words. "But how are we going to work at your house?"

"I have a word processor. We'll haul the files up, and with the phone we'll be set. Look, Karen, I know this bomb thing is shocking, but we've got a business to run. The Faire concert is just around the corner, and we've got ten other assignments before then."

"But you're hurt! The newspaper said—"

"I'm fine," Catherine interrupted, trying to ignore the ache in her finger and the throb in her head. "The only thing that's weak right now is my memory for next week. Can you give me a quick overview of what's on tap?"

"We've got the beer people Monday. And your interview with *People* magazine starts Friday. Are you going to be able to go up in the balloon?"

The beer people! Catherine had let Niagra Brew's kick-off of Niagra Light slip her mind. They were launching a promotional giveaway at the Rose Bowl game on Saturday, and she and Mickey were scheduled to do publicity shots on Monday's practice ride.

"Don't worry, that's fine. But that's one other call you can make. Get ahold of Mickey and see how things are going out in Agoura. Explain why I didn't get over to see him last night and have him give the go-ahead for the cable repairs. Remind him about the balloon shoot Monday."

"Okay. I'll stop at his studio tonight."

Karen was being unusually cooperative, Catherine thought. Maybe she was one of those types who were flaky until the chips were down. "Thanks. I'll see you Monday."

"Right. But I've got an audition Monday at nine o'clock. I'll be at your house by eleven."

So much for the chips. "Fine. Come prepared to stay late." Catherine gave Karen a few more directions, then hung up wearily. She had no concussion from the blast, but every muscle in her body complained when she tried to do anything more strenuous than yawn.

Her sister's frown had grown larger the longer Catherine's conversation with Karen continued, and the young girl's voice now sounded exactly like their mother's. "Mom wants you to come home and let her take care of you."

Catherine closed her eyes. "I know. She and Dad were here until all hours last night. I told her I have too much to do."

"Can I help?" Cheryl asked.

"You have." Catherine opened her eyes and tried to smile at her sister, but her face felt numb and puffy and stiff. "Did you get the newspapers?"

Cheryl nodded and laid a stack of them on the hospital tray table that jutted across Catherine's bed. Cheryl helped herself to one of the sections. "It's a circus. This Brennan Richards guy was once some big deal, huh?"

Catherine was skimming the front page of the Los Angeles *Times* article. "Ten Grammies, four platinum albums. Yes, he was a big deal."

"Well, he's not bad-looking for an old guy, either." Cheryl grinned. "He got headlines in all the local papers. I wonder how he got out of jail so fast? The *Valley News* says he was out by midnight."

"Money. It buys quick justice." Her retort sounded cynical to her own ears. "He shouldn't have been in jail in the first place," she amended. Then she groaned as she read the captions in the second paper. "'Rock Star's Room Bombed,' 'Look-alike Actor Nearly Murdered in Concert'! God, they're connecting the two incidents." Somehow the paper had found a picture of Johnnie Lord. Both Johnnie's and Brennan's faces stared off the newsprint at her.

"I know. I went down like you asked and visited Johnnie Lord a little while ago. He was talking to someone from *Entertainment Tonight* about doing a live interview from the Faire."

"Wonderful." Catherine's mind recoiled from the thought of how happy this latest bout of violence should make Sydney Carr. "Did Brennan call again?" She heard the strain in her voice, and her pulse beat strongly when she thought of how he'd acted last night when he'd phoned. Her father had taken the call and wasn't going to let her talk to him. She had insisted and was shocked at the intensity of the ex-rock star's concern. His voice was worried. Caring. Guilty. She wondered, not for the first time, if he had more to feel guilty about than he was admitting, but she pushed the dark thought away.

"Twice." Cheryl grinned. "He sounds hunky on the phone. And real sweet. He said to tell you he would be by this afternoon."

"He's not coming here," Catherine gasped.

"He said he was. What's wrong?"

"There are networks, radio stations and other newspeople camped out in front, according to the floor nurse. If he comes here it will be a mob scene."

Cheryl smiled, young enough to like the idea. "This is great. Johnnie Lord is one floor down. You and Brennan's attorney are on this floor. It's like *General Hospital.*"

"Right. And the leading actors are being pursued by snipers and bombers," Catherine retorted. "Let's hope the police are as interested in our little soap opera as the fans."

"I'm sorry I said that. Are you scared, Cath?" Cheryl came closer to the bed and touched her big sister's shoulder. "I am. Why would someone send you a bomb, anyway?"

"That's the sixty-four-thousand-dollar question, isn't it, miss?"

The question boomed across the room from the doorway. A man who looked to be in his mid-fifties held the door open with a splayed hand, his quick, small eyes perusing the room with a professional air. "Miss Grand, I presume?"

Catherine struggled to a sitting position. "Who are you?"

"Charles Gutierrez, L.A.P.D." The man flipped out a worn brown leather badge case and flashed it at the two women. "May I have a few minutes of your time, Miss Grand?"

"My sister is resting." Cheryl stood straighter, her voice protective. "If you would leave now and—"

"It's okay, Cheryl." Catherine motioned for Gutierrez to come into the room. "What is it you'd like to see me about?"

"I would like to ask you a few questions about Brennan Richards, Miss Grand." The policeman closed the door quietly and moved to the end of the bed.

"I don't know what more I can tell you people."

Gutierrez's face was impassive, but his eyes remained intent. "Do you know where he's staying?"

A small chill made Catherine cross her arms over her robed chest. She had no intention of telling this Gutierrez that information. The protective feelings that stirred inside her were unnerving. "I'm surprised your people didn't get that information when they arrested him yesterday."

"They did. He said he was staying at the Sheraton. But he's checked out."

Catherine felt her face twitch. "Does that surprise you? With all the publicity, he could hardly stay in a hotel."

"I assume he's rented a house. Do you know where it is?"

"No." The lie sounded like what it was. Nervously she added, "I mean, I don't know exactly. He said he had taken a place at the beach. In Malibu. Somewhere." Knowing where Brennan was apparently wasn't going to be easy, Catherine realized.

Gutierrez's smooth face tightened. "And when did he say that? This morning?" He turned to Cheryl. "Has he been here this morning already?"

"He's coming later." Cheryl blurted out the information then looked nervously at Catherine.

"Is there anything else, officer?" Catherine asked.

The policeman advanced another step and folded his thin arms. "How well do you know Richards?"

"She doesn't know him at all," Cheryl interrupted.

"Let's let Miss Grand answer that." Gutierrez stepped closer. "How well do you know him?"

"Hardly at all," Catherine replied. She yawned and pointed toward her injured hand. "I really am going to have to ask you to leave."

"Let me show the way," Cheryl added, then walked purposefully across the room, nearly brushing the cop's arm as she passed. She opened the door. "I'm leaving, too, so my sister can rest."

Gutierrez kept his gaze on Catherine. "Are you dating him?"

"No!"

"Who do you think sent the bomb to you?"

"I have no idea, which is what I told you all last night."

"Why did they send it? Trying to get you to cancel the concert? Or trying to get more publicity for it?"

Catherine inhaled deeply, catching his implication. "It's a mystery to me. Now if you'll excuse me, I really do need a nap."

Gutierrez sounded angry. "Brennan Richards is a marked man, Miss Grand. I would stay clear of him if I were you."

"Mr. Gutierrez!" Cheryl bellowed. "It's time you left."

Gutierrez and Catherine locked glances. She felt her cheeks flush. "If he's a marked man, I guess it's your job to protect him. Not harass me."

"Do you know where George Jesse is?"

Catherine opened her mouth in surprise, then closed it with a click of teeth. "I have no idea. Goodbye, officer," she replied coolly.

Gutierrez took yet another step closer. "Stay out of this, Miss Grand. Brennan Richards isn't as innocent as he appears to be." Before Catherine could respond, Gutierrez inclined his head, which was full of thick, graying curls, and turned away. He hurried toward the door. Cheryl grimaced and followed, mouthing, "I'll be right back."

With a swish of air, the door closed. Catherine closed her eyes and tried to relax, Gutierrez's words echoing in her mind. Before she could sort through any of them, the door opened again. She turned toward it nervously. A tall man with a beard, wearing a deliveryman's shirt that read

"Fauna's Flora," sauntered into the room. He carried two enormous vases that held tiger lilies and white roses.

"Delivery for Miss Grand." He set one vase on the rolling meal table by the door and walked toward Catherine. "Where do you want these?"

"Please put them next to the bed. They're gorgeous! Is there a card?"

"No card. But the man who ordered them said to include a singing telegram for Miss Grand."

"Oh?" Something about the man was very familiar, but she couldn't quite place him. "What song?"

The man grinned, white teeth glinting. "Whatever you like. I've a bit of a repertoire."

At that moment she noticed the blue eyes and earring. "Oh? That's great. How about Tone Loc's 'Wild Thing'?"

The man drew his hand up to his chest in mock surprise. "You like rap music?"

"I like a variety of music. But if that's too hard, how about some Beatles?"

"Great. Boys close to my own heart." He sat down on the edge of Catherine's bed and winked. "Which tune?"

At that moment Catherine relaxed, sure now of her visitor's identity and enjoying the easy banter. "'Yellow Submarine'?"

"Nah, too whimsical. You need something more restful. How about 'Norwegian Wood'?"

"Too sad."

"How so?"

"The singer wakes up in the morning and the girl is gone."

The man frowned and scratched his beard. "That is sad. Ditto 'Hey Jude'."

"How about 'Michelle'? I'm a big fan of a good ballad."

"Are you now? Well, you're a smart girl."

"Thank you." Catherine nodded at the uniformed florist and read the name from his shirt. "José, is it? Please sing 'Michelle' for me, José."

"Certainly, madame." The man stood and faced the window then turned to her and folded his arms. The melancholy first line of the song came out of his mouth, rich and evocative. The words flowed in a mellow, lyric stream from the singer, filling the room with the passion and anxiety of new love.

Catherine was stunned by the beauty of the man's voice. It was richer than she remembered, colored by life now in a way it had not been when he was younger. She closed her eyes to put some distance between her emotions and the man staring openly at her, but that made the song even more intimately invasive. The voice, husky and demanding, prodded her to share Brennan's vision of the song.

When he finished, she opened her eyes. "That was beautiful. Very beautiful. Thank you."

"I'm glad it was to your liking."

"It was perfect, Mr. Richards."

Brennan grinned. A second later he tugged at his beard. Half of it came off in his hand. "Can't fool you, eh? Thought maybe you'd think I was a Brennan Richards lookalike."

She bristled. No matter how lovely the song, Catherine recognized the old animosity in Brennan's voice. "I've always been able to distinguish between the fakes and authentic versions."

He had the decency to look uncomfortable. "I'm sure that's an important asset in your profession." The joking, easy manner of seconds before evaporated. The two of them stared at each other. Brennan pulled off the other half of the beard and peeled a bushy mustache away. "Are you really all right, then?" he finally said.

Catherine tapped her forehead lightly. "Knock on wood." She swallowed and tried to quell the nervousness she felt. "How is Mr. McKinney?"

"Good. I'm taking him to the house I've told you about for a bit of rest. Hotel living is out now. My sister's coming into town, too, so the house will be—" Brennan stopped himself, unwilling to say easier to protect "—more convenient."

"Is she bringing her children?"

"No."

"I've been worried about them, since the bomb..."

"Thank you for that, Cath. But there's no need to worry." His warm hand caressed her arm, and the intensity of his gaze held her eyes. "I've hired more people, alerted the locals. Thanks to your help, I think I've covered all my bases."

Catherine moved her legs out from under the covers and put on her slippers. Lying prone was no way to receive a visitor. She stood, pulling her robe closer, and winced with the effort. "We can go see Sydney Carr tomorrow. Early. He's leaving for London at five."

"You talked with him?"

"His secretary called to find out if I was okay."

"Does he know I'm coming, too?"

"No." Catherine managed a weak grin. "It seemed like a good idea to surprise him, as we'd agreed."

Brennan moved one of the visitor's chairs close to Catherine, and she slumped into it. Despite the ordeal she had been through, she looked good. Very good, he found himself thinking. Then he felt an enormous rush of guilt. Was it because of some pyscho's vendetta against him that

Catherine Grand was in the hospital? he asked himself. "That was nice of Carr," he said.

"I'm sure he was only worried about the concert," Catherine said curtly. "When I suggested to his secretary that it might be a good idea if Mr. Carr postponed the concert, she laughed. I doubt we're going to be able to change his mind, Brennan."

"Well, then, can I change yours?"

"Sorry, no. Johnnie Lord is delighted by all the publicity. He was up and about and talking with the press this morning."

Brennan's blue eyes glinted. "Maybe I should drop in and sing him a tune."

"He wouldn't recognize you." Catherine suddenly felt tired.

"He's made it clear he's going on with the concert. I might as well tell you now.

"He's a fool."

She shrugged, agreeing with him but feeling too tired to say it aloud. "Where did you get that disguise, anyway?"

"I've got lots of them. Used to be a rock star, you know? We objects of love have to be pretty cagey if we want to go about without a squad of bodyguards."

"Well, you're still quite a star, if the publicity is any indication." She glanced at the papers. "What are we going to do about the police now, Brennan? I think I should tell them everything." She swallowed hard. "I think you should talk to them, too."

He didn't want to encourage her by telling her he had nearly done that yesterday. "I disagree, Catherine. I think it's more important than ever that we lay low and wait for the guy ourselves. These bombs change things, but not much. Someone's out to get us, and we'll have a better go at him if we work behind the scenes. Let the coppers look for a bomb sender and a sniper. You've told them about your letter. We've got to concentrate on the letter writer."

"It would appear to me that they are one and the same person."

"Probably. But you never know. Maybe you have an enemy, too, one unconnected with me?"

Catherine had wondered the same thing a hundred times. The falsified invoices pointed to a more personal grudge against her, but her intuition told her that her woes could be laid to rest at the feet of the man standing beside her. "I may have."

"Care to tell me about them?"

"Not right now."

"Okay, then." He stood up and slapped his thighs, full of nervous energy. "When can I take you out of here? Now?"

Catherine looked shocked. "Take me out? I'm going home, but my folks are coming later to take me."

"No, you're not. Since you're sure I'm the cause of this mess you've gotten involved in, I think it would be better if we're under the same roof for a while. We can work out our strategy much better. I've got security men hired. And a flower truck outside. You put on your disguise, I'll reglue my whiskers, and the press boys won't know what hit them."

"My disguise? I don't think—"

"Exactly. Don't think, just get dressed. I'll be right back."

"Now wait a minute. I can't just run off—"

"Yes, you can," he argued, his voice hard. "And I really think you'd better. It's not safe out there, Cath."

She gulped, remembering the warning Gutierrez had given her. If she wasn't safe, was it smart to go off and hide with a marked man? she wondered. A man who might not be as innocent as he seemed? "The police said—"

"I'll take care of you better than they can." He put his hand on her face, and his voice softened. "Just for a couple of days. Besides, you can iron things out with Liam about the lawsuit, meet my sis and rest. I've made some contacts and got a lead on Jane Scarlett, so we can work on that together. Now get dressed."

She watched silently as the broad-shouldered Irishman headed for the door. Though unused to being ordered around, Catherine found she wasn't offended by his proprietary tone. *Why not go with him? And get to know him better?* a little voice in her head whispered. Answers to those two questions seemed best avoided until she felt stronger. Catherine slipped off her robe and began dressing with an eye to using Brennan's disguise.

When Cheryl returned, Catherine was humming. Against all her sister's protests, Catherine gathered her things and promised to call, reminding her sister that, despite her advanced age, she still had some adventure left in her after all.

Chapter Eight

Catherine chuckled as the delivery van whizzed down Pasadena Avenue, past the throng of reporters and sound technicians hovering in front of the hospital. Brennan had been right. Because of their disguises, he had managed to wheel her by the media without anyone giving them more than a bored look.

Liam McKinney was ensconced in the rear compartment of the van, wrapped in blankets and napping from the effects of his ordeal. Even though the attorney seemed to be sleeping, his presence made Catherine feel self-conscious. She put down the blanket-wrapped baby doll she had been clutching. "Good job, Brennan. Ever think of becoming a spy?"

"Nothing to that." He grinned. "I learned a long time ago that people see only what they expect to see. The news hounds weren't looking for a new mum. Only an attractive bomb victim."

She nodded agreement. "Was that my description on the news?"

He winked. "I would have said very attractive."

Catherine liked his compliment even though it made her feel foolish. She looked outside and searched for a new topic. "Where did you get this truck?"

"Bought it. Money talks in the U.S. of A. like nowhere else I've ever seen. The florist was looking me over suspiciously until I flashed cash at him. In a fast minute he signed over his ownership to one Liam McKinney."

"Before you became a florist, you were impersonating your attorney?"

"Yeah, I guess I was and still am. Want to hire me?"

She ignored the dig. "Don't you think the florist will figure out who you were?"

"Nah. Like we just proved, the odd detail escapes everyone's attention. Too much telly watching has made the public numb."

Catherine pulled off a fluffy blond wig and shook her head. "That's an interesting theory." Craning her neck to peek through the cab window into the air-conditioned back compartment, she winced in pain. Though only her finger had been broken, the rest of her body felt sprained. Liam McKinney was lying still, but his eyes were open. "He looks pretty good. No broken bones?"

"Not a one. His hands were burned a bit but there's no permanent damage. Liam's a tough old bird. Just needs some rest and my sister's cooking and he'll be good as new."

"He and your sister are an item?"

"Not so anyone can get them to admit it, but they are. From the time my brother-in-law was killed, Liam took every possible opportunity to shield Ellen from publicity—the lawyers, press, everyone. He even got into a scuffle with some fans once. Knocked a bloke on his bum who was trying to snap pictures of the kids. When he bought a summer place and started spending half his time in the U.S. and half at home, it seemed clear to me that they were going to get married. But so far they haven't."

"You all seem very close."

"We are." Brennan reflected on his easy admission of that. Something about Catherine Grand made it easy to admit things about himself, even those things he generally felt self-conscious about. "He's a good man, Ellen always says. Loyal as the day is long."

"Did it ever bother you to be approached by your fans on the street?"

"Nah. I expected it, even welcomed it when it happened. Surprisingly, most folks didn't recognize me without my patch."

Catherine pictured him with the black satin patch, sure she could now pick him out anywhere, even in a crowd. "Is that the reason you made it part of your performing costume?"

Brennan was quiet a long moment. "No. That wasn't the reason for the patch," he finally said. Then he changed the subject. "You held that baby doll very convincingly, by the way. Ever plan to have kids?"

"No immediate thoughts that way." Catherine wondered why he had sidestepped her query. "How about you?"

He made a wry face. "Have you ever been married?"

"You're good at answering questions with questions," Catherine replied. "Is evasion another skill rock stardom taught you?"

Brennan surprised her by laughing. She realized that she'd never really heard him laugh. The sound was rich, dense and full of music and spirit. "Touché. Okay, I'll answer your questions. I chose to wear the eye patch to make a political statement. My folks were innocent bystanders, killed by an errant bomb in Ireland. When I started to get very big, I thought the patch could be a symbol of protest."

"I see. Well, it brought a lot of comments from the press."

"Only about how sexy it made me look." Brennan shook his head. "Mine was the typically naive, half-baked idea of a young person. I had good intentions, but none of it turned out like I intended."

Catherine remained silent, registering the grief in his melodic voice.

"As to whether or not I want children," Brennan continued, "the answer is yes. *More* children. I regard my niece and nephew as my own kids, and someday, when they're grown, if I'm not too decrepit, I'd like a baby of my own. I do hope to marry, too. But it's hard to know who'd want an old rock and roller like me." Brennan grinned and stopped with a squeal of tires.

"I can't believe you have any problem attracting women," Catherine said.

"No? Do I attract you?"

"Me?" she sputtered, caught off guard as the van sped up and merged into the snaky flow of traffic on the Pasadena freeway.

"Ah, no fair answering a question with a question." Brennan laughed again, obviously enjoying her embarrassment.

"I'd say you're off limits."

"Off limits? Why's that?"

Because you are rich, famous and too handsome to trust, she thought in irritation. "I don't get involved with industry people," Catherine said lamely.

"I'm not in your industry," Brennan said. "I'm a real person, remember? The authentic thing."

Stung but refusing to take the bait, she crossed her arms over her chest. "Let's just say you're not the right type."

"I see." Brennan didn't sound the least bit hurt. "You've really got yourself hung up on this right way and wrong way to live, haven't you?"

"I have certain standards, yes."

He chuckled, glad to see he'd ruffled her composure a bit. "You've also quite a wicked tongue, Catherine Grand. Are you part Irish?"

"I have no idea. I'm adopted." She immediately flushed at her flip reply. It wasn't one she had made before in her life. Before the recent revelation that she wasn't blood relations with her family, she would have rattled off her parents' lineage in characteristic American fashion. "Half Irish, half Scottish on Mom's side, all very proper British on Dad's side of the family" was what she'd said a million times growing up. And it had been a lie.

"I see." Brennan's voice was soft.

"No, you don't."

"Then why don't you explain it? Sounds like it's bothering you some."

He was right. "I'd rather not go into it."

"Odd thing to be sensitive about."

"You know nothing about it!"

At her harsh rejoinder, Brennan cleared his throat. She was right. He didn't know much about her. Certainly not as much as he would like to. But if he was going to learn more, it wouldn't be by bludgeoning her with questions. Catherine Grand made that clear. She answered them only when she was ready to. "I'm sorry I said that, Cath. You're right. But if you'd like to talk, I'd like to listen."

"Thanks. But I don't want to talk." Catherine hugged her arms tighter to herself and closed her eyes. For a moment she remembered the shock, and it felt fresh and new. When Cheryl had needed blood after surgery, and when the blood bank informed her that hers didn't match that of the members of her family, her parents were forced to admit she was adopted. It was simple, yet complex.

It took her a week to feel angry, but once she did, Catherine had been unable to forgive them for their deception. Logically she understood the reasons they had lied, but emotionally she was unable to shake the sense that they felt something was wrong with being adopted, and consequently that something was wrong with her.

Catherine closed her eyes tighter and tried to think of something else. It was over an hour's drive to their destination in Malibu. It would be best spent avoiding idle chit-chat with Brennan Richards. Suddenly, she wasn't in the mood to share this neurosis about herself. Besides, Catherine told herself, Brennan Richards *wasn't* her type.

He cleared his throat as if he'd read her thoughts. "I'm trying to get a line on Jane Scarlett. And I spoke with George Jesse, or tried to, I mean."

Grudgingly she opened her eyes. "What happened?"

"He's missing."

Catherine sat up, remembering Officer Gutierrez and his intense questions. "Missing? Really missing?"

"Well, no one at his club has seen him. Or admits to it."

"For how long?"

"I called around yesterday trying to get a fix on him, but no one had seen him since Thursday night's shooting. Coppers are looking for him, too, it seems."

"I know. Did Gutierrez talk to you, too?"

Brennan hit the brakes, and Catherine was nearly thrown against the windshield. The baby doll flew off the seat and crashed onto the floor. "Who did you say?" Brennan demanded.

"Gutierrez. Charles Gutierrez, an L.A.P.D. cop I understand you know. Take it easy, Brennan," Catherine scolded, rubbing a sore spot on her elbow.

"Put your seat belt on, then tell me how you know Charles Gutierrez," Brennan ordered.

"He was in my room not ten minutes before you came."
She struggled with the seat belt, finally clasping the two ends
together and leaning back. She had no idea why Brennan
was so worked up over the mention of Gutierrez's name.

"That's impossible," he said quietly. "Describe him."

"What?"

"Catherine!"

She swallowed, panicking because she and Cheryl had
been alone with someone who raised such a negative reaction in Brennan. "Well, mid-fifties, with gray, curly hair, a
long face and small eyes."

Brennan swore and shook his head. "This is nuts!"

"Why?"

"Gutierrez is dead. He was the cop who investigated the
murder of my brother-in-law. He was killed on the job a
couple of years ago."

Catherine sat back as if he'd struck her. "There's got to
be some mistake."

"I went to his funeral. Sent flowers. Kissed the widow.
There's no mistake. On my part."

Catherine tasted fear and tried unsuccessfully to swallow
again. She wished she was still in the hospital and could ring
for some drugs to block out all the assorted pain and fatigue she felt. "But that's absurd. The name must be a coincidence. Two cops must have the same one. In Los
Angeles, there are probably several—"

"Or maybe you're not the only person in L.A. hiring im-
posters," Brennan rejoined forcefully.

Catherine's growing sense of unease increased. "He did
ask where you were staying, Brennan," she replied with a
tremble. She felt cold in spite of the late summer heat pour-
ing through the wide windshield.

"What did you tell him?"

"That I didn't know the address, but that you had rented a place at the beach." She finally navigated around the lump in her throat and swallowed, trying to recall the conversation. "I might have said in Malibu."

"What? I told you not to tell anyone—"

"I forgot! I'm sorry. Besides, I'm sure he's a legitimate officer. He gave me a number to call."

"Call it." Brennan's brusque command was accompanied by a narrow-eyed nod toward the cellular phone that sat in an aluminum case at her feet.

Catherine fumbled in her pocket for the scrap of paper Gutierrez had given her, then reached for the car phone. Gingerly, careful not to hit her splinted pinky, she dialed the number.

Six rings, then a click. "Hello?" It was an elderly female voice.

Catherine's spirits sank another notch. "Hello. I'm looking for Charles Gutierrez. He's a policeman with L.A.P.D. Is this his home?"

"Who?" the woman snapped. "What number did you call?"

Catherine repeated the number slowly, praying she had misdialed. After a moment she hung up, staring at the traffic ahead. She felt Brennan's eyes on her, then flushed as he made a noise halfway between a growl and a moan.

"Great. Just great!" Angrily he swerved into another lane and swore under his breath as a car cut him off.

Catherine's voice rose a notch. "Now look. I've kept all kinds of information from the police because you asked me to, despite my better judgment, and—"

"Where was your better judgment today?" Brennan interrupted, fuming over his own lack of it. "I should have never told you any details. You had no need to know anything." He rapped his hand against the steering wheel. "Damn."

"I did, too! Or do you think I would simply check myself out of the hospital and let you carry me off?"

"I don't know you enough to tell what you'll do!"

Despite her angry tone, Catherine felt more guilty than hurt. Brennan was right. She should have used better judgment. For a moment she felt she had let him down, but she stubbornly fought against that. "How was I supposed to know the guy was a fake? If he was. Maybe he wrote down the number wrong. Sometimes I don't remember my home number right...." Her voice trailed off miserably.

"I don't doubt that in the least." Brennan gunned the van, his body language grim. But his anger was directed more toward himself than her. The danger he had downplayed could have easily gotten her killed if the bomber was also into assuming identities and cockily passing himself off as a cop.

Catherine sighed and huddled against the door, her sore finger throbbing. She crossed her legs and felt something bulky under her foot, then leaned down and retrieved the doll from the floor. Holding it on her lap self-consciously, she fumed about Brennan's arrogant reaction. Good grief, she thought. Would she always be on the defensive with this man?

Ten minutes later he broke the thick silence. "I'm sorry I tore into you like that, Cath. But you've got to be careful. We're dealing with a psychopath. It's not going to be safe to be as trusting as a lamb with folks."

At the sound of his voice, Catherine stiffened. "I know that."

"I know you do. I just want you to take care of yourself." He did, too. And the feeling was more than one of general goodwill, he suddenly realized.

His hand patted her leg, and the sensation was one of warmth and strength. Catherine moved her knee away from the distraction. "I'm a big girl, Brennan. I don't need a lecture from you."

He grinned, the anger evaporating from his voice. "Of course you don't, but you got it anyway. Now why don't you rest. We've still got a bit of a drive. I'm not going to worry about your phantom cop visitor. There's no way anyone can find out which place in Malibu I've rented. We'll be safe enough."

She met his glance, relieved the combativeness had fled from his demeanor and her own heart. "I'm sure we will. When is your sister getting in?"

"This afternoon. I'll get you and Liam settled then go into L.A. and meet her flight."

"Who is staying with her children?"

Brennan glanced at her quickly then turned away, but not before she saw the flash of doubt in his eyes. Suddenly she realized his chivalric offer to keep her safe and out of harm's way at his beach hideaway might merely be an attempt to keep an eye on her.

"Don't bother answering," Catherine snapped before he had time to reply. "I really don't need to know."

THE BROWN FORD PINTO kept well back of the florist's van. The Pinto's radio had broken years ago, but the driver kept up a steady stream of bebop, singing in an eardrum-shattering soprano to the old Frankie Valli song "Sherri," which wailed away on the portable cassette recorder in the back seat.

The recorder, an ancient, bulky General Electric model sold in Great Britain in the late 1960s, was perched in the middle of a tangled pile that held the suit, tie, shoes and wig Officer Gutierrez had worn.

The rifle used to shoot Johnnie Lord was also in the car, hidden in the trunk along with a much-worn favorite white silk suit.

The interview with Catherine Grand had gone pretty well, the driver thought while waiting for "Big Girls Don't Cry" to come on. Grand had shown no inkling she was talking with someone she knew by another name.

"My boyfriend will be proud of me over this one," the driver said. And even more proud, and willing to compensate, when Brennan Richards's exact address was found.

Gunning the stick-shift vehicle, wailing the opening lines of the old tune, the driver smirked as the florist's van took the beach off ramp and headed toward the ball of orange-red sun that baked the late summer landscape.

When the rocker got to his place, it would be easy to set up the next shot.

CATHERINE STOOD when she heard Brennan and his sister coming through the front door. She had been lolling, nearly asleep, in the lumpy upholstered chaise by the window, re-hashing the strange events of the past week but making no sense of them. The two phone calls she had made, to her mother and to Karen, had only served to make her feel more paranoid, for neither woman disguised her shock over the fact she had gone off with Brennan Richards.

When she thought it over, Catherine realized grimly, she felt a little bit shocked herself. What had seemed a good idea some hours before seemed the epitome of the ridiculous now. How much safer had she made herself by running off with the man who was surely the mad bomber's number-one target?

Just as that thought faded, Brennan bustled into the living room, his arm around a vividly smiling female version of himself. "There you are, Cath. This is my sister."

"Hi." Catherine offered her hand to the slim, dark-haired woman with the familiar sky-blue eyes. When she remembered her splint she smiled and let her arm drop to her side. "I'm Catherine Grand."

"Hello, my dear. I'm Ellen Chapin, Brennan's sister." Ellen gave Catherine a quick hug, then looked at her closely. "Brennan told me about your ordeal the past couple of days. We both appreciate the help you're giving us. How are you feeling?"

"I'm good. Tired, but good." She looked at Brennan. "Liam hasn't come downstairs. I checked on him a while ago and he was sleeping." Catherine glanced at Ellen again. "We had quite a job getting him to rest when we got here, but I promised I would wake him when you arrived."

"Fat chance we'll be doing any such foolish thing as that!" Ellen retorted, then squeezed Catherine's arm. "I'll look in on the old dear then head to the kitchen. We'll put some nourishment into all of you, then sit down and decide what to do about this nonsense."

With that, Ellen marched down the hallway without asking for any directions from Brennan. Catherine was impressed with the woman, even more so when she realized why she had looked familiar. She turned an amused look at Brennan. "The Satin Dolls. I remember hearing her album. She was once a great singer!"

Brennan let himself relax for a moment. "She'll be mortified that you recognized her. But I agree, she was a good singer."

"Why'd she give it up?" Catherine asked.

"Lots of reasons," Brennan answered tightly. "She's a bit bossy, but very kindhearted. And she's a great cook," he offered.

"I'm sure. She seems very capable."

"That she is." He crossed his arms over his broad chest and stared out the window. The house he had rented was typical of those in Malibu's chic private developments. Security guards had checked them in, and the steep and anonymous front facade had shut off any view from the street.

The long, tiled foyer opened into a high-ceilinged expanse that offered a floor-to-ceiling view of the Pacific. A deck stretched from the house across the smooth, white sand. Pots of pink azaleas, straggly by L.A. standards, hugged the perimeter of the sliding glass doors, their petals sticking to the glass in the salty air.

Suddenly Brennan felt restless. "You been out there yet?" he asked.

Catherine glanced at the turquoise-tinted water, its foamy edge spilling onto the sand. "No. But I was planning to take a walk and work off some of this stiffness. Want to join me?"

"Thanks. I will." Brennan took her arm and they went onto the deck. In both directions a few people could be seen sunbathing and swimming. It was shocking to see so much sand with so few bodies, but where they were staying was private. The hordes of teenagers and hot suburbanites who blanketed the public beaches from Zuma to Del Mar were nowhere in sight.

Catherine set a brisk pace that Brennan didn't object to. Silently they skirted the water, their shoes leaving a trail of marks. "So what do you think?" Brennan finally asked after they'd been walking for ten minutes.

"Think? You mean about the bomb?"

"The bombs. Everything. Got any ideas about why someone would do it?"

Catherine slowed and was aware her heart was racing. She was out of breath and waved Brennan to a stop. "I'd say it's obvious. Someone doesn't want your impersonator to perform. Someone, I'd say, connected to the attack ten years ago. As to who that person is, I was hoping you'd fill me in." Catherine shaded her eyes against the glare and stared at Brennan.

"I told you it was most likely a disgruntled band member. Or George Jesse."

"Do people really kill because they lose a job?"

"According to the papers, Americans kill for any number of reasons."

"Americans aren't the only ones with so little respect for lives," she retorted.

"You're right there, my girl." Brennan sat heavily on the sand and wrapped his arms around his knees. A gull screamed above him, dive-bombed toward a half-buried beer can a couple of feet away, then floated over toward a steep sand dune next to them. A breeze blew, but both of them had sweat on their foreheads. "It makes no sense to you, either, I see. The cop who died, Gutierrez, remarked ten years ago that a crime like the one that killed Ellen's husband was generally a crime of passion."

Catherine joined him on the hard-packed sand, dusting her hands off as she faced the rolling waves. "I'm no cop, but I agree. The tone of the letter I got was very intense... personal. So was the vandalism at my home. And to send a bomb! That would require nerve and..."

"And what?" Brennan asked.

"Passion is the right word, I guess. You have to put a lot of energy into those kinds of actions to pull them off." The question that had occurred to her several times could no longer be avoided. "There's no old romance in your past that would account for this?"

His brow creased with concentration, but he slowly shook his head. "Think this shows a woman's hand?"

"That's a cliché, a woman scorned and all that. But I think it does show someone who's been deeply hurt. Anyone come to mind there?"

"No. I can't imagine—" His words stopped. A small, high-pitched whistle sounded, followed by the smack of metal against metal. An object flattened the beer can in front of them.

Before Catherine knew what had happened, Brennan threw her facedown into the sand and jumped on top of her.

"What is it?" she gasped.

"Be quiet and stay down. Someone just took a shot at us."

Catherine felt a jolt of fear and clenched her teeth. Out of the corner of her eye she saw a wisp of black smoke waft over the dunes and heard the screams of two gulls who took flight into the blue sky.

Chapter Nine

For the scant seconds Catherine lay against the sand, the light faded and night seemed to fall unnaturally fast. Moments before the sun had shone against the water; now it slipped into the horizon, and the evening shadows smothered her like a blanket. Catherine felt Brennan's heart pumping blood in the same frantic tempo as hers and wondered in shock if she had been shot.

"Can you see anyone?" she whispered to Brennan, feeling him tense as she spoke.

"No. Just lie still. The sniper is probably gone, but no use giving him a better target by standing up."

As her body signaled that she was, in fact, not wounded, it occurred to Catherine that they were sitting ducks. But she didn't move. After another full minute, Brennan's weight was lifted off her, and she got on her knees. Her finger throbbed, and she tasted blood from where she had bit the inside of her mouth. Her lips were covered with sand, and she blinked to dislodge a grain from her eye. But she wasn't dead. And from the look of the hole in the sand-filled beer can, she could have been.

"We've got to go for the police," she shouted after Brennan, who was scaling the soft side of the dune.

He stopped and put his hands on his hips, his eyes dark in the dusky light. "Don't be a fool, Catherine. They'll never find him." Brennan turned and disappeared over the ridge. The soft grasses bent sideways from his tread.

Clumsily Catherine followed, holding her arm protectively against her. Down the beach she saw a young couple throwing a piece of driftwood out to sea. A huge Irish setter splashed after it. Maybe they had seen something, she thought, but dismissed the idea quickly. If they had noticed someone firing a rifle on the beach, they surely wouldn't still be here.

Catherine caught up with Brennan on the other side of the dune. They were in a small valley of deep sand. Faint footsteps led off to the right. Leaving Brennan kneeling and looking at an object that glinted in the last rays of daylight, she followed the marks and peeked over to a small paved lot that abutted the dunes. Three cars were parked there, a Volvo with tinted windows that were rolled down, a silver Corvette with Nevada plates and an old Pinto. All were empty, their drivers nowhere to be seen.

Exasperated, Catherine looked at Brennan. He was still staring at the sand. "What is it?"

Slowly he picked up the object and carried it over to her, a scowl on his face. "It's this." He held a five-inch-long bolt of some kind. The end was nicked and twisted.

"What is it?" Catherine repeated.

"I don't know for sure." Brennan answered through clenched teeth. "But I'd guess it's what killed my brother-in-law ten years ago."

"What?"

"I saw its twin during the murder investigation. These bolts held the scaffolding that fell during my last concert." Brennan's blue eyes sparked as he stared at her in the half light. His face was twisted with pain, and his voice shook. "It looks like I've been left a message."

"We've got to call the police, Brennan!"

"It's not going to do any good, Cath. I'm going to have to find this guy myself." Enraged, he threw the bolt a hundred feet into the ocean, then swore.

"Why did you do that? The police could trace it. Get fingerprints!"

"Can't you see? He's baiting me! First the kids, then Liam, now you. He's challenging me in a game of cat and mouse. The police have no place in the game."

Furious at his stubbornness, Catherine grabbed his arm. Her voice was shrill. "This isn't just about you, Brennan Richards! I appreciate your vendetta with the past, but I'm now very much involved. I've been sent threats, had my house broken into and my office bombed. One of my employees was almost killed, and now I've been shot at. So don't tell me not to call the police. They are the only ones capable of sorting this mess out."

"And if they have as much success as they did last time? Are you willing to risk the safety of my niece and nephew?"

"You're the one who's risking their safety, Brennan. Because of your pride."

Her words aroused his fury, and he stepped toward her. "It's because of your damn impersonator that this has happened." Brennan caught her roughly as she turned away and pulled her close to him. His mouth was set in a tight line of anger. "Don't judge me so harshly, Catherine, not until you've had to live night and day with the kind of guilt I have. Because of me, my brother-in-law lost his life. My sister's kids have no father. I understand you're upset, my girl. But you can't—"

"Don't tell me what I can't do. I will call the police now." She pushed violently away from him. The rush of the surf was the only sound Catherine heard as Brennan let go of her and morosely turned away.

"Do what you have to, then. *I* intend to."

She watched him walk over the side of the dune and head toward the cars parked below. There was little she could say to comfort him. Besides, her anger at his self-centered obsession with righting an old wrong kept her from really wanting to comfort him. Resolutely she headed toward the house.

The shock of the night's events made her feel weak-legged, and the truth of Brennan's words heaped frustration on top of her. He was right. If she had never taken the assignment from Sydney Carr, Brennan Richards and his family would still be living the anonymous lives they wished for.

But it was too late for regrets. What she had helped set in motion she had to take steps to stop. She hurried down the beach shivering. It was fully night now, and the stars shone weakly above. She passed a man who lay quietly on a blanket, a huge tape recorder sitting next to him on the sand. The breeze picked up, and Catherine heard a snatch of music. Her mind responded to the old lyrics forcefully as she took a swipe at the hot tears that fell.

"Big girls do, too, cry," she said, hoping the police would come before Brennan returned.

WHEN SHE OPENED the sliding door and went inside, Catherine found Ellen sitting on the sofa, two teacups and the remains of sandwiches on the glass table in front of her. The smell of roasting chicken permeated the air, and Catherine felt her stomach crumple with hunger pains.

"Hello," she offered, pushing her windblown bangs aside.

"Hello, Catherine. Can I get you some tea? Liam and I have been sitting here like a couple of fat cats relaxing." She started to stand. "I'll just go get the pot—"

"No. Please just sit. I have a couple of things I'd like to ask you. If you don't mind."

"About Brennan?" Ellen's eyes twinkled. "He seems rather smitten with you."

Catherine couldn't stop the "Humph!" from escaping. "I think he must hate me. He blames me so for the look-alike thing. The threats—"

"Don't let him." Ellen replied hotly. "Honestly, he is the most bullheaded man I've ever met sometimes. He gets on his high horse, decides he knows what's best for everyone, then forces them to go along or he pouts." Ellen picked up her teacup and sipped at the dregs. "You know, I raised that boy when our folks were killed. We're as close as a sister and brother can be. But sometimes I barely recognize him. He goes inside himself. I can't reach him."

Catherine watched helplessly while Ellen's eyes filled with tears. "He cares so much for you. And your children."

"Too much." Ellen slapped the teacup into the saucer and sighed. Her eyes sparkled with unshed tears, and a great sadness seemed to rob the youthful prettiness from her face. "The boy needs to get on with his life. Have babes of his own. I told him that the kids and I can manage without him, but he doesn't listen."

"He knows you're very strong. I think he just wants to help."

"I am strong. I've made many hard choices, Catherine." The blue eyes glinted, and a single tear slipped from the corner of one eye. "But I don't second-guess myself. I go forward. I gave up my singing career to raise Brennan. Took my children on the road so they could be with their father.

And made lots of mistakes along the way. But I forgive myself. It's something my brother needs to learn."

Catherine sat back, drained of all ability to act. She enjoyed listening to Ellen's common sense, enjoyed feeling the love the woman and Brennan shared. "Do you know, my mom's got your album. You've changed very little over the years."

"Not the Satin Dolls!"

"Yes. I can still see the cover. You're blowing a kiss and your partner is hiding behind a fedora and glasses, hands on her face. It's very campy and ahead of its time."

"Don't forget the satin dresses. What a collector's piece. Do I still really look like that naive girl on the cover?" Ellen mimed blowing a kiss and grimaced.

A tiny idea flickered in Catherine's mind as she recalled the cover. It was something about the pose, about the way Ellen and her tall, mannish-featured partner looked, and it reminded her of something she knew was important, but couldn't quite get hold of.

"Ellen. Where have you put my jacket? I need to go out and get some cigarettes." Liam McKinney strode into the room, then stopped and stared at the two women.

"You're not going out. And you're not smoking. Sit down and finish your tea."

"Ellen—"

"Sit, Liam. Or I'll make you go to bed now. Alone."

Ellen grinned, and Catherine was again struck by how much she and Brennan resembled one another. "You're looking much better, Mr. McKinney. Are you feeling that way?"

"Yes, thank you." His formal reply was followed by his pointed look behind her. "Where's Brennan?"

"He'll be in soon." Catherine thought better of mentioning the gunshot. While the lawyer did look better, he was still very wan, and she didn't want to bring on a relapse. Lord knows, Catherine thought, I'm responsible for enough already.

"I've got a chicken in, and some rolls. We'll eat soon." Ellen's announcement was followed by a big smile, but she couldn't disguise the look of concern about her friend's health.

"Good. I'm famished." Catherine sat on the edge of the white linen chair opposite the couple. "Is there somewhere I can use the phone? I need to call my secretary again."

Liam sat beside Ellen, and the two exchanged a quick glance. "In the guest room next to you there's another phone," Ellen said.

"You know not to give out the exact address," Liam interjected roughly.

"Of course she does," Ellen cut in. "Stop being such an old bear. You and Brennan have put the poor lass through enough the last couple of days."

"Now, Ellen, you know as well as I do that if she wouldn't have insisted on that fool impersonator—"

"I'll just go make that call." Quickly Catherine got up, her face flaming. Several emotions were charging through her system. Were they right? she asked herself. Was she responsible for bringing a madman out of hiding? No! she answered silently. As she had told Brennan, if she hadn't taken Sydney Carr's contract, someone else would have. Then some one else would have had to deal with this, she thought.

She hurried down the hall. As she passed the entrance, the bell rang, stopping her in her tracks. "Should I answer that?" she shouted toward the living room.

"No," came Brennan's deep voice. Three seconds later he hurried through the dark hall and appeared at her side. His hair was spiky and damp from the ocean breeze, the color in his cheekbones high. He walked by Catherine and looked out the peephole.

"Who is it?" she whispered.

"No one." Swiftly he yanked open the door and walked out.

Catherine hung on to the door frame and peered outside. No car, no people, and finally no psycho with a gun, which was what she had expected to find, she realized.

"Who is it?" Liam demanded from behind them. Ellen was beside him, her blue eyes huge with worry.

"No one's there. Maybe the doorbell malfunctioned." Catherine's remark sounded lame, even to her. "Why don't we call down to the guard's shack and find out if anyone has asked about us?"

"I'm sure they didn't. They know right where we're staying." Brennan walked into the house with these words. He was holding a small manila envelope he had retrieved from the walkway. His knuckles were white with the restrained energy in his hands.

"What's that?" Ellen and Liam asked in unison.

But Catherine didn't bother to question him. She saw the black letters that spelled her name and silently held out her hand for the latest communication from the deadly missive writer.

In the dim hallway light she tore open the envelope and read aloud:

"Dear Cath:
Stop the Brennan Richards concert now or your favorite blond impersonator will not be as lucky as you just were. No police, Cath. Brennan can remind you what happens if you call them."

"Catherine?" Brennan's voice was harsh.

"Now he's threatening *my* family!"

"What?"

She sagged against the door frame. "My sister. Cheryl. She's one of the actors I use. She impersonates Madonna." The letter crumpled in her hand. "This is too much to deal with alone. We've got to go to the police. Tonight! Now!"

Brennan grasped her by the shoulders firmly. "I know this is hard for you, Cath. But you've surely got to see he's watching us. If the police show up, none of us will be able to do anything to stop him."

"Then what can we do?"

"We'll have to make Sydney Carr stop the show. Go call him now. See if we can visit him tonight or first thing tomorrow. We've got to find out what he knows about this, and if he'll consider pulling out of the Faire."

As Catherine hurried from the room, Ellen reached out and touched her brother's arm. "It's going to be all right, Brennan."

"Is it?" he asked harshly. "Is it ever?"

AFTER A SLEEPLESS NIGHT, Catherine met Brennan in the kitchen at eight o'clock. Her agreement to approach Sydney Carr and try harder to get the concert with Brennan's look-alike temporarily postponed, if not canceled, filled her with nervous energy.

For his part, Brennan had grudgingly agreed to go to the police with the bullet he'd retrieved from the beer can and the latest anonymous letter. Unfortunately, the bomb at her office had destroyed the other two letters. In silence Catherine and Brennan drank cups of tea, then walked out to the florist's van for the drive to Carr's beach house, which was several miles up the coast.

The morning was gray and overcast. A chilly breeze, kissed with mist, dampened the trees and shrubs and made the car handle slide under Catherine's grasp. It was uncommonly humid, and the sky threatened a storm.

She got in the van, and Brennan slammed his door. They didn't speak. He gunned the van's motor and they started out, past the guard's shack and down to the Pacific Coast Highway. The traffic was light, the road slick.

"What's Carr's address?" Brennan finally asked, twenty minutes into the trip.

"Nine Seabreeze. You have to go through Santa Monica and past the pier."

He glanced at his watch. "He knows we're coming this early?"

"Yes. You're going to be his morning surprise." Carr's secretary hadn't sounded pleased by her request, but Carr had okayed it. Catherine met Brennan's eyes, but they both quickly averted their glances.

Brennan watched the scenery with no appreciation, aware of his mental comparisons of California to where he'd grown up, but not really tuning in to anything but his anger. He'd paced his rented house most of the night, called the guards watching the children in Minnesota, then paced some more. Several times he'd stopped in front of Catherine Grand's closed bedroom door, but he had resisted knocking and waking her.

Their talks seemed to only go one way anyway, and that was badly. It had not seemed unfair to urge her to drop the concert. But the danger she and her family found themselves in *was* unfair. His inability to protect his family, and now this lovely, hardworking woman, was too bloody much to bear.

He hit the steering wheel with his fist. "Damn."

"What is it?" Catherine asked, startled. "Did you miss the turn?"

"No."

She studied his profile, wondering what he thought. In the dreary light he looked older. His beard was not shaved close enough nor was his mood relaxed enough to allow his handsomeness through. But even in turmoil, Brennan Richards was compelling. Catherine felt her emotions stir, and was amazed that being beside a rock star could still make her feel like a schoolgirl.

Especially this rock star. The memory of him singing "Michelle" to her seeped into her mind, and she smiled. Talent was power, and his charismatic voice and personality were forces to be reckoned with. Her smile faded. It occurred to her that she was abandoning good sense. She'd gone along with Brennan's request to see Carr mainly because Brennan had charmed her. "Rats," she said.

"What?"

"Nothing," Catherine snapped, grateful for her returning equilibrium. "The street's there. Turn right and follow it to the gates. There's a speaker."

He sped up, then swerved, slowed and proceeded to climb the steep hill. At the top he followed the narrow private road. They arrived at two massive steel gates. After a moment a disembodied voice asked their names. "Catherine Grand and associate," said Catherine, then watched as the gates slid smoothly aside.

A minute later Brennan stopped the van in front of the house that Knight Records had built and let out a whistle. Catherine decided it wasn't a whistle of appreciation or envy, but one full of the same sentiment she'd felt on her first visit. Brennan also felt awe. How could so much money be spent on so much ugliness?

Sydney Carr's home was custom built for him. Its gaudy exterior of massive flagstones painted yellow above turquoise blue siding proclaimed a man of great wealth and great lack of taste. "He's named it Carousel. Said it reminds him of the circus called the music business. I guess he thinks of himself as a ringmaster," Catherine finally said.

"Its horrible," Brennan remarked simply. "Let's go in."

A gorgeous Latin woman dressed in a simple maid's dress opened the door. "Señor Carr is on the patio. He said for you to join him for breakfast." She turned prettily and led the way. The inside of the house was done on the same massive scale. There were huge pieces of furniture that did not look comfortable, upholstered in shades of purple, teal and red.

Outside was a rock garden and newly laid deck. Beyond rolled an acre of grass and flowers and a pool with a waterfall. The majestic Pacific gleamed dully in the distance, cloudy and leaden under the blanket of clouds.

Carr sat at a glass table laid with five places. He wore a lime green cashmere turtleneck sweater and did not stand as they followed the maid outside.

"Your guests are here," the woman announced, then disappeared.

Sydney turned to them. His florid face reddened slowly, from chin to forehead, like a thermometer. Finally he removed a thick cigar from his mouth. "Hello, Catherine. What a surprise you've brought with you. Brennan, it's been too long. Come and eat. There's plenty."

"Sydney." Brennan nodded curtly, then held out his hand indicating that Catherine should walk ahead of him. He stayed close behind her.

"Good morning, Mr. Carr," Catherine added finally, aware that her guest had shocked her host, but unable to tell to what extent. She went around the table, distracted by a figure off to her left. Whoever it was jumped into the pool. She was startled at the tangible animosity apparent between the two men. Somehow she'd imagined that the years had healed the pain of their business troubles.

"Can I pour you a Bloody Mary? There's Tabasco, if you can stomach the stuff." Carr replaced the cigar in his mouth and smoothly talked around it. It was unlit.

"No, thanks." Catherine reached for the orange juice at her place. "This is fine."

"Brennan?" Carr made the one word sound like a challenge.

"I don't drink," Brennan replied.

"Right. I forgot. Liquor's hard on the voice, although that's not the consideration these days, I guess." Carr laughed and Brennan stared.

Catherine gulped down half her orange juice. "Mr. Carr, I appreciate your seeing me. As you can imagine by my bringing Brennan with me, we both have some concerns that must be addressed."

"No problem, Catherine. We've got a lot to discuss about the Faire concert. How are you feeling, by the way? You look okay. No bomb damage."

"Fine." She tried to swallow her anxiety and waved her pinky. "Minor injury."

"Catherine was very lucky," Brennan added quietly.

"It seems." Carr removed the cigar and rolled it between his thumb and index finger. "So? What can I do for you?"

Catherine took a deep breath. "Brennan asked to see you to tell you about some things that have happened lately. You heard about the bomb left in my office and—"

"I did," Carr interrupted. "Bloody awful world we live in. Can't even trust a package."

"Mr. Richards's attorney also received a mail bomb, and we've both gotten rather nasty letters, warning of more trouble if the Knight Records concert goes on. So I thought it might be good if we postponed, even canceled, the Brennan Richards impersonator, at least until things calm down." Catherine finished in a rush, surprised that Carr did not seem the least bit shocked by her suggestion. If any-thing, he seemed amused.

The corpulent man turned to Brennan, and sucked on the cigar again. "Is this what you want, Brennan?"

Brennan had fought to hold his tongue during Cather-ine's speech. She'd sounded meek and apologetic, not at all full of the vim and spunk she'd shown with him. Carr al-ways made people feel at a disadvantage. He was a king at that, Brennan well remembered. "Yes, Syd. It certainly is."

Carr reached for his Bloody Mary and stirred the thick red drink with a celery stalk that protruded from it. "Okay."

Catherine's stomach seemed to curl into a knot, and she felt like shaking her head to steady herself. "You'll do it?" she blurted.

"Of course." Carr drank, then stuck the cigar in his mouth. He folded his pudgy hands and beamed at Bren-nan. "I'll do it on one condition, that is. We'll kill the im-personator, in a manner of speaking, if *you* perform." Carr's grin got bigger. The cigar made a rigid slash against his puffy face. "Knight Records presents the return of Brennan Richards! I love it."

Catherine felt the blood drain from her face. Suddenly a terrible possibility occurred to her. Perhaps Sydney Carr had been behind the whole mess, from the letters to yesterday's gunshots, in order to pull off Brennan Richards's return. She opened her mouth to speak, but Brennan cut her off.

It was clear the rock star had shared her thought. "You bastard." The Irishman stood, his muscles bunched into fist-size balls under his white shirt. "You manipulating, sleazy— If you think you can pull this off, you're even crazier than I thought."

Carr blinked and swished his drink. "That's the deal, folks. If you don't like the terms, I still have a contract signed by this little lady that's iron-clad." He grinned

NO RISK, NO OBLIGATION TO BUY... NOW OR EVER!

CASINO JUBILEE
"Match'n Scratch" Game

Here's how to play:

1. Peel off label from front cover. Place it in space provided at right. With a coin, carefully scratch off the silver box. This makes you eligible to receive one or more free books, and possibly other gifts, depending upon what is revealed beneath the scratch-off area.

2. You'll receive brand-new Harlequin Intrigue® novels. When you return this card, we'll rush you the books and gifts you qualify for ABSOLUTELY FREE!

3. If we don't hear from you, every other month we'll send you 4 additional novels to read and enjoy. You can return them and owe nothing but if you decide to keep them, you'll pay only $2.49* per book, a saving of 30¢ each off the cover price. There is *no* extra charge for postage and handling. There are *no* hidden extras.

4. When you join the Harlequin Reader Service®, you'll get our subscribers-only newsletter, as well as additional free gifts from time to time just for being a subscriber!

5. You must be completely satisfied. You may cancel at any time simply by sending us a note or a shipping statement marked "cancel" or returning any shipment to us at our cost.

YOURS FREE!

This lovely Victorian pewter-finish miniature is perfect for displaying a treasured photograph and it's yours absolutely free — when you accept our no-risk offer!

*Terms and prices subject to change without notice. Sales tax applicable in NY.

CASINO JUBILEE
"Match'n Scratch" Game

SCRATCH HERE

CHECK CLAIM CHART BELOW FOR YOUR FREE GIFTS!

YES! I have placed my label from the front cover in the space provided above and scratched off the silver box. Please send me all the gifts for which I qualify. I understand I am under no obligation to purchase any books, as explained on the opposite page.

(U-H-I-10/91) 180 CIH ADE5

◀ DETACH AND MAIL CARD TODAY! ▼

Name

Address   Apt.

City   State   Zip

CASINO JUBILEE CLAIM CHART

WORTH 4 FREE BOOKS, FREE VICTORIAN PICTURE FRAME PLUS MYSTERY BONUS GIFT

WORTH 3 FREE BOOKS PLUS MYSTERY GIFT

WORTH 2 FREE BOOKS

CLAIM N° 1528

HARLEQUIN "NO RISK" GUARANTEE

- You're not required to buy a single book — ever!
- You must be completely satisfied or you may cancel at any time simply by sending us a note or a shipping statement marked "cancel" or by returning any shipment to us at our cost. Either way, you will receive no more books; you'll have no obligation to buy.
- The free book(s) and gift(s) you claimed on the "Casino Jubilee" offer remains yours to keep no matter what you decide.

mirthlessly. "Despite this big bad tale of bombs and letters that go bump in the night."

Catherine stood and gripped the edge of the table. "Mr. Carr. You don't understand. My family's been threatened. And Johnnie Lord's been shot."

"Is someone talking about me?"

Catherine and Brennan swung around. In the doorway stood Johnnie Lord, his arm in a soft sling, his hair in a ponytail. With his blue eyes, he looked for all the world like Brennan Richards's younger brother.

"Hello, Miss Grand. Did you get my message? I called Karen and let her know I was staying here until the performance." He walked to the table and poured a drink. "Mr. Carr made me an offer I couldn't refuse." His gaze focused on the ocean. "Isn't this place amazing?"

Brennan looked stunned. Catherine crossed her arms and exhaled. "Well, this is quite a surprise. I guess you've decided to perform despite the danger?"

"Oh, yes. This is going to be my big break." Johnnie grinned at Brennan. "I do you well. Very well, I might say. You should come hear me. Maybe give me a pointer or two."

Brennan raised his hand and pointed at the younger man. "I'll give you a pointer, my boy. If you perform—"

"Don't, Brennan." Catherine's voice rose. She grabbed his arm and stood in front of him. The whole scene was becoming impossible. Brennan looked like he was going to commit murder. "Brennan, calm down. There's got to be a way we can all discuss this rationally. Mr. Carr, you can't go on with this."

"Oh, I think I can, Miss Grand." Carr lit his cigar. "And I intend to. And I think Johnnie boy here would agree to work with any agency I hired. So if you back out, I'll owe you for finding such a great look-alike, but I'll still sue you into the ground.''

Revulsion filled Catherine, and for a moment she wondered if she were capable of strangling another human being. Forcing control, she turned to Johnnie. ''Is that right, Johnnie? You know I have an exclusive one-year deal with you.''

''I wouldn't want to, Miss Grand. But I am committed to this. I always wanted to be Brennan Richards, you know.''

Before Catherine could answer, a woman's voice broke in from behind. ''Sydney, you really are being a pig. Have Geraldine bring out the eggs. Everyone must be famished.''

Catherine turned toward the pool to meet the eyes of the woman who spoke. She was short, sleek and full-bosomed. Beneath a black silk caftan, a slim black swimsuit dripped water down her suntanned legs. A single diamond the size of a small marble rested on a chain between her breasts. She took off her sunglasses, and her green eyes glinted coolly. The crooked teeth gleamed with droplets of pool water. ''Miss Grand, would you pour me one of those Bloody Marys before Sydney sucks them all down?''

Dumbly Catherine reached for the pitcher, wondering how the blonde who had offered her $10,000 to drop the concert wound up on Sydney Carr's patio.

Chapter Ten

Catherine didn't have to wait long to find out.

"This is my wife, Siobhan, Miss Grand." Sydney smiled. He removed his cigar and blew a huge blue smoke ring. "You remember Siobhan, of course, don't you, Brennan?"

"Of course he does, Syd. Don't push things here," Siobhan replied, standing on tiptoes to give Brennan a chaste kiss on the cheek. "No man ever forgets his first lover. Especially when she was his true love. Right, Brennan?"

"Catherine, let's go." Brennan took her arm and pulled.

Johnnie, Sydney and Siobhan Carr all stared at Catherine, who felt as if her sanity had slipped a notch. "None of you understand. There's someone dangerous out there."

Carr smiled around his cigar and puffed. "That's show business."

"Don't worry about me, Miss Grand. I'll be fine. What time is that *People* magazine interview on Friday, by the way? Eleven at the Sheraton?" Johnnie squeezed her arm and fell into the chair next to her. His blue eyes looked feverish, and Catherine was struck by the thought that he was high on pain medicine. He certainly was in no shape to make a rational decision.

"I'm canceling that, Johnnie. In view of all that's happened—"

"Don't!" Carr ordered. "Think of the great publicity!"

"SLOW DOWN or stop and let me out!" Catherine shouted her request as the van skidded nearly out of control on Sydney Carr's driveway.

Brennan glared at her, but hit the brakes gently and slowed to a reasonable speed. They passed through the gates and exited Carr's property.

"I told you it was a mistake asking Carr for help," Brennan bellowed.

"You also told me you had no simmering, fatal-attraction type love affairs in your past. Did you forget about Siobhan Carr?"

"Siobhan and I were never in love."

I'll bet, Catherine mouthed to herself. Brennan could call what he and Carr's wife once had whatever he wanted, but it was clear to Catherine that Siobhan had once been very much in love with him. And if her body language and tone of voice were any clue, Siobhan had never quite gotten over it. "Whatever you say, Brennan. But the point is this. I think we need to consider Siobhan Carr capable of being behind all that's happened lately."

Brennan braked at the light at the Pacific Coast Highway, then headed toward Malibu with a squeal of tires. "You think so? Why?"

"Remember when I asked you about the woman and the offer to cancel the impersonator concert?"

"It was Siobhan?"

"In the flesh."

Brennan's blue gaze concentrated on the road ahead, but his hands wrung the steering wheel as if it was someone's neck. "But why? Why would she try to kill the concert?"

Catherine crossed her arms and counted silently to ten. God, men were so dense sometimes. "I can think of several reasons. One, she wants to tick off her husband, for whatever marital give-and-take agenda. Two, she wanted to protect you, for old times' sake. Three, she's working for someone else who wants to get Carr."

"Someone else? Like who?"

"Like half of the people in show business, for instance. Most have good reasons for despising him. Or—" The thought ambushed her, and Catherine sat back to try to get her equilibrium.

"Or?" Brennan pressed. A light rain began to fall, clouding the windshield and covering the asphalt with a glittering rainbow of colors where the gasoline and oil mixed with the water. He glanced at Catherine impatiently, startled to see how pale she was. Without thinking, his hand covered her left knee. "Cath? What's wrong?"

She kept her eyes focused on the road. "Nothing. You better slow down even more, the asphalt's like Teflon in this weather." Her brain was buzzing with the turmoil the newly realized possibility had created.

"You were saying Siobhan could be working for someone. Who did you think of? Who would she likely be working for?"

Catherine felt her pulse lurch. "You," she answered softly. "I'd say it would be possible she's working for you."

"Don't be absurd!"

"Is it absurd?"

"Of course it is. Do you think I would scare the hell out of my sister and hurt Liam McKinney just to get my way?"

Catherine didn't think he would do that, but then again, she really didn't know him. "I don't know."

"Yes, you do," he argued. "For crying out loud, Catherine, you've just slandered me. Can't you do me the common decency of explaining?'' In his anger he stepped harder on the gas.

The van lurched as Brennan's hand slipped from the wheel. Before Catherine could even scream, the van careened off the asphalt, bounced into a trench of muddy debris then banged into a telephone pole. She smashed her left hand hard against the dashboard as the van slid into the ditch and the engine died.

A moment later Brennan was unsnapping her seat belt and pulling her into his arms. ''Bloody hell! Catherine, I'm sorry. Are you all right?''

Gulping for air, Catherine pushed away from him, but not before she experienced a second of comfort from being held gently in the strongest arms that had ever been wrapped around her. ''I'm fine. Though I think my other hand took a knock.'' She flexed her fingers and looked at him. ''How about you?''

''I'm okay. But an idiot.'' He touched her lip. ''You've bit yourself. Does it hurt?''

Meeting his glance, Catherine felt her skin warm. She was amazed by how gorgeous he was, how sexy and tender and male had wrapped themselves in a dizzy ball of contradiction the world knew as Brennan Richards. A unique, one-of-a-kind man, a man who drove her crazy. She had a mad impulse to nibble on his earring, but stopped herself. ''It doesn't. And you're a terrible driver.''

He smiled at her. ''I know. I've never got a license, either. So I best hurry out and see what the damage is before the law shows up.'' Brennan opened the car door to a whoosh of rainy air, then slammed it shut.

Catherine heard a siren in the distance and grimaced. Great, she thought, just what they needed. Another round with the police. They would surely haul Brennan off to jail if they found him in this fix. A tiny bit of fear pricked along her neck, and she shivered. Glancing nervously out the window, she looked for any sign that they were being watched. After all, she had been warned not to go to the police or her sister would be in danger.

She jumped as Brennan slammed the hood and came around to the door and opened it. "It's no good. The radiator's leaking like it took a direct hit, and the tire's flat. Let's go into that coffee shop across the street and call a tow truck. That is, if you don't think it's too dangerous to have breakfast with me."

"Don't be sarcastic, Brennan. When I said you and Siobhan could have arranged things together, I was thinking out loud. Don't take it so personally."

He surprised her by raising a long-fingered hand to her face and brushing back her hair. "I'm starting to take things very personally with you, Cath. I don't want you to think I'd hurt you just because you won't use good sense and cancel the damn concert. I'm not mad, you know."

His Irish brogue got thicker when he was being gentle, and Catherine felt herself tremble as he slipped an arm around her protectively. "I never said you were mad, Brennan. But you have to admit Siobhan's offer of $10,000, followed by your personal visit, looks suspiciously like a two-pronged attack."

"I think you're right there. But two-pronged to hurt me?"

"What do you mean?"

Brennan stopped her at the curb, waiting for the traffic to pass. "Maybe we're jumping to conclusions here. Maybe the reason for the letters, the bomb, everything, has something to do with you and your business."

She saw the flash of hope in his eye, but couldn't let him mislead himself, not even for a minute. "And the shot on the beach? That was for me?"

His blue eyes clouded. "Of course not. Come on, let's get some coffee and get to a phone."

They crossed the busy highway together, trying unsuccessfully to beat what had turned into a full-fledged California rainstorm.

Brennan held open the door to Bobo's Bar and Grill, and Catherine hurried inside to the smell of fresh coffee. Bobo's was a small, diner-type establishment that reminded Catherine more of New York than southern California.

The sign outside, bordered by light bulbs, pictured a white mongrel with an enthusiastic look on his face staring at a plate of food. Inside was a wide, shiny counter on the street side of the building. Several booths were on the far wall. In between the seats lay the open kitchen, which consisted of two long grills and several worktables and sinks. Old color lithos of Norman Rockwell paintings covered the walls, and the cook wore an L.L. Bean T-shirt and cords. Brennan nodded to the man, who said, "Take any table." Brennan led the way to the ocean side of the restaurant. The two slid into a booth.

"This place isn't very busy," Brennan warned. "With a dog on the sign and all, maybe we should stick to coffee and wait for breakfast until we get home."

"It's too early on a Sunday morning for the party crowd," Catherine replied. "I've been by here several times at lunchtime and it's packed. The dog looks well-nourished, so since I'm famished, I'm eating."

"Whatever you want, Cath." His voice held a lot of emotion, none of it related to eating.

She made no reply, but opened a menu and studied it. She really was starving. She'd been unable to eat any of Ellen's lovely chicken dinner after getting the letter. And the juice she'd had at Sydney Carr's gurgled impolitely in her stomach. She wondered if it would be tacky to order both pancakes and waffles.

"I'm going to go see about a wrecker." Brennan rose and searched in his faded jeans for a quarter. "Order me coffee and scrambled eggs, will you, please?"

"Sure." She watched him walk through the door marked Rest Rooms, Telephone, then looked around, suddenly nervous. The first siren she had heard belonged to an ambulance that had passed them as they waited to cross the highway, but another could be heard close by. Catherine craned her neck to see out of the front of the restaurant, just as two black-and-white California Highway Patrol cars screamed by, red lights flashing.

In this weather, half of Malibu was stuck on the Pacific Coast Highway and the other half had malfunctioning burglar alarms. No one was going to stop for a florist's van in a ditch.

With that comforting thought she ordered, then gulped down the coffee a young redheaded waitress brought. The strong brew helped her focus on her predicament. Simply put, if she dropped the concert, Carr would sue her, she would lose her business, and someone else would stage the show while Johnnie Lord went ahead and performed. If she kept to her contract, Brennan, her family and herself were in danger. Physical danger.

With a bang Catherine put the coffee mug down, unenthusiastic about the food that was being unloaded on the table.

"Well, that's set then." Brennan slid onto the bench across from her and grabbed his mug.

"The wrecker is coming?"

"Yes. He'll be here in twenty minutes to a half hour." He picked up his fork and skewered his eggs. "So eat up." After two bites he saw that Catherine wasn't eating. "What's wrong? Are you hurt, after all?"

"No. I'm just not hungry." She leaned across and touched his arm. "I'm trying to see a way out of this, Brennan. What am I going to do?"

He chewed solemnly. "Seems clear, Cath. Don't do the concert."

"I'll lose my business! You heard Sydney!"

"I'll help you get started in a new one."

"Please. I don't need your money."

Brennan shrugged. "Taking some help from me seems a better choice than losing your life. Or your sister's. Or even mine."

"Don't make me responsible for yours, Brennan," she snapped. Then she buried her face in her hands. Around them the restaurant was filling up fast. Catherine registered the mumblings and laughter at the surrounding tables, but blocked out the noise in an effort to concentrate. "The police are already looking into the bombings, so I'm going to wait until they find out something before I take them more information."

"And in the meantime?"

"In the meantime, we'll keep trying to solve this ourselves. Tell me about you and Siobhan."

"Why?"

Her hands came down and she stared at him. "Brennan, I have to understand this mess better. Maybe I can come up with something if you fill me in on the background. Something that can help us find out for sure who is after us."

He looked unconvinced but abandoned his food. Brennan could see the turmoil and anxiety Catherine was suffering. He felt it, too, but kept telling himself there was a way out. Deluding himself might be a better description, a voice in his head whispered. "There's not much to tell. She was a sound technician on the 1981 tour. We got involved. I liked her, but she seemed to want some kind of major commitment right off the bat. In L.A. in 1981 I was having a rough time and wasn't interested in anything long term. Then Ellen found out Siobhan was involved in delivering drugs. Ellen told her husband, Mitch, my stage manager, and he fired Siobhan. When I axed the singer Siobhan was selling to, Ellen's old mate, Jane Scarlett, my relationship with Siobhan ended.''

"Siobhan must not have been too fond of Ellen. Or Mitch."

"She wasn't. If you're thinking she's a suspect in Mitch's death, rule it out. The police were all over that. She had an airtight alibi. She was at a party in Brentwood during the concert with Sydney. A *private* party."

"So he was her alibi?"

"Right. And shortly after that became her husband."

Catherine nodded, deep in thought. "Seems an awfully quick rebound for someone who was in love with you. Maybe Carr blackmailed her."

"His silence for her love, you mean?"

"Could be. From what I know of Carr, it wouldn't be out of character."

Brennan squinted, then glanced around.

Two teenage girls were huddled together in the booth behind them. One was pointing at Brennan. "It is him. I saw his picture in the paper." She giggled.

Brennan scowled and turned to Catherine. "Seems a bit farfetched. When I sued Carr to get out of my contract after the accident, Siobhan never tried to contact me. And she's stayed with him all this time. She doesn't strike me as the kind of woman one could blackmail for very long."

"Not even if there was a murder conviction hanging over her head?"

He sat back heavily. "That's a hard one for me to believe. Although I once thought of her in connection with the first letter. I thought I remembered that she had been in my dressing room, waiting to see me one last time, before I found the note. But I couldn't be sure."

"Could she have found out you've been living in Minnesota?"

"Don't think so, my girl. No one knew about that, except Liam."

There was a piece of information nagging at the corner of Catherine's brain. "Ellen told me last night that when she broke up her girl group Sydney Carr threatened to sue her, then backed down. Why was that?"

"I don't remember ever knowing. I was only ten when that happened, you know. Jane Scarlett may have had something to do with it, though. She had a thing for Carr, if I remember. Maybe she appealed to his better side."

"Now that I hear this, it really amazes me you hired Carr when you started to get big. Did Ellen approve of that?"

"Not really. But Ellen never really got involved in my career. And despite her personal feelings about Sydney, he was the best."

"Why did you hire Jane Scarlett as a backup singer?" Catherine was pressing him and she wasn't sure why. But it seemed to her suddenly that the close-knit little group of players, Ellen and Jane Scarlett, Sydney and Siobhan Carr, Brennan and George Jesse, all had to be connected to the mystery that embroiled them now.

"For old times' sake, really. Jane had always been a bit of an odd duck. Solitary, weird, I guess you'd say. Secretive. But she was a hell of a harmonizer. We heard she was trying to get some work, and even though she had a reputation as a druggie, Ellen felt some loyalty for the old times. When she tracked her down, I hired her for the tour."

"How do you do that?" Catherine asked. "Get hold of someone in the business?"

Brennan blinked, trying to remember. "There're lots of agencies that handle talent, but it seems like Ellen heard about Jane from George Jesse."

"George. Another missing link." Catherine folded her hands together, then winced as her splinted pinky banged against the plate. "We've got to run him down and try to get a line on Jane Scarlett. We've got to find out if she's heard from Siobhan in the last ten years. I really think there's a connection to the past that has to be found."

"You and Gutierrez. He thought so, too."

"He did? He thought your brother-in-law was murdered by one of them?"

Brennan was interrupted before he could answer. "Excuse me, could you sign this for my mother?" A young man wearing a U.C.L.A. T-shirt came and stood next to their table. He held out a paper napkin. "You are Brennan Richards, right? My mom's got all your albums."

Brennan glared at the boy. "I don't have a pen. Sorry." He gestured to Catherine's plate. "If you're not going to eat, I think we should go back to the van to wait for the tow truck."

The boy shoved the napkin closer, and a couple in their forties joined him. "Can we get an autograph, too, please? We saw you in San Francisco in 1978. Are you going to come out of retirement?"

Brennan got up quickly, nearly knocking over one of the teenagers behind him. The rudeness of the other diners had made them bolder.

"Are you a rock and roll star?" one girl asked, hanging on to Brennan's arm. "Do you know Sting? He's British, too."

"No. Sorry, I'm a florist. An Irish florist." He put a hand out to steady the girl, and had to use force to get her to let go. She giggled louder.

"Hey, Brennan! Where's your patch, man?" a boy standing with a group near the front door shouted across the restaurant.

Brennan grabbed Catherine by the arm and led her from the table toward the back exit. The general noise level increased dramatically as several people shouted for Brennan to stop.

"Is it always like this?" Catherine gasped, struggling to get by the waitress. Brennan pushed a twenty dollar bill into the waitress's hand. She looked at it like it was something magical.

He used his shoulder to shove the door open and yanked Catherine into the rain. "No. For several years I've been anonymous. I got my private life back. Until—"

She read the look in his eyes and the tone of his voice and finished the rest of his sentence. "Until Catherine Grand ran an ad that said, 'Be Brennan Richards...'"

"You've got it about right, Cath."

Numb from cold, worry and fatigue, Catherine let him hurry her around the side of the restaurant. What she wanted more than anything was some peace and quiet and a phone. Tracking down Jane Scarlett would lead them closer to the truth, her intuition told her.

"Damn!"

Catherine came to an abrupt stop next to Brennan, wondering what he was swearing about. Following his stare, she blinked twice when she looked across the street, but her eyes didn't lie.

There was an Automobile Club of Southern California tow truck pulling up, followed by a highway patrol cruiser.

Chapter Eleven

Siobhan Carr left the Rolls in the rambling open parking lot outside Bullocks Department Store in Pasadena. She kept her dark glasses on and entered the store, glancing at nothing and no one as she made her way to the tearoom-style restaurant.

She waved the hostess away with a curt, "I see my party," and sauntered through the sunny room to the single occupant waiting at a table for two by the window.

"Hi, Siobhan. How did it go this morning?"

Siobhan sat and weaved her long-nailed fingers into a tight double fist. "How did it go? How nice of you to ask, considering that you've screwed things up so well."

Her companion drew back as if slapped. "I've screwed things up? How? I did everything you said. Sent out the phony invoices, planted the phony press releases, paid off that construction worker so that it would look like an accident—"

"Just shut up!" Siobhan snapped. She straightened her glasses and leaned forward. "Despite your assurances to the contrary, Catherine Grand is not going to be persuaded out of the Knight Records contract by a few minor stunts like that. What we need to do is something that will stop her cold."

"I don't like this, Siobhan. You should have told me at the beginning there was more to this. I could have been in the office when that bomb went off! Didn't you think about that when you sent it?"

"Don't be a fool. I didn't send it," she replied coolly.

"What?" her tablemate gasped. "Well, who did?"

Siobhan knew full well who had, but she saw no need to tell the person across from her any more information than necessary. "I don't know. Maybe Brennan Richards did it to try to get her sympathy. Or scare her to death. But the point is that it didn't work. Now, tell me what Catherine Grand has planned this week so I can arrange things."

"You're going to kill her, aren't you?"

Before Siobhan could respond, the elderly waitress assigned to their table arrived with glasses of water and place settings. The waitress smiled vacantly, then left them without a word. The question that had been uttered prior to her appearance seemed to hover above the table precariously.

"Well, are you?" the nervous conspirator demanded.

"Don't be an ass." Siobhan hissed the last word. She had no intention of being responsible for another murder. The one already on her conscience was weighty enough.

"I won't be a party to it. I care about Catherine."

"Don't get on your high horse now, my dear," Siobhan replied. "You betrayed Catherine Grand for money and my promise to introduce you to some people who could help your career. Now you're damn well going to deliver what you promised. So tell me what the owner of Grand Illusions has planned this week so I can get on with it."

Haltingly, a summary of Catherine's planned appointments was given. Siobhan took particular note of the Niagra beer shoot and a *People* magazine luncheon. Both would give her ample opportunity to stop Catherine Grand. She'd create so much bad publicity that Catherine would have to pull out of the Brennan Richards look-alike concert. And with Catherine Grand out of the picture, Siobhan was sure the concert would be so delayed it would be impossible to stage.

The waitress returned with order pad in hand. Silently she stood, pencil poised above the small tablet.

"Go ahead and order. I'm not eating." Siobhan stood and smiled. "And thanks very much for the information. You'll be hearing from me soon."

"But you haven't told me which appointment you're, ah, keeping," the person across from her whined.

"I know." Siobhan smiled, then winced. Her bruised cheek, which was hidden under makeup and the huge lenses of her sunglasses, was made painful by any movement. "You'll hear from me this week. Goodbye."

Siobhan returned to the Rolls and headed back to the ugly Santa Monica house, a house that was full of evil secrets. Once she stopped Catherine Grand, Siobhan told herself, there would be time to repay the man who waited there, the man who had this morning so heartlessly struck her, the man who knew she couldn't strike back without going to prison.

The blonde smiled wanly at the thought of prison and put on the cassette tape of Brennan Richards's first album. As the singer's voice filled the car, a tear rolled down her cheek and fell onto her cashmere jacket, evaporating with a glimmer in the warm sunlight.

"IT'S MIRACULOUS," Catherine said.

"What is?" Brennan replied.

She sat back against the van's seat and chuckled. "Your stardom, or whatever you want to call your reputation."

Brennan flipped on the blinker and got through the traffic light then flashed her a smile. "You mean because the cop didn't arrest me when I told him I had not yet got an American license?"

"Didn't arrest you? Not only did he not arrest you, he and the tow-truck driver fixed the radiator, towed you out of the ditch and refused to let you pay a cent!"

"Yeah. Well, now you've seen two sides of the cost of celebrity. There's a bit of a riot when they don't get their bloody autographs, and then they fix your car and won't take a thing but thanks."

"I'd say the guys who fixed your car were your real fans."

His smile faded. "It's the stuff about me in the media that's caused the ruckus. No one would have recognized me if it weren't for those stories about the bombs."

"The price of fame! But isn't it nice being so loved?"

"Don't kid yourself. I would rather have had breakfast in peace. Besides, the closer they get to me, the more danger Ellen's kids are in."

"Why?"

"The publicity. Before you know it, some enterprising young reporter will be snapping candid pictures, then we'll have no peace at all." His voice sounded weary.

"I see."

"I'd give it all up, the past glory, everything, if I could only be anonymous now."

His answer sounded sincere, and Catherine was amazed. She knew so many people who sought fame. He was the first who truly seemed to shun it. "Really?"

"Really." Brennan's voice was firm. "Now, what do you say we take a trip out to Glendale and check out the address I got for George Jesse? Are you up to it? Or do you want to go find someplace else to eat?"

"No, let's go to Glendale. I think I'll stick to take-out food with you from now on."

"Oh, I think we'd be safe most places."

"Maybe." And maybe not, Catherine found herself thinking. There was no disputing it. Brennan Richards was a bona fide star, still alluring even though he'd retired. The folly of her plan to use a look-alike to rekindle his magic mocked her once again, and for a moment Catherine wondered if it would be all bad if her business *was* shut down.

But then what would she do? Go back to work at a large company on the bottom rung, and report to a boss forever?

Catherine and Brennan rode in companionable silence for several miles. The sky still looked threatening, but the rain had dried, leaving the San Gabriel Mountains clean and the air fresh. Brennan rolled down the window and took a deep lungful of air.

"A penny for your thoughts, Brennan."

"I was thinking about Ireland."

His answer surprised her. "Do you miss it?"

"Not usually. But today, looking at those purple mountains, makes me realize that I've not been back for a long time. Maybe I should take Ellen and the kids for a visit."

An unexpected disappointment filled Catherine. She and Brennan had spent a lot of time together in the past week; his problems had occupied much of her energy. But she *wasn't* part of his life, and once they ran down the psychopath, he'd be gone. "That's a good idea. Maybe you should go now. Let the police handle everything."

"Wouldn't want to leave now, Cath."

"Why? It would be safer."

He heard the edge in her voice and silently cursed himself. Catherine Grand had a savvy, smart exterior, tough even when it came to her business, but he was beginning to see that it masked a very vulnerable woman. In the bits she had offered about herself, he had learned she was at odds with her family, even though she was also devoted to them. With a pang of conscience, he realized how much she was risking, both emotionally and professionally, by helping him.

Repaying her by pointing out that he had a full family life was insensitive, Brennan realized. And while no one had ever described him as sensitive in the Alan Alda mold, being an arrogant boor wasn't his style, either.

Brennan cleared his throat. "Let me be direct, then. I wouldn't want to leave you, Cath. In fact, I'm hoping when this is all past us that you'll relax a bit and let me get to know you better."

"This isn't the time for any long-range plans." Catherine's voice had a tinge of misery to it, but she remained in control.

He felt surprisingly wounded by her reply. "And I'm not your type, right?" he shot back.

Something told her he knew that wasn't true, but she decided to avoid any discussion of the matter. "I'm nothing if not practical. You live, quite happily, fifteen hundred miles away from my home. You have a busy, involving family. You hate my business, and..." Catherine faltered, embarrassed and unsure suddenly what it was she was arguing against. After all, the man had merely offered an increasingly friendly relationship. He hadn't asked to marry her, or even to take her to bed. That thought made her cheeks color.

"And?"

"And nothing. Let's drop this and discuss what happened ten years ago. I asked you before if the police thought Jane Scarlett could have been involved in your brother-in-law's death."

"I thought I was the one who evaded questions," Brennan said. "Sometimes you do a good impersonation yourself, Catherine. Of an iceberg."

"Excuse me!" Her voice rose. "Okay. I'll answer. I don't think we have anything in common other than a madman,

Brennan. And I just can't see complicating things by be-having like a star-struck groupie in order to have a one-night stand with you!''

"Is that what you think I just offered you? Honestly, my dear Miss Grand, you jump the gun at every opportunity.''

"That's your opinion,'' she huffed.

The Irishman made a sound like a dismissive snort. "Good American expression, that.'' He rolled up the win-dow and looked in the rear-view mirror. Brennan didn't like what he saw. There was heavy traffic, but it was his reflec-tion that made him cringe. His eyes had a haunted, lonely expression. Suddenly he felt lonely. It had something di-rectly to do with the aggravating young woman beside him. "Why are you so afraid of getting to know me? Of me get-ting to know you?''

"I'm not!'' Catherine crossed her arms. "It's just not— not tenable.'' She uncrossed her arms and looked out the window. *And you're rich and famous and too sexy for thought, much less actions.*

"You've no way of knowing that, Cath. You're judging me by some preconceived notion of who I am.''

"I'm not judging you at all,'' she answered quietly. "I just don't think there's any reason to become better ac-quainted. Since my marriage ended, I—'' Catherine inter-rupted herself, "Look Brennan, we've no common ground.''

"You're a woman. I'm a man.''

She tried to sound witty. "As I said, we've no common ground.''

"Help me here. We'll go out tonight, have a proper date. Would that help?''

"You want to go out on a date?'' Catherine realized sud-denly that she didn't know what he did with his life. "After what happened at breakfast? I don't think so.''

"This is weird for me, Cath. I don't know much about dating. There were always a lot of women around, available, when I was performing, but I never had much to do with them. How did you meet men before you married?"

She shrugged. "At work. At school. I don't know."

"Do you date much now?"

Catherine felt like telling him it was none of his business, but the vulnerability in his tone stopped her. "No. I've always hated dating. My husband and I were roommates. We fell in love, or whatever it was, by living together with a mutual friend." She clamped her lips together after that, cursing herself for sharing anything about her ruinous marriage with him.

"Very modern love story. What happened?"

"I wasn't important enough to him. He wanted a career, not responsibilities to another person."

"And now you're the one who wants a career?"

"That's not fair!" Catherine retorted. "Besides, you're no one to judge. You never even got married."

Brennan didn't reply, just shook his head and steered the van. Five hundred yards later he came to a complete stop. A line of traffic a quarter of a mile long stretched before them.

Catherine was embarrassed by what she had said to him and cast around for an unemotional topic. "Looks like a truck jackknifed. We're stuck for awhile."

Brennan looked at her. Her hazel eyes were warm, her mouth naked of lipstick and soft looking. The circle of argument they'd just engaged in was hiding something, he realized. Suddenly it seemed to him that the only thing to do was kiss her. He put the van in park, then calmly reached behind her and pulled her toward him. Then he kissed her, thoroughly.

Catherine's lips were hard with surprise, then they relented. Never a believer in chemistry, she was stunned by the physical reaction to the touch and taste of Brennan Richards. Her injured hand rested against his chest, and she felt his heart racing. His hand rubbed her leg, then moved over her hip bone and released the seat belt that constrained her. Both his arms went around her possessively as his tongue filled her hungry mouth.

Heat flashed down her chest, and as she kissed him for all she was worth, Catherine discovered Brennan Richards was not the rich, aloof, hands-off ex-rock-and-roll icon she had judged him to be. He was a tender and sexy male she very much wanted to know better, and he was offering her a chance to take a chance.

A horn blasted behind them. Brennan took his time releasing her, then kissed her eyelids and nose before turning to the steering wheel. "Well, that's settled then."

"It is?" she whispered.

"Yes, it most certainly is. We're going to have a date." He laughed.

Catherine smiled as the deep, hot, honeyed sound of his voice poured over her. But as good as she felt, she knew they couldn't take the luxury of forgetting about the mystery that spun its web around them. "I really don't know what you're talking about, Brennan. Now, about Jane Scarlett..."

Brennan's laughter stopped, but when he caught his reflection once again in the mirror, the lonely look had been replaced by something that looked suspiciously like hope.

CATHERINE'S BACK TENSED when Brennan parked the van in front of the rambling white house in Glendale that supposedly belonged to George Jesse.

The owner of Pretenders, Brennan's ex-manager, lived in a yuppie district of fifty-year-old houses on small lots in the $300,000 plus price range. Despite the affluence, Jesse's house looked abandoned. Heavy drapes were pulled across the front windows, and several weeks' worth of throwaway circulars and newspapers were scattered over the rutted and brown front lawn.

Catherine was grateful that Brennan helped her out of the van and kept his arm across her back. As they walked to the front door, she had a premonition of danger and a sudden disheartened feeling that their amateur sleuthing was no match for the problems at hand.

Brennan's knuckles rapped against the peeling front door.

They waited a full minute, then Catherine tried the doorbell. She heard no echo of chimes that might indicate whether the bell worked. "Well, that's one dead end," she finally said.

"Come on." Brennan dropped his arm and walked onto the lawn, heading toward the backyard.

Catherine followed. Out of the corner of her eye, she caught a movement at a window. When she stopped to stare more carefully, nothing was there, but the curtain seemed to be slightly ajar.

"You coming, Cath?" Brennan called.

"Yes." She skirted some bushes and looked nervously in the direction of the neighboring home, but could see little through the thick shrubbery. Brennan held a sagging redwood gate open, and Catherine walked through it into the backyard.

A swimming pool was ringed by a four-foot chain-link fence, which was locked with a huge padlock. The pool took up most of the space in the backyard. The water was green and polluted with moldering leaves, trash and the remains of a floating lounge chair. The water was so filthy that it was impossible to see even a few inches down.

The deck surrounding the pool was also covered with debris. Several pizza boxes were piled around, and full green trash bags sat in heaps. Several were ripped open like huge, sleek fish, the contents spilling out.

"This is unbelievable," Catherine said. "I bet the neighbors aren't very fond of George Jesse."

Brennan surveyed the mess with his hands on his hips. "Odd, too. George was always scrupulously tidy, even on the tour bus. The guys in the band always kidded him about his favorite line, 'a place for everything and everything in its place.' He must have changed."

At that understatement, Catherine crossed the deck and went to a back entrance of the house. The French doors were locked and covered with the same heavy curtains that covered the windows. "No one covers French doors in California. Did George Jesse have a skin problem or something?"

Brennan stood next to her. She looked up and saw a stunned expression on his face. "What's wrong?"

"Why did you ask that about George?"

"The curtains." Catherine nodded at some more of the windows. Heavy, wide-slatted blinds as well as the heavy curtains covered them. Similar blinds covered the garage windows. "There are blinds and curtains everywhere. And the pool looks like it's never been cleaned. Or used. I thought maybe he couldn't go outside or something."

"George never had anything wrong with him." Brennan turned and walked toward the garage. "But I know someone with an eye problem who couldn't take the sun. Always lived in dark rooms and kept her skin covered up. Wore shades at night, and not just to look cool."

"Who was that?" Catherine asked.

Brennan turned. "Jane Scarlett."

Catherine whirled around, her hand on the garage's side door. "You're kidding!"

"No. I told you she was weird. That was just one of the things that enhanced that characteristic."

"Was she always like that?" Catherine remembered the album with Brennan's sister and Scarlett. Jane had worn glasses that had pointy black frames and orange-tinted lenses.

"No. It started after a bad love affair, I think. She got obsessive—became almost a nut really—over an American singer. Followed him around to all his concerts for six months, begging to be a backup singer."

"Who was it?"

"Frankie Valli. You know, 'Sherri' and 'Big Girls Don't Cry'?"

"Yeah." A nagging memory dug at her mind, but she couldn't capture it. "She had an affair with him?"

"No. She tried, he wasn't interested, and when she came back to England, she was a recluse with the dark clothes and all. No one really got a straight answer why she acted like that."

"You're right. She certainly sounds weird." Weird enough to send bombs in the mail? Catherine wondered. She tried the garage door and it wouldn't open. Squinting, Catherine bent over and looked through the slit of window not covered by the blinds. A car filled the garage. A dark, seventies model Ford of some kind.

"See anything?" Brennan asked.

"Not much. There's a car, a lot of boxes. The usual garage junk." Just then her eye glimpsed something leaning against the back door of the car. "My gosh!"

Brennan's hand squeezed her arm. "What is it?"

Catherine turned to face him. "You'd better look. But I think it's a rifle!"

THE PHONE RANG three times inside Sydney Carr's den before it was picked up.

"Yes?"

"I'm glad you answered. I'm in trouble."

The receiver of the call calmly moved the phone to the opposite ear. "Calm down. Where are you?"

"I'm in Glendale. At the house. And Brennan Richards is outside! He's got that Catherine Grand woman with him, and they're poking around the garage. What are we going to do?"

"Shh. Now calm down. They're not going to break in, so just stay inside until they go. Then come here. I'll meet you at Bobo's in an hour."

"But what are we going to do? I left the gun outside. What if they see it and call the police?" The caller's voice rose hysterically.

"Listen to me. Lower your voice or they'll hear you. Just stay quiet until they leave then bring the gun with you. You're going to need it this week anyway, and I'll keep it here until then."

The caller giggled nervously. "Okay. Bobo's, huh? You like that place?"

"It'll do just fine. Now remember, stay calm. Don't blow everything now."

"Okay, okay."

"I'll see you in an hour. And because you're a little upset, I promise to bring you a present."

"Thank you. Thank you so much." The anticipation of drug-induced rest was thrilling. "Tell me one more time where to go."

"Bobo's, on the beach. And remember, don't forget the gun. If you do, I'll be very unhappy."

"I won't. I promise. Oh, thank you." Jane Scarlett hung up the phone and peered out through the edge of the kitchen blinds. "Oh, no," she whispered in horror.

For several dizzy seconds she watched as if mesmerized. Brennan Richards was breaking into the garage. When he walked outside seconds later with the rifle in his hand, Jane Scarlett grabbed her mouth and covered the scream of panic that escaped.

Chapter Twelve

"What are you doing?" Catherine yelled. "You shouldn't touch that!"

"It's okay." Brennan held the rifle up. The butt and trigger section were covered by white cloth. "I used my handkerchief. Now come on. I don't want to be here when George comes looking for this." He grabbed Catherine's wrist with his free hand and marched her through the gate and toward the van.

Elation and fear mingled inside her. "Are we going to the police? I'm sure if they get prints they can—"

"We're not going to the police. We're going home."

"No!" Catherine pulled her hand free and dug her heels in the hard ground. "You are removing what could very well be evidence in an attempted murder, Brennan. There might be other clues in there. If the police come out now, they might have enough evidence to arrest someone."

"I'm going." He pointed to the van.

"I won't be a part of this."

His blue eyes darkened to a stormy shade. "You are a part of this, like it or not. I'll give this gun to the coppers eventually. Right now I'm just getting it, and us, out of harm's way."

"You're gambling with my life, Brennan!"

Her comment stopped him. "Look, Cath. If George comes looking for the gun and finds it gone, he'll know someone's on to him. Maybe it will be enough to stop him."

"Or it will be enough to make him stop *us*. For good!"

"I'll risk it." Brennan's voice was quiet but deadly. "Now come with me. I don't want a neighbor to come out and see us arguing in the front yard with a rifle. I'm liable to get shot at by some self-defense nut."

"Wherever Jesse got that rifle he can get another, Brennan. This isn't going to accomplish a thing."

Her words made sense, but Brennan's pride wouldn't allow him to admit the logic in what she'd said. "You've got to go along with me, Cath. Come on home. I'm sure Ellen's cooking dinner for us. We can both use some food."

"We're not doing the right thing, Brennan." It was futile. A second later she walked to the van and got in. She certainly couldn't argue with him here. Maybe Ellen or Liam McKinney would be able to make him see that acting like an Irish Matt Dillon was going to lead him into trouble, if not prison.

"Fasten your seat belt, lass." Brennan squeezed her leg and started the van.

Catherine moved away from him and pulled the restraint across her lap. As she did, her attention was again drawn to the windows. One side of a curtain was ajar a good two inches. A chill passed up her spine and made the hair on the back of her neck rise. "Brennan—"

He put the van into reverse, looking behind them to navigate the twisting driveway. "What?"

The scene that would result from a face-to-face meeting between Brennan and whoever was inside flashed through her mind. "Nothing," Catherine replied as the house disappeared from view behind the overgrown foliage.

It was time to stop asking his opinion and take control of her own life again, Catherine realized. Her marriage had taught her that she could seldom reform or lead other people toward a course of action against their will. It was a lesson she had ignored with Brennan Richards, allowing herself to be swept away by the forcefulness of his personality.

Well, it's time to stop acting like a groupie, she ordered herself. Let him drive to the beach. She could call the police and tell them about the gun and the bullet from the sniper's attack on the beach.

Brennan's melodic voice interrupted her thoughts. "I can't believe Jesse is involved in this. Even after finding the gun at his house, I just can't believe he would try to harm me or anyone else."

"Why not?"

"He was my friend for such a long time."

Honestly, logical motivation did seem to be beyond this man, Catherine thought. "Before or after you fired him as your manager?"

Brennan looked sharply in her direction, his mouth drawing into a tight line at her sarcastic tone. "Meaning what?"

"Meaning I'm not surprised. After all, you fired him when you were one of the top draws in the business. I'm sure it cost him a lot of money. Money is a prime motive in violent crimes, I understand."

"But he and Ellen—" Brennan stopped short, frowning at the growing tangle of traffic.

"He and Ellen what?" Catherine prompted.

"He and Ellen were so close."

Catherine digested this latest information. This new piece of the puzzle of the past might solve the current mystery.

"Money and sex," Catherine said softly. "I'd say George Jesse had the two biggest motives."

ELLEN DIDN'T HAVE DINNER waiting for them when Brennan and Catherine returned to the rented beach house. Silence greeted their arrival, and they found a note propped up on the kitchen table.

The ride had become an ordeal of strained silence. Brennan had sworn at the unusually heavy Sunday traffic, and Catherine had felt she was having a relapse. Her finger throbbed and her head ached.

Without asking Brennan's permission, she picked up the note and read it aloud. "Brennan and Catherine, took Liam back to Huntington Memorial Hospital. He had a terrible headache and blurred vision. The doctor is meeting us there. Call when you get in. Ellen."

Brennan bolted to the wall phone and called information, then hurriedly punched in the hospital's number.

Catherine paced. Anxiety worsened her hunger pangs, making her forget her aching hand.

"Ellen! Finally! What's happened?"

At his words, Catherine met Brennan's gaze. The lines around his eyes and mouth were very pronounced, and dark circles hollowed the shape of his cheekbones. It was obvious to her he loved Liam McKinney and was feeling a great deal of guilt over the man's injuries. After all, the bomb had been meant for him.

"How is he?" she whispered, touched by his affection.

Brennan shook his head and held up a finger for her to wait a moment, but his face relaxed. "Well, good enough. You give the old lion my best and I'll be there first thing in the morning." He listened intently. "Good, if you've already talked to the children, I'll wait and call them tomorrow. Okay, love. See you then." He hung up and sighed.

"Well?"

"It's okay news. The doctors say he's still suffering from the force of the blow, but they're confident he'll be fine. He has to stay flat for forty-eight hours. Ellen's staying with him tonight."

"Good. You can drop me at my apartment before you go by there in the morning."

"Your apartment?" Brennan echoed. "You're surely not thinking of going back there? Not now, anyway."

"I most certainly am. I have a full week of work ahead of me, complicated by the fact I have no office supplies, no office and a unreliable secretary who fancies herself the next Julia Roberts." Catherine opened the refrigerator and yanked out a bottle of wine.

"What's the real reason you want to go?"

"That is the real reason." Even as she muttered the words, she knew she was lying. "If I had been thinking clearly I would have had you take me there when we left Jesse's house." But since I need to get the rifle and call the police first, tomorrow will be fine, she thought. This plan, which had seemed sound before, now seemed fraught with danger. Catherine struggled with the cork in the wine bottle, wondering how violent Brennan's reaction would be when the police showed up.

"Let me help you with that." Brennan moved swiftly and took the icy Chardonnay from her. He rummaged in the drawer for another opener, found one with two long tongs and pried out the cork.

Brennan poured two glasses, aware that Catherine's eyes were on him and aware that her demeanor had changed since the incident at George Jesse's garage. "Cheers," he offered.

"Thanks." Catherine sipped, growing nervous over the fact that they were alone. The afternoon kiss replayed itself in her memory, and uneasiness slid over her like a second skin. The thought of calling the police when Brennan was so worried about Liam suddenly seemed like betrayal.

"Hungry?" he asked, watching her over the rim of his glass.

"No. This is fine." Catherine waved her drink at him then turned away, hurrying down the hallway and escaping into the living room. She needed some time to straighten out her thoughts and get her emotions in control.

Wearily Catherine curled up on the sofa. Outside, the final rays of afternoon light mottled the surface of the ocean, and the blowing sand was empty of beachcombers. She sipped the cold wine. It somehow felt like she and Brennan Richards were the last people on earth.

Brennan entered the room. Behind her, she heard the radio come on. Blasts of jerky static and hints of songs filled the air as Brennan tuned in a mellow oldies station. He continued to turn the radio dial.

The next second the room was filled with the sounds of Michael Jackson wailing the lyrics to "Billie Jean." Catherine closed her eyes and lost herself in the beat, willing away the confusion of her life and the attraction she felt to the man who was now beside her on the couch.

"Like Michael, do you?" Brennan asked.

"Yes. He's very..."

"Passionate?"

"Among other things, yes." Catherine opened her eyes and took another sip of the wine, feeling more light-headed by the moment. She had to eat soon or the consequence would probably be a swoon more appropriate to a southern belle than a businesswoman. "Interesting song, 'Billie Jean.' I guess it's common for rock stars to be leery about fans and phony paternity suits."

"I guess it is."

"Did you ever go through that?" Catherine asked, wishing Brennan had not moved closer. She noted the swell of his thigh muscles under the soft denim of his jeans and felt her confusion, as well as her attraction to him, double.

"No. I never did. Ellen made pretty sure I was responsible in that department."

"She was a good parent to you."

"The best." Brennan drained his glass and sat, his arm stretching behind Catherine and resting on the sofa. "When my folks were killed I was away at boarding school. She'd been touring around, Germany and spots in England, mostly, and I hadn't seen her for several months. During that time away from us she had got pregnant. She was planning on keeping the child, but then my folks were gone and I was only ten...." His voice trailed off. "I never knew about the child until she had put him up for adoption. Said she was just a kid herself, and taking care of the two of us would be more than she could handle."

"She didn't want to marry the father?"

"No. I started to tell you that in the car. George Jesse was the father."

Despite her attempts to control it, a gasp escaped. "My gosh, and you still signed with him as a manager?"

"I never knew this story until a couple of years ago, or I never would have subjected Ellen to having to work with Jesse."

Catherine was moved by the tenderness and pain in Brennan's voice. "You must have been horribly shocked."

He reached up to stroke her cheek. "I was. I felt, well, even a little betrayed that she had kept such an important secret from me. I was pretty hard on her over that, but she finally made me see it had nothing to do with me. I had to respect her choice. She did the best she could in a lousy situation, and it was unfair of me to second guess her."

Unaccountably Brennan's speech brought tears to Catherine's eyes. She felt her throat close in a sob.

"Hey, Cath. Don't be upset." His arms circled her shoulders, and he pulled her to him. "Since we're playing true confessions, why don't you tell me what's happened with your folks? It might help."

For several moments Catherine cried harder than she remembered ever doing before. She was mortified that she was crying in Brennan's arms, but some part of her felt relief at the opportunity to talk. "They lied to me."

"About what?" Brennan's voice was gentle, but his hand was warm and strong on her cheek.

"I was adopted. They never told me. Seems they never thought they'd be able to have kids. And when they finally did, they were afraid I'd feel left out. So, since they'd never faced up to the delicate task of telling me before, they conveniently ignored the truth and decided to never tell me. Then last year when my sister got sick, they had to." She cried silently now, letting the tears stream down her face. "I know what you feel about being betrayed. I just haven't been able to put it aside like you have."

Brennan pulled her closer and held her tight against him. The fact that he didn't offer any comment was comforting to her. His silence didn't make her feel foolish or petty, merely understood.

After a couple of minutes, Catherine wiped the back of her hand across her eyes and drew away from him. "Well, enough of this. Let's get something to eat. I've got some things to do."

"You're going to end up back in the hospital if you don't slow down. So sit and relax and I'll fix some dinner."

"Did she ever try to find the child?" Catherine asked.

Brennan looked deeply into her eyes. He was aware that her own pain was behind the question. "No. Liam handled the adoption, through an agency in London. Neither knew the identity of the parents, only that they were upstanding, religious people. They were working folks who'd been unable to have their own children. Ellen told me she had her share of torment after giving the child up, but she trusted that she'd done the best thing for the baby. She placed the child with people who deeply wanted him.''

Catherine's tears fell again, and she hugged her face to her knee. "I've never had the slightest doubt in my heart that I'm loved every bit as much as my folks' natural children. It's the secretiveness that stings."

"The secretiveness?"

"Yes. Like you said you felt betrayed a bit by Ellen not telling you about her pregnancy."

Brennan hugged her and gently kissed the side of her face. "Don't be too hard on yourself, Cath. It was a big shock. Give yourself time to digest it."

Catherine held on to his hand as she gave in to an impulse. "Instead of you cooking, why don't we go on that date you suggested earlier?"

"You want to go out?" His face, inches from Catherine's, reflected his surprise and disappointment. Sitting next to her, holding her in his arms, Brennan suddenly had no wish to go anywhere for a long, long while. "Well, if we're going to do this date thing right—"

"What's right to you and right to me could be very different things."

Catherine tilted her head back and looked into his clear blue eyes. The light and teasing words she had just spoken seemed inappropriate to the way Brennan Richards was looking at her.

Gently he crossed the inches that separated them. His lips brushed hers, then pressed, opening to claim her mouth with more urgency than was in his earlier kiss.

Despite every brain cell's urgent call to order, Catherine allowed the kiss to deepen. Concern for her business and their safety, as well as her plan to contact the police, retreated to a far corner of her consciousness. Suddenly Catherine cared only for herself, and she responded hungrily to her need to be close to this enigmatic stranger who had so dramatically walked into her life.

It was useless to deny she was attracted. It was useless to tell herself that he was rich, famous and too sexy to risk the hurt she'd feel when he retreated to his secluded life. It was useless not to kiss him. Though Brennan had begun the kiss gently and in an undemanding way, Catherine allowed her body to demand.

When he slipped his hand under her blouse and found her breast, Catherine felt her skin heating down her body. She reveled in his touch and used her own to explore the muscles and wide expanse of his back.

Brennan undid her blouse and ran his tongue over her collarbone, then down her chest. He nibbled and nudged with his lips. "Your skin is gorgeous," he murmured.

A noise from somewhere in the house distracted Catherine. Her eyes fluttered open and she concentrated on it, but only heard her racing pulse and Billy Joel's voice plaintively singing on the radio. Catherine focused her attention on Brennan. His dark hair curled in heavy circles around his ears. His eyes were warm, and his mouth was slick and hungry looking.

She buried both hands in the luxurious tresses and pulled him closer. "Your hair is gorgeous."

Brennan smiled. "I want you, Catherine. Come into the bedroom with me."

Catherine experienced a jolt of pure, sexually charged delight. "What's wrong with right here?" Her voice was husky, and her bones felt weak with excitement.

"There's a right way and a wrong way to do everything," he intoned, a note of teasing in his voice. "And I want our first time to be perfect." His hand trailed along her thigh, then rested on her hipbone. He rubbed her leg with long, caressing strokes. "Come on," he whispered.

Brennan stood and pulled her to her feet, kissing her long and deep as if to seal a bargain, then led her toward the darkened hallway. He snapped off the radio and checked the lock on the front door, then took her arm. Only a faint glow from the skylight and curtainless French doors in Brennan's room at the end of the hallway lit their way.

Catherine's mind was whirring, but she shut out all arguments against what she was about to do. It was freeing and joyous to simply feel. She glanced sideways at Brennan, reveling at the sight of his well-defined chin and the curve of his eyelashes. He was gorgeous. Even though her common sense yelped from a repressed corner of her mind, she was delighted he wanted her as much as she did him.

They crossed through his doorway. He turned and kissed her again as she draped her arms around his neck, standing on tiptoe to fit her body next to his. His hands fumbled with the snap on her jeans, then on his.

Catherine took a deep breath, finding a sudden shyness descending as he stared hot-eyed at her. When they were both undressed, he surveyed her, then kissed her again.

Breaking the kiss, Catherine moved away enough to let her glance move down his body. His wide chest was covered with soft blue black hair that curled into a silky mat on his abdomen. He was aroused and unembarrassed about that obvious fact.

After several moments Catherine reached out and stroked his chest. "I want you, too, Brennan."

He hugged her tight against him, then lifted her onto the bed. Somewhere in the distance Catherine heard a familiar song. Out the open window the words from a radio on the beach became louder. It was Frankie Valli. Singing "Sherri." Catherine opened her eyes for a moment. But Brennan's lips found a soft spot on her stomach, and she closed them again. Whoever was on the beach listening to golden oldies suddenly held no interest for Catherine at all.

Chapter Thirteen

Catherine woke with a start that jerked her neck painfully. Her vision focused and she saw the clock on the nightstand beside her. It read 3:23 a.m.

Beside her she heard Brennan. His arm was draped over her and he lay completely still. The deep, satiated snores of contentment made her smile. They had made love three times in four hours, taken two showers and eaten the left-over roast chicken. Her smile grew wider with satisfaction, but a second later she froze.

There was a man in a white suit standing and watching them from a corner of the room. And before she could stop the scream, she saw that he had George Jesse's rifle raised and pointed directly at them. Brennan leaped out of bed at the sound of Catherine's scream, completely disoriented. The dreamless, contented state he had surrendered to did nothing to prepare him for the hallucination staring him in the face.

The French doors leading to the bedroom's private deck stood open. Moonlight poured into the room, providing a backdrop that was no longer romantic.

Facing him at the end of the bed was a man. He wore a brilliant white suit and mirrored sunglasses, and his long blond hair streamed down his thin shoulders. The intruder held a rifle pointed directly at Catherine.

The creature spoke, dashing Brennan's fleeting prayer that it was only a nightmare. "Hello, Brennan. Coming out of retirement despite all the advice to the contrary?"

The man's face was hidden in shadow, but his voice held a slight British accent and sent chills down Brennan's spine. "Put the rifle down and we can talk," he ordered, wading through his memory to put a name with the familiar voice.

"Ah!" the intruder gasped melodramatically, "was that an order, boss man?"

Goose flesh crawled along Brennan's upper arm as something familiar itched his brain. Standing in nothing but his boxer shorts, he was cold, but he knew it was dangerous to move too quickly. Slowly Brennan folded his arms across his naked chest. "No. It wasn't an order. Just a sound suggestion. I think we need to talk. About the past, if that's where your grudge against me lies."

The white-suited man giggled. The sound was incongruous and jolting. "Reminds me of a song, Brennan. Remember 'Talk Too Much'? Silly little song. Silly little suggestion." The rifle barrel shifted, so that it was pointed at Brennan. "I need the bullet you picked out of the sand. Where is it?"

Brennan looked at Catherine. She was hunched against the headboard of the bed, her bare legs smooth and vulnerable-looking. Her hazel eyes were wide with shock. Brennan turned to the gunman. "It's in the top drawer of the dresser you're standing next to."

"Come get it, Brennan. My hands are a little full right now."

"I'll get it," Catherine's nervous voice broke in.

"Stay put!" Brennan commanded as he saw the rifle barrel jerk uneasily in her direction. "Just point that back over here. Catherine's not going to do anything dumb."

"I'd say she already has. Hooking up with you wasn't real bright." The sunglasses shook as the man laughed mirthlessly. "I told you he was dangerous, Miss Grand. You should have listened to me."

For a moment Catherine couldn't breathe. The voice of the man holding the rifle had changed effortlessly to that of the curly-haired policeman who had called himself Gutierrez.

"Who are you?" she whispered, fear pounding inside her.

"I'm the ghost of Christmas past, honey. But my beef's not with you." The voice changed back to the flirty, faintly British accent. "Now get the bullet, Brennan. It's time I was going."

Brennan moved deliberately toward the dresser. He opened the drawer with his right hand, his mind considering all the options. If he rushed this maniac, the gun could go off and hit Catherine. He couldn't risk that, he decided. His fingers found the cold steel of the bullet. At the same time, he realized that the rifle probably wasn't loaded. Brennan had checked it himself earlier, and he doubted that the gunman had brought ammunition with him.

A second hunch grew stronger each second as his earlier recognition finally connected itself to a name, and he came to a startling conclusion. *The man dressed in the white clothes and sunglasses isn't a man at all.* Brennan held the bullet in the palm of his hand, remembering that "Talk Too Much" was the number-one hit on Ellen's album. "Is this what you wanted, Jane?"

Catherine gasped, "You're Jane Scarlett?"

The available light was reflected off the sunglasses. "Very clever, singer boy. But Jane Scarlett is a person of the past.

Now I'm anyone and everyone I want to be." The blond head swiveled in Catherine's direction. "Get any jobs for me yet, Catherine? Now that you can see for yourself how grand my illusion ability is, I bet you'll try harder to book me."

"What are you talking about?" Brennan demanded. He took a step toward Jane, crushing his fingers into a fist around the bullet.

"Tell him, Miss Grand." The blonde threw off his sunglasses. He removed his wig, revealing dark, slicked-back hair.

Catherine shuddered and flattened herself against the headboard of the bed. The intruder's voice had changed yet again. Catherine was stunned. As she spoke the name, it seared her throat. "Tommy? My god, is it you, Tommy Lyle?"

"What the hell is going on here?" Brennan yelled.

No one moved as the breeze softly came through the room. Finally Catherine spoke, hoarse with fear. "This person is one of my look-alike models. Tommy Lyle. He did a stint as John Travolta for a clothing manufacturing show." Catherine felt suddenly ill. The situation was truly strange. "Why are you doing this, Tommy?" she whispered.

"Why are you, Jane?" Brennan yelled. Despite the slicked-back hair, Brennan could only relate to the creature in front of him as Jane Scarlett. The fact that his ex-back-up singer was masquerading as a man didn't surprise him. He was too numb from looking down the barrel of a gun for something like that to sink in. "What can you possibly gain by carrying on a ten-year-old vendetta against me?"

"Oh, I don't live in the past, Brennan. This isn't *my* vendetta. I'm just hired help. Now give me the bullet."

Brennan clutched the lead slug tightly. "Who are you working for? Siobhan? George Jesse?"

"Give me the bullet or I'm firing this gun." Jane's voice dropped again, sounding like Jack Nicholson's. "And in case you're thinking of testing me, just remember how good a shot I was when I took Johnnie Lord out."

"Give it to him, Brennan," Catherine pleaded.

Brennan's features were set into a stubborn glare. "You are sick. You need help. Put the rifle down and I'll see that you get it. But this nuttiness is going to stop now. Tonight!"

"I'm no nut!" Jane hollered. The rifle was raised and the voice grew deadlier. "You always were very judgmental, Brennan. Ten years ago, just because you didn't approve of my little habits, you tried to put me away! I think you're the one who needs some help."

"I do need some help, Jane. I need help understanding what it is you want. If it's a promise that I won't perform, you've got it."

Jane's mouth tightened. "No matter what you say, I know what you'll do. You'll perform. Or the look-alike will perform. The deejays play your records. Your fans say they still love you. The bottom line is that it's not fair, Brennan. You don't deserve your life! You're not entitled to it!"

All the muscles in Brennan's back bunched together, ready to act. "So what do I do, Jane? What do I do to square things with you?"

The laugh emitted by Jane Scarlett was bitter. "Give me the bullet, Brennan. And just relax and play along. After all, you wouldn't want Ellen's kids to be orphaned a second time."

At that moment Brennan decided to act. He hurled himself directly at Jane. The gun's hammer exploded as the barrel spewed fire and smoke across the dark room.

"No. My God, no!" Catherine screamed as she watched Brennan leap across the room toward the figure in white. He made contact with Jane, and they both crashed into the wall.

Wildly, Catherine looked around for a weapon as the two people on the floor grappled and swore and threw punches that landed with sickening thuds. She picked up the empty Chardonnay bottle and rushed to them. Swinging for all she was worth, she connected with the head of the white-clad intruder. The bottle didn't break, but merely bounced off. A pair of powerful legs kicked at her, tripping her in the darkness. Catherine smacked her head against a nightstand as she toppled against the bed.

"Catherine, get away!" Brennan hollered.

I have to call the police. Get help! Catherine tried to stand. She'd do anything to get to the doorway and safety. A hand clawed at her leg and she screamed again, kicking frantically. Finally, she freed herself. She pulled herself to her feet, jarring her broken finger and crying out as she ran toward the door. She tried to think of where the nearest phone was, decided on the kitchen and hurried faster. When she stepped into the hall, the gun went off behind her. Catherine turned just as the rifle belched destruction a third, and final, time.

THE BINOCULARS WERE trained on the back entrance of the rented house. The watcher looked through them again, then cursed as Jane Scarlett came running, arms flailing, across the deck. The white suit was easy to see in the moonlight, as was the fact that Jane had the rifle with her.

The watcher removed the binoculars and walked to the Rolls. It was hidden in the scrub eucalyptus that had blocked the Pinto from view. *Something went wrong. Everything went wrong.* These realizations were sobering and potentially deadly. If Jane had killed Brennan Richards and

Catherine Grand, things were going to be much more complicated.

It was time to switch to Plan B. Quickly Jane's coconspirator opened the trunk of the Rolls and removed the cardboard box, walked to Jane's car and placed it gently on the Pinto's back seat floor. Moments later Jane scampered up the sand dunes, out of breath and wild-eyed.

"I shot him! God, I think I killed them both!" she cried, then collapsed against the side of the Rolls.

"Get hold of yourself. I want you to get into the car and go home. Now, Jane!"

"I'm going to go to prison," Jane sobbed. "Maybe even to the gas chamber."

A strong hand grasped Jane's heaving shoulder. "No, you're not. Get in the car and go. I'll go back for the bullet. There's nothing to tie you to this or the shooting at Pretenders. Nothing. But you've got to leave now!"

Jane stared, glassy-eyed, at her companion. At Bobo's an hour ago the plan had seemed so simple. But now she didn't believe it was. Now Jane realized for the first time that something more complicated, something she didn't understand at all, was going on. And she was smack in the middle of it. "Can't I stay here until I see that you got the bullet? If I don't know what happened, I'll never sleep."

"Sleep is the last thing you need to worry about. Now get going. There're only two guards on duty at the front gate, but if someone sends them down here to the sand dunes we won't get away. You have to go now!"

Jane looked around nervously. "Okay. But be careful."

Her companion laughed sarcastically. "Why, Jane. I'm touched."

A pang of remorse stabbed at Jane. She had never hated Brennan Richards, despite the part she had willingly played ten years ago in bringing about the end of his career. And she had never wanted anyone to die, especially not Ellen's husband. He had once been good to her, better to her than anyone else had ever been. "Will you call me? As soon as you get home?" she begged.

"You'll hear from me."

A shudder traveled through Jane as the shock of the evening began to set in. "But if I killed him—"

"You don't know that you did."

"He knew it was me. If I didn't kill him, he'll tell the police."

The other person stopped dead. Brennan Richards knowing Jane Scarlett was involved in the letter writing campaign was bad news. But not fatal. "If he's alive, I'll call 911 before I leave. Now don't argue anymore. We don't have time. Drive straight home. Be sure to go the speed limit. And get rid of that suit. It's got blood on it."

Jane looked at the white trousers and cried harder. "Okay. Will you call me soon?"

"Yes. Now get going."

Jane crawled into the front seat of the Pinto and started it. The engine noise sounded like a scream in the thickening night air. Quickly she pressed the button on the bulky tape recorder beside her, and the comforting sounds of "Sherri" drowned out the noise of the car as well as her thoughts. She grasped the steering wheel with shaking hands. Jane didn't feel like her legs were strong enough to press the gas pedal, but she forced herself to concentrate and the Pinto moved around the Rolls. Jane waved through the window, but got no response.

After two minutes of tense waiting, the Rolls's ignition fired up the big, quiet motor. A quick glance at the car's clock showed 4:01 a.m. In nineteen minutes the bomb would go off. By then, the conspirator estimated, both the Rolls and the driver would be safely home. Jane Scarlett would be a handful of dust in the wind.

The driver smiled as the voice of Brennan Richards filled the rich interior of the car. The Rolls gracefully followed the path to the Pacific Coast Highway, back to the house full of secrets in Santa Monica.

CATHERINE TRIED TO STAND, but when she put weight on her left leg she toppled to the carpeted floor in agony. "It can't be broken," she said aloud, trying not to cry when she felt the swollen area around her ankle. Gamely, she pulled herself onto her knees and started to crawl into Brennan's bedroom. She had played dead as long as she could stand to. She had to get to the phone, but first she had to check on Brennan. If Jane Scarlett or Tommy Lyle or whoever the killer was still waited for her, then so be it.

A pain in Catherine's right shoulder made her moan, and her broken pinky throbbed. She crawled the few feet to the bed, dizzy with pain. The bullet fired at her had somehow missed, but she had run headlong and fallen into a heap on a massive oak table in her panic to escape. It seemed she had been unconscious for a few minutes, but in her shock over tonight's attack, Catherine wasn't sure.

Holding her injured right hand palm up and like a claw, she managed to get to the center of the room. It was then that she found Brennan. He was lying on his face, his left arm flung out as if he'd tried to grab at a lifeline but failed.

From three feet away Catherine could not tell if he was breathing, but the dark smear on the beige carpet near his head confirmed her worst fear. It was blood. A lot of blood. "You've been shot!" she sobbed, then pulled herself forward. "Brennan. Brennan, don't die."

"Cath?"

Catherine stopped and listened. "Brennan? Can you speak?"

"Cath? Are you okay?" His dark head moved slightly, and his left arm moved tentatively toward his face. He tried to prop himself up, but faltered and fell back.

Covering the distance separating them, Catherine reached her left hand out and grasped Brennan's right wrist. The pulse was slow but steady. She put her head on his back, partly to comfort him, partly to comfort herself and allow a moment of joy that he wasn't dead. "Stay still. Tell me where you've been shot."

He grasped her leg with his left hand and squeezed. "Are you okay?" he demanded hoarsely.

"Yes. I've wrenched my ankle, but I'm fine. What about you?"

At that moment Brennan turned his face to her. Despite every desire not to, she cried out. Blood dripped down his forehead and ran in disfiguring rivulets across his ears, nose and cheeks. His bottom lip was split open and swollen.

"I'm great." He tried to smile and failed miserably. Tentatively he touched his scalp. "I guess the bullet nicked me."

"There's so much blood!"

He pulled her close and hugged her arm reassuringly. "Head wounds bleed a lot. I'm okay, really. I was deaf for a few moments, but I'm okay now." Suddenly he thought of the fear he had experienced. Despair and anger had welled up in him right before he had jumped Jane. Despair that Catherine was going through this, and red-hot anger that he could do nothing to spare either of them.

Catherine sat up and cradled her hand in her lap. "I'm going to call 911. We'll get to the hospital and talk to the police there."

"No police."

For the first time in her life Catherine knew what people meant by living a nightmare. "You're crazy." She began to laugh. It was a mirthless, hysteria-edged sound. "You're absolutely crazy! You've been shot, Brennan! I probably have a broken hand and ankle."

Brennan tenderly reached for Catherine and pulled her close. He knew she was in shock. He probably was, too, he realized. But he could think clearly enough to see that calling the police would only send Jane Scarlett into deeper hiding. He'd tried to find her ten years ago, as had the authorities. "The police won't be able to find Jane, Catherine. You saw her little show tonight. She'll simply change her identity and hide. She'll do who knows what to me and you and our families if we let the media and police turn this into front-page news."

"What do you suggest we do?" Catherine demanded. She felt like slugging him for talking so calmly. She felt like crying because she knew what he said was true. "You're hurt. I'm hurt."

"Well, let's see first how hurt we are. Can you bend your fingers?" Brennan asked gently.

Except for the splinted one, she could.

"How about your ankle? I know it's sore, but can you stand on it? Come on, let's try."

They grunted and groaned and stumbled against one another, but finally stood. Her body hurt, but not as badly as it had a few minutes before. Catherine glared at Brennan in the soft light. "I broke my other ankle in high school. Running track. This doesn't feel anything like that."

"Good." He weaved a little with dizziness and leaned against the dresser. "Let's go into the kitchen. You can check out my pupils to see if I'm concussed, and if you can stand it, I'd appreciate a bandage." Brennan gestured toward his scalp. "Good thing I've a hard head, my girl."

"Good thing for who?" she asked ruefully, then led the way to the kitchen.

They located alcohol and peroxide, swabs, bandages and an elastic bandage for Catherine's ankle. After a half hour of working on one another, they made their way into the living room. The first rays of sunrise were glimmering off the dark blue water, and the horizon was peach and purple and gray, like a kindergartener's first chalk drawing.

Catherine stared hard at Brennan. His bruised face was as multicolored as the sky. His blue eyes were dark and fatigued. "Okay, now what?"

"We've got to find out who Jane's working with."

Catherine shakily reached for the steaming cup of tea in front of her and brought it to her mouth. "It must be George Jesse, don't you think? She was living there. We found the gun there. Johnnie Lord was shot at George's club."

"You might be right."

"But why would Jesse do it? Does he hate you enough to try several times to kill you? To kill someone just because he looks like you?"

"I don't think so," Brennan answered quietly. "And that's something that bothers me. Why am I still alive?"

Catherine sloshed tea on her hand and stared incredulously at Brennan. "Excuse me? You're complaining that you're still alive?"

"No. But don't you think it's rather odd that I am? A bomb is left for me, but it's not powerful enough to kill me. A shot is fired at me on the beach, but it misses by a mile. Now Jane Scarlett has every opportunity to blow me away, and she doesn't. Why?"

"It doesn't make a lot of sense, does it?" Catherine frowned and tried to sit more comfortably on the couch. "And look at what's happened with me. I get a bomb, which did enough damage to kill me. Someone breaks into my house and leaves messages, sends out phony invoices and press releases to ruin my business—''

''What invoices?''

Quickly Catherine filled Brennan in on the details. ''What occurs to me, Brennan, is that someone is looking for publicity.''

''But why ruin your business to get it? That doesn't make sense.''

''I don't know.'' Catherine buried her aching head in her left hand. ''None of it makes sense. We should dump it all on the police, Brennan. Really.''

''I can't risk the kids, Catherine. And besides, if we go to them, the amount of publicity will double or even triple. Something tells me that's just what Jane Scarlett and her friend want. Though I don't know why.''

''What was all that nonsense about you having the life you don't deserve?'' Catherine stared at Brennan. ''Didn't that strike you as odd? Like Jane was jealous of you.''

''It's all odd.'' Suddenly Brennan felt too weary to breathe, much less talk. He leaned into the soft cushions and closed his eyes. His arm reached for Catherine, and he pulled her close. ''We've got to find George. He's got the answers, I know it.''

''I'm glad someone does.'' Catherine didn't want to, but she reveled in being held again in Brennan's arms. The man had turned her life upside down in one short week, but she couldn't say she would change anything. ''It's nearly six. We should head to Pasadena before the traffic gets terrible.''

Brennan turned to Catherine and winked. ''Have car, will drive. You want to stop for breakfast?''

''No.'' She unwound herself from the couch and stood. ''I'll change and pack. We should clean up the bedroom, too, before Ellen and Liam get back.''

"You're right." He continued to sit on the couch. "We should dig out the bullets and paint, too. Have the carpet cleaned."

"Don't be smart, Brennan."

Her words put a ghost of a grin on his face. "I'm just teasing, Cath. You're always so eager to do the right thing, even now."

"The right thing would be a shower, makeup and a phone call to the police. But instead I'm listening to you. So much for me doing the right thing," she shot back.

"Even banged up and bruised and with no makeup on you look beautiful, Cath. You are beautiful."

"You are nuts."

"I'm falling for you. Hard."

Brennan's words made her want to cry with frustration. "Get up."

He did. Wearily. "Does this mean the date's over?"

Catherine uttered a one-word curse that delighted and surprised him. As she limped down the hallway, Brennan followed, agreeing silently with Catherine that he might well be nuts.

Chapter Fourteen

The ride to Catherine's apartment started smoothly, but twenty minutes into the trip Catherine and Brennan came upon a solid wall of stopped vehicles.

"Now what?" Brennan said.

"A wreck. We better get off the freeway."

"And go bloody where?"

Catherine sighed. It was going to be a long drive. They were both exhausted, sore and preoccupied with doing something to end the quagmire of danger they were sinking into. "Don't worry, I know how to get home on the side streets. If you'll just drive by the rules—"

"I don't need to hear a lot of bunk about my driving." Brennan slammed on the brakes to avoid piling into the station wagon in front of them. His neck was blotched red, and he kept his eyes averted from Catherine's.

"Please just get off the freeway at the next exit and go right." Before he could argue she flipped on the news station. The announcer was warning everyone away from the roadway interchange where they now sat.

A plume of smoke ahead marked the site of the trouble. The radio announcer added the details "The single-car collision caused a spectacular fire to tie up traffic in both directions. There appears to be one fatality, although firefighters and rescue workers at the scene have made no further identification. A passing motorist who stopped to help reported to police that he heard a tremendous explosion before the car, a brown American-made sedan, burst into flames." Catherine snapped off the radio.

"After you go right, drive two miles and turn right again," she said. "There's a drive-through doughnut place at the corner. We can get some coffee."

"You're sure?"

"Yes."

For the next ninety minutes Catherine directed Brennan through six suburb communities, but the side-street maneuvering in the Monday morning traffic was tense and exhausting. By the time they got back on the freeway in Encino they had endured three disagreements about driving rules and two near collisions.

Catherine spotted the Allen Avenue ramp and breathed a sigh of weary relief. Never had she been so glad to see home.

"These bloody roads should be bombed," Brennan snarled between clenched teeth.

"They're better than in a lot of places. There are just too many people using them who don't know how to drive properly."

He let her challenge pass. "It seems all we've done is drive for the past bloody week."

"Welcome to L.A.," Catherine replied. "Land of fruits and nuts and gridlock."

Brennan grumbled something unintelligible, swung the van around a stalled Toyota and gunned the engine. For two miles they were silent.

"I'll be back to pick you up after I get Ellen and Liam," Brennan announced. He pulled in to the driveway that led to her apartment complex.

"No, you won't. I told you last night I'm staying here. I have a full week of work." *And a lot to do to prepare for the Johnnie Lord concert.* It was a topic she couldn't stomach discussing with Brennan. It was a topic she didn't even want to think about.

Brennan turned off the ignition and hobbled out of the van. Catherine sat and waited for him to open her door. He surprised her by reaching up to assist her, his big hands sliding around her waist as he lifted her.

"Keep your weight off that ankle."

Her glance met his eyes. Catherine smiled. "Thanks, I will. Why don't you go ahead and go to the hospital to pick up Liam and Ellen. While you're there, maybe someone could look at your scalp—"

"Hospitals automatically call in the police for gunshot wounds, Catherine."

"I know." She wished she could take the words back the moment she uttered them.

He released her and frowned. Catherine turned and tried to reach for her bag. "I can manage the duffel. Really, why don't you just get going."

Brennan gave her a look that said he was mad and defiantly yanked the overnight bag out of the van and slammed the door. They walked uneasily together through the narrow parking lot. "When should I plan to see you again?" Brennan asked.

"Is that a request for another date?" she shot back. "Neither of us is well enough for that."

"I don't want you staying here alone," Brennan responded. "I won't have it, Cath."

"I can take care of myself."

"I doubt that. Jane Scarlett and her partner are out there, remember?"

A shiver accompanied the sudden, vivid memory. "Well, if you'd let me call the police, they wouldn't be!"

"We can't do that," Brennan replied. "You know why."

Ignoring the urge to scream, Catherine turned away from him and headed down the sidewalk to her door. Honestly, she fumed, the man was impossible. Spoiled, hardheaded, authoritarian. But deep inside she knew he was right. The publicity resulting from police involvement would cripple her business and endanger Brennan's niece and nephew and her own family.

"I'll take Ellen and Liam home then come back here later this afternoon," Brennan said. "Then we can go check out George Jesse's house again."

"No."

"No? Are you feeling okay, Cath. I know this has been an ordeal, but—"

"I've got work to do! Mountains of it. A photo shoot at the Rose Bowl at three o'clock! Will you please listen to me? I've had enough of this mess. I shouldn't even be involved. I *wouldn't* be involved, if it weren't for you. So don't ask me to do any more sleuthing."

Catherine stomped up to her front door and fished the key out of her purse. She didn't look at Brennan, but could imagine the hurt and guilt in those sky blue eyes.

Hurriedly she unlocked the door of her apartment and flipped on the lights. Sally the cat blinked from her perch on the back of the sofa, then stretched and meowed and sauntered across the living room to greet her. The feline turned tail and ran at the sight of Brennan.

"Do I look that bad?" Brennan asked, depositing the duffel bag of clothes on the sofa.

Catherine stared at him. "Yes. Your face is fifteen different colors, your eyes are so bloodshot that I can hardly see the blue, and your hair is sticking up in spiky curls."

"You don't look the picture of fashion, either. But then that's my fault, isn't it?"

His testy tone surprised them both, but Catherine laughed out loud, glad for any break in the tension. "Thanks a lot. One date and the honeymoon's over." She limped into her bedroom and threw down her purse and cosmetic case, careful not to hit her hand again. When she caught her reflection in the mirror, her good humor disappeared. "God!"

Three sets of black circles vied for space under her eyes, a green-and-blue bruise edged her bottom lip, and a darker bruise marked a one-inch circle of discoloration on her neck. Catherine moved closer to the mirror. "What in the world?"

"We call them love bites in Ireland."

Catherine whirled from the mirror to glare at Brennan, who was leaning against the door frame. "I can't believe you did this to me." When did he do this to me? she asked herself, flushing as the details of their amorous evening rolled through her memory.

"You have an incredibly luscious neck." His eyes strayed to her breasts. "And if I'm being taken to task for losing control, there are a couple of other places—"

"Don't you have to be somewhere else?" Catherine grabbed the front of her blouse with her uninjured hand as if she could protect herself from his stare.

"Do I?"

"Yes. Ellen's expecting you. Remember? It's already nine o'clock."

"Throwing me out again, are you?"

"Yes."

"Maybe I should deliver another singing telegram. Do you like Leon Russell?"

The lyrics from "You Are So Beautiful" began to roll out in Brennan's rich voice. The words made her body hum, and not with pain, Catherine realized. With need. She covered her ears with her hands. "Out!"

Brennan stopped singing and crossed his arms over his chest. The hazel-eyed woman with the bouncy good looks in front of him was frazzled and bruised, her chestnut hair a mess of tangles and curls. Brennan realized at that moment that he was falling in love. The timing stunk, his technique was more than rusty, and she didn't seem very keen on loving him back, but Brennan didn't care at that moment. "I don't know what our lovemaking meant to you, but to me it meant just that. I care about you. I want to get you out of this mess I've gotten you into. But most of all I want to take you to bed again and convince you that the honeymoon is anything but over."

His words ambushed her, taking her emotions by surprise. "I—I don't know what to say, Brennan. Last night meant a lot to me, too. I don't ever fall into bed with—"

"I know, industry types."

"I wasn't going to say that." She stopped and straightened her shoulders. "But this isn't the time for a romance. We've got to find Jane and stop her. Our lives are too screwed up to even be considering romance!"

Brennan took two steps toward Catherine and grasped her arms. "Does everything have to be cut and dried and by the book with you? Cath, you can't schedule appointments for love. You can't slough me off because I've not come into your life at a convenient time! I didn't mean for this to happen any more than you did, but it has. Stop denying the truth just because it's untidy!"

His words brought tears brimming to her eyes. "I don't even really know you! How do I know if I can trust you? This is all so fast. You're rich, famous—"

"And not your type?" Gently Brennan shook her. "Stop it! I'm rich, yes. I used to be famous. I can't help that! But I'm no liar, Catherine Grand, and I'm—"

Catherine brought her sore fingers up and placed them over his lips. "Shh, don't say any more. Let's just leave it alone."

"Okay. I'll let it go for a few hours. I'll be back by three this afternoon."

That was the time the balloon-ride pictures for Niagra beer were set, Catherine remembered. Her voice had a catch in it. "I'll be busy."

They stared at one another for a few seconds. "What's going on with us, Cath? Are we enemies again?"

Before she could answer, the distinct sound of her front door opening came to them. Brennan grabbed her and pulled her close, holding his finger to his lips. Catherine's heart pounded madly as all the fear of last night returned in a wave.

"Catherine?" came a loud voice from the living room.

She relaxed and grinned at Brennan. "Hi, Dad," she hollered. "I'm coming." Catherine walked out of her bedroom and found both her parents standing by the front door. Her mother crossed the room to hug her, but stopped short. "How are you, dear? You look awful! You've got more bruises now than you did in the hospital."

Catherine grabbed her neck and smiled weakly. "I'm fine, Mom, really."

Catherine's father, Leonard, frowned as Brennan walked out of Catherine's bedroom behind her. "And you have visitors?" he asked. "Don't you think you should get some rest, Cath?"

"I have work to do," Catherine said more sharply than she had intended. Realizing their discomfort, she kept talking. "Mom, Dad, this is Brennan Richards. Brennan, this is my mother, Dorothy Grand, and Leonard Grand, my dad.''

Brennan held out his hand and smiled, looking surprisingly well all of a sudden. He turned on the charm that had been lacking most of the morning. "Hello, folks. Mrs. Grand." He smiled more broadly. "Mr. Grand, sir. Nice to meet you."

"Brennan was just going," Catherine started.

"It's okay, Cath. I'll stay and chat a bit with your folks." He chuckled to himself over the daggerlike look she sent his way and walked to the ottoman beside the couch. "Why don't we all sit?"

Leonard Grand gave Catherine a searching look, then followed Brennan and sat down in the chair beside him. "Been reading quite a bit about you, Mr. Richards. I understand you've been involved in things like this before."

Brennan drew back. Leonard Grand wasted little time getting to the point. It was something Catherine had obviously learned from him. "Yes, sir, I have. It's unfortunate that Catherine's business is suffering from it. I'm sorry she was hurt."

"Don't apologize, Brennan. Honestly, Daddy, don't start attacking the man."

"Cath, don't misunderstand your father," Dorothy Grand interrupted, "it's just that he's so worried about you. This morning there were two reporters on our doorstep. Cheryl chased them away in her pajamas!"

"Reporters?" Brennan's voice was angry. "I'm so sorry for that. Those vultures will go after every—"

"Stop apologizing!" Catherine rose and put her hands on her hips. They all stared at her with concern, which further tried Catherine's patience. "Look. Everything is under control. Just tell the reporters I'm not really your daughter if they come around again."

"Cath!" Dorothy Grand went pale at the words.

Feeling like the class fool, Catherine bit her lip. She hadn't meant to say anything that pointed, but now that it was out, the sting of her words overwhelmed her.

Brennan saw the pain in Catherine's face; it was the same type of bone-deep hurt that shone from her mother's. Leonard Grand had paled, and his fingers were tensed around the arm of the chair.

"So, Mr. Grand," Brennan boomed out heartily, "Catherine tells me you helped her finance her business. I bet you're very proud of the success she's made for herself."

"Her mother and I have always been proud of Catherine, Mr. Richards," the older man replied stiffly.

The tension between the four of them thickened like cold gelatin. Catherine caught Brennan's glance and smiled wanly. She knew he had interceded to help. It wasn't his fault that nothing would help the strained relations between her and her folks right now.

"So, Mr. Richards," Leonard finally said as he relaxed a bit in the chair. "You're the first rock star I've ever met. Cheryl, my other daughter, told me yesterday when we came to feed Sally that you gave up quite a successful career. Don't you miss it?"

"Not a bit." Brennan smiled at Mrs. Grand. She was a lovely woman, and her huge, dark eyes reminded him of Liza Minelli's. "It was not as glamorous as it's made out to be by the news folks."

"Plenty of girls after you, I bet," Catherine's father interjected.

Brennan smiled. "Some."

"Don't embarrass Mr. Richards, Lenny," Dorothy Grand said. She sat on the sofa and patted the spot next to her. Catherine joined her. "Tell me what you've been up to. Did you two have a restful weekend?"

Catherine made a face at Brennan, telling him to mention nothing about their anything but quiet weekend. "It was fine, Mom."

"I bet it was warm at the beach," Leonard said.

"Yes, it was." Several moments passed before Catherine decided to forgo the pretense of being a hostess. She addressed her father. "Thanks for having my business lines transferred over. Did you bring my car?"

"Yes. It's outside," Dorothy answered.

"I had my mechanic check it out," her father added. "No problems, but there's a scrape along the driver's door. Probably from some flying lumber." Mr. Grand looked closely at Brennan, then leaned back in his chair. "Did you hear anything from the police, Mr. Richards? About suspects, I mean?"

"We didn't hear a word, Dad." Catherine jumped up, too nervous to allow this volatile mix of people to have another second of conversation. "Well, Brennan, I know you're anxious to go. Mom, Dad, thanks for bringing the car by. Are you off to have lunch somewhere?"

Her parents and Brennan looked at one another and a short, embarrassed silence fell.

"It's nine-fifteen," said her father. "A little early for lunch, wouldn't you say?"

"Are you sure you should be out of the hospital?" Dorothy added. "I know they said you didn't have a concussion, but—"

"Your girl is fine," Brennan cut in. "And I do need to be going." He shook both their hands and winked at Catherine. "I'll be seeing you folks again, real soon."

Catherine watched Brennan leave with a feeling that was one part relief and three parts regret.

"He's very handsome, Cath."

Catherine blinked, then smiled weakly at her mother. "He is. If you like that sort. Now, you two run along. I've got tons of work to do." She waved at her desk where the answering machine sat, it's red light blinking furiously. "I haven't checked for messages, though I'm sure there are tons of them."

"I collected a few things from your office." Leonard's voice was gruff. "Address book, what was left of your Rolodex, tax returns, pictures. Small stuff. Can I get them out of your car for you?"

"Thanks, Dad. But then you guys should go. Really, I'm okay."

Her parents hugged her without another word. Dorothy collected her purse while they waited for Leonard to bring the supplies up from the parking lot. "I'll bring some dinner later, okay?"

"Don't bother, Mom. But I'll be by tomorrow, I promise." Catherine gave her another hug, hating the look in Dorothy's eyes, hating herself for putting it there with her own cold, snippy behavior. But she couldn't help it, Catherine told herself. It was taking all her stamina just to walk and talk. Someday she would have to explain how she felt to her parents. But not today.

Ten minutes later Catherine was alone. She pulled on her oldest running suit, took the elastic bandage from her ankle, which her parents had thankfully not noticed, took three aspirin and made tea. She sat down at her desk to listen to messages, wondering suddenly about Mickey.

"Rats," Catherine muttered aloud. She had forgotten all about the pictures he had wanted to show her. Could they somehow be connected to what had happened to Johnnie Lord at Pretenders?

Before she could press the button on the answering machine, her doorbell rang. She glanced at the clock. It was ten minutes to ten. Was Karen early? she wondered.

Catherine peered through the peephole, then drew back as if she had been stabbed in the eye. Her stomach clenched and her mind went suddenly blank as the adrenaline rushed through her system.

Slowly, without making a sound, she leaned her head against the door and tried to decide what to do. The person outside knocked hard on the door, and the vibrations against her forehead made her jump. Catherine waited several moments, then looked through the peephole again. There was no sign of a weapon, and the man standing there looked as nervous as she felt.

Catherine turned the knob and opened the door. "Come in, Mr. Jesse. Brennan Richards and I have been looking for you."

George Jesse took a step back in surprise. "I've been trying to reach you, too, Miss Grand. Is Brennan here?"

Ardently wishing he was, she told the truth. "No. But he will be later. Come in."

"I'd rather you came with me then, Miss Grand," George replied. "Neither one of us is safe if Brennan Richards is coming back."

"What are you talking about?" Catherine snapped.

George put his hand into his jacket pocket. Catherine blanched, but George was in such a panic that he didn't notice. He pulled out an envelope and handed her a folded letter.

She recognized the cut-and-paste-job, and her hands began to shake. The message was long, colorful and exceedingly cruel.

"George. Give this to Miss Grand and tell her love is the biggest illusion. Cancel the Faire concert or Cheryl Grand will learn firsthand that relatives are sometimes dangerous people."

Numbly she read it again.

"You better see what came with it, Miss Grand."

She looked at him. "What?" Catherine demanded.

George Jesse held out a photo. It was a picture of Brennan Richards standing beside a huge motorcycle. The bike was parked in the lot behind Pretenders. The sign was clearly visible in the top left corner of the photo.

"I don't understand." Catherine's voice faded as she scanned the picture again. This time she did understand George Jesse's words. In the photo, Brennan Richards was holding a rifle.

Chapter Fifteen

"Where did you get this?" Catherine demanded. Her hand was trembling, mirroring her sudden lack of confidence in Brennan Richards.

"I got it at the club yesterday. I've been staying there, in a room no one knows about behind the office. You know, since the shooting." George Jesse ran a hand through his thinning hair. "I need to talk to you about some things, Miss Grand."

"What things?"

"About what happened to Johnnie Lord."

Catherine swallowed the lump that had formed in her throat. "Come in, Mr. Jesse. I'll make you some coffee."

The man looked nervously over his shoulder, then came in.

Shaken by his gesture, Catherine checked the path to her front door, but no one, particularly not a blonde in a white suit, was in sight. She shut the front door and waved her hand toward the sofa. "Have a seat."

"Thanks, Miss Grand." George collapsed as much as sat.

Catherine wondered how long it had been since he'd slept. While the circles under her eyes were dark, his were black. "Can I get you something to eat? Some coffee?"

"If it's no trouble, that would be very nice."

A few minutes later Catherine watched silently as George polished off the last of the Pepperidge Farm cookies. They had made small talk while he ate, but now she knew it was time to get to the real topic.

"Why did you bring me this picture, Mr. Jesse? Why didn't you take it to the police?"

He wiped his fingers on the yellow paper napkin several times, struggling with his answer. Finally he balled the paper up and closed his fingers around it. "You know, Miss Grand, I'm not sure. I just thought that maybe if you canceled the contract for the look-alike performance, things would get back to how they were."

"Who are you trying to protect?"

"Ah, no one. I don't know what you mean."

His tone told Catherine that he knew exactly what she meant. "You are protecting Jane Scarlett, aren't you?"

Jesse blanched at her direct question. "I care about Jane, Miss Grand. But you know, she's been sick. Jane isn't real right in her head now, and I don't think calling the police and digging up the past would help very much."

"But by bringing me this photo you're saying you think Brennan Richards *would* shoot someone?"

"I don't know. But people do strange things when they're desperate."

"I'll say. Look how strange what you're doing is. Basically you've admitted you would let Brennan Richards go unpunished for trying to kill Johnnie Lord rather than dig up the past." Initially, the photograph was jarring. Still Catherine didn't believe what she saw in the photograph proved anything about Brennan's guilt. For argument's sake, she was going to pretend she did.

"Well, you know, I guess I would. Brennan's no killer. I think he was just trying to scare the boy off."

"Some scare."

"Well, Brennan's capable of making the big gesture," Jesse offered quickly.

Catherine immediately thought of the hasty purchase of the van, the disguise and the house at the beach. Those gestures had seemed so innocent and caring until Jesse's words fell on her ears. Uneasily she sat back in the chair. "Why don't you tell me what happened between you and Brennan ten years ago?"

"You mean when he fired me?"

"That, but mostly what happened between him and Jane Scarlett."

A guarded look entered George's eyes. "Well, she was caught taking drugs, and Brennan got it in his head that I gave them to her. You know, Brennan can be pretty stubborn when he thinks he's right."

"You didn't give Jane the drugs?"

"No."

"Who did?"

Jesse coughed and squirmed. "I don't know for sure."

"But you can guess."

"Yeah. If I guessed, I would say it was Siobhan Carr. She was known to do stuff like that. And she had a personal grudge against Brennan, if you get my drift. One I think she was trying to get Jane to help her pay off."

That was an interesting topic, but Catherine didn't want to cover that ground secondhand. She would call Siobhan Carr later and try to set up a private meeting. "Did you have a grudge against Brennan?"

George blinked. "I'm not sure what you mean, Miss Grand."

Catherine took a deep breath. She was fishing, trying to connect a hundred bits and pieces of information about the past into one coherent picture, and she hoped George could help her. But her intuition told her that if she made a wrong move, George would clam up. "I know you and Ellen Richards once had an affair, Mr. Jesse. Did Brennan hold that against you? Did Ellen or her husband?"

George recoiled in surprise. "That was more than twenty-five years ago, Miss Grand. Ellen was a kid. So was I. Brennan didn't even know anything about it when it happened."

Catherine noted the increased tension in George Jesse's body. She had a hunch that she was on the right track, but wasn't sure where the track would lead. "What's your relationship with Jane Scarlett now, Mr. Jesse?"

"Why do you keep asking about Jane, Miss Grand? She doesn't have anything to do with this."

The memory of Jane dressed as Tommy Lyle, a rifle aimed at her, whirred inside Catherine's mind. "I think she does. Now why don't you tell me why you're protecting her?"

After several moments, the club owner sighed. His face collapsed into a frown, and he looked every one of his fifty years. "It's time to give it up, I guess, Miss Grand." His bleary eyes met hers. "Jane Scarlett is my wife."

That news stunned Catherine. She sat back and stared at the man. "Where is she now?"

"I don't know. After Johnnie Lord was shot she started to act real weird. The cops were real hard on her when Brennan's concert was sabotaged ten years ago, particularly a guy named Gutierrez. Jane started to cry when she heard about Lord and was nearly hysterical by the time I got home that night. She said Gutierrez was going to come back and get her. Put her in jail."

"You mean Gutierrez thought she killed Ellen's husband?"

He hung his head again. "No, she had an alibi for that. But ten years ago that cop made it real plain he thought she was the one who cut the bolts on the set. Her fingerprints were on the scaffold.'' His bloodshot eyes met Catherine's gaze. ''But that didn't prove anything, Miss Grand. Lots of people's prints were on that equipment. Brennan's were, too.''

His words raised goose bumps on Catherine's neck. ''Where was Jane when Johnnie Lord was shot?''

George started to look angry. His shallow face reddened. ''She wasn't at Pretenders. She was home, though she left that night and I didn't see her for two days. When she came around Saturday I made her stay with me at the office, but Sunday she disappeared. She does that a lot, you know.''

Catherine thought of the gun, the Pinto and the swaying curtains at Jesse's residence. ''Why weren't you two staying at your home?''

''I didn't want to see the police. Look, please don't drag Jane into this, Miss Grand. What I didn't want to bring up is that Jane was probably staying with her boyfriend. She's seeing some guy that lives around here.''

''Jane has a boyfriend?'' Catherine couldn't hide the skepticism in her voice.

''Why so shocked? It's 1991.''

Catherine measured her words slowly. ''I know about Tommy Lyle, Mr. Jesse.''

George looked defensive, then embarrassed. Finally he bowed his head and ran his stubby-fingered hand through his hair. ''Her pretending to be a guy isn't how it looks. You know, I guess to other people that's weird. But you've got to know Jane. She's an actress in one side of her heart, and a hermit in the other. She's mostly just mixed up, Miss Grand.''

''Does she own a rifle, Mr. Jesse?''

George's eyes got huge and he started pulling on his fingers to crack his knuckles. ''No. Why would you ask that?

It's Brennan Richards who owns the rifle, I'd say. That picture is proof of that.''

They both looked at the photo on the coffee table. Catherine felt another jolt of doubt.

Her previous conviction that she was in over her head returned in a rush. "I'm not going to the police now, Mr. Jesse. But you should go to them. I'm bound by contract to stage the concert for Sydney Carr, and besides, I'm not going to do something based on threats in an anonymous letter."

Catherine stood. George Jesse blinked once, then picked up the photograph and replaced it in his jacket pocket. "Thanks, Miss Grand. But I think you should know someone else—''

His words were cut short by the shrill ring of the telephone. Catherine ignored it. "Yes, Mr. Jesse?''

"Nothing. You're probably right, Miss Grand. I think I will go to the police. Thanks for your time.''

Catherine shook his hand as the telephone was answered by the machine. The volume was too low to hear who it was, but Catherine told herself she didn't care. Karen could sort out the messages when she got to work.

After she closed the door on George Jesse, Catherine leaned against it for a moment. Did she have several more pieces of the puzzle to fit together? Or was the solution suddenly very clear? Had Brennan orchestrated it all, including bombs and Jane's bizarre appearance in their bedroom? After all, no one had been killed. The bomb in her office had destroyed her place of work, but maybe that was the real reason for it. And the shots Jane had taken at them—had she deliberately missed? Both on the beach and when she had had the point-blank opportunity to kill them? And even though Jane had said she'd shot at Johnnie Lord, had she? Or was that a smokescreen to protect the real trig-german?

Was Brennan Jane's partner? And was that twisted rela-tionship the legitimate reason Brennan had not wanted Catherine to go to the police? But if it was, what was the point? Was Brennan so intent on protecting his privacy that he would blow up her office? Shaking her head, Catherine took a step. *Have I made love to a madman?* Before that equally troubling thought could be digested, the doorbell sang out, forcing her back to the present. She looked out the peephole.

"Hello, Karen!" Catherine called through the door, then pulled it open to admit her secretary.

The redhead walked with her usual saunter, stopping first to study Catherine. "God, you look terrible!"

"Thanks, Karen."

"Is that a hickey?"

Catherine slapped her hand against her neck. "No, of course it's not. Now, can we get to work? It's nearly eleven." Her foul mood escalating, Catherine pulled the box of doc-uments her father had brought off the desk and walked to the sofa. "Take down the phone messages first, please, then call Mickey and see how things are going out at the Faire site."

"You're not still going through with Johnnie Lord's ap-pearance!"

"Yes," Catherine replied patiently, "I am. Next, would you please call and check with the Niagra beer people about the shoot today."

Karen sat at the desk and pressed the button to replay the answering machine messages. "I think you're making a big mistake," she muttered.

Catherine ignored her and tried to concentrate on her paperwork. She was glad her father had thought to bring this stuff. Opening her accounting ledger, she saw that money was tight. Over ten thousand dollars' worth of invoices were past thirty days late, and another eight thousand for September remained unpaid. For several minutes she blocked out the sound of Karen talking as she organized the accounts. The twenty-five thousand dollars she stood to make on the Johnnie Lord concert was looking more and more important to the survival of her business.

"Did you get the stuff from the printers?" Catherine asked Karen when she heard her hang up the phone.

"They'll have it all tomorrow."

"Good. I think we're going to have to send duplicates of all the August and September bills with a note saying that Grand Illusions is still in business and would like to be paid."

"That's a lot of typing."

Catherine scowled and held up her injured hand. "Slow as I am, I'll help. As long as the mysterious fake bills don't keep going out, the two of us can handle it."

Karen shot a quick look at Catherine, then pursed her lips. "Sydney Carr didn't go to Europe. He called twice. You want me to get him on the phone?"

"No." Catherine stood and picked up the box of documents. "I'm going to sort through these then make some calls on my private line in the bedroom and write out some checks. Call and get some pizza delivered for lunch pretty soon, would you?"

"Yeah. Mickey wasn't home, but he left a message saying he'd see you in San Dimas at three." Karen pushed back the curtains and looked out at the sweltering sky. "You guys are going to fry in this weather."

"We'll be fine."

Before Catherine got out of the room, Karen shouted one last message. "Oh, someone left a message for Cheryl on your tape. You want me to call her with it?"

Catherine swung around. "What's the message?"

Karen picked up her pink pad. "It came in at seven this morning. A man called, didn't leave his name, but said, 'Tell Cheryl that Jane sends her regards and plans to spend some time with her soon.'" Karen snapped her gum and made a face. "Sounded like a weirdo to me."

The box slipped out of Catherine's hands and crashed to the floor. She rushed to the desk and pointed to the answering machine. "Let me hear it. Play it back."

"Catherine, what's wrong?"

"Just play the tape, Karen!"

The redhead raised her hands in the air. "I can't. I erased the tape. Why would I save it? Was it something important?"

Without a word Catherine turned and went to her room. She shut the door and collapsed on the bed. It was foolish, she realized, to think she could ignore this mess and it would go away.

It was time to find Jane and her ubiquitous boyfriend, time to stop hiding from the fact that someone was willing to do anything to shut down Grand Illusions and the Brennan Richards look-alike concert.

BRENNAN HANDED the salesman his credit card and wheeled the motorcycle out to the street. He strapped on his helmet, signed the receipt the bug-eyed young clerk brought him, shoved it into his leather jacket and took off.

The roar of the bike's pipes was satisfying, as was the bite of the wind on his bare face and the warm power of the engine underneath him. He'd left the van with Ellen. Liam was going to stay in the hospital until the late afternoon when the final test results would be in.

Brennan was determined to make some headway on resolving the identity of Jane Scarlett's partner within the next few hours. Then, he was going to go out to Catherine's photo site and convince her to come back to Malibu with them. Until Jane or Tommy Lyle or whatever she was calling herself was behind bars, none of them were safe.

He turned onto the freeway, amazed as always that no matter what time of day or night he found himself on the paved monster the traffic was staggering. He smiled as he remembered Catherine's remark, ''That's L.A.'' Then he pursed his lips as he thought about his feelings for the hazel-eyed American woman who had stirred his heart so quickly.

Catherine was soft and yielding in his arms, but went toe to toe with him otherwise. Brennan grimaced, then chuckled. She had spirit, she was stubborn, and most of the time she was on her guard. Against who and what, he wasn't sure. But he was going to take it as a good omen that she had let it down with him. He realized at that moment that he wanted this relationship with Catherine Grand to grow and evolve. The truth of how badly he wanted her shocked him. He pushed the bike faster, weaving around cars and back and forth in lanes.

What that desire for her would do to his life was clear. It would turn it upside down. He had a low-key life in Minnesota, where he worked on small projects for pet charities, wrote music no one heard and acted as a father to his sister's children. He couldn't abandon those commitments, and the sudden clenching in his guts warned him that Catherine Grand wasn't likely to abandon her life to be with him.

''Damn!'' he shouted, egging the bike on faster. Would he never get what he wanted? Twenty minutes later Brennan roared up the street to George Jesse's home. Before he could turn into the drive, he saw the commotion and stopped abruptly across the street.

A crowd of neighborhood people stood in two gossipy groups at the end of the driveway. Three police cars blocked the way. An ambulance, its back doors gaping open, was parked on the drive next to the house.

Brennan pulled off his helmet and walked slowly toward the larger group. "What's going on?" he asked quietly.

An older woman turned to him. Her voice was animated. "It's horrible. My husband, Weston, and I went over to Mr. Jesse's house with the police. They'd come to give him some terrible news about his wife but couldn't get him to come to the door. They forced the door and found him inside!"

"Dead!" a second woman said, pushing back her wire-rimmed frames. "I heard the one policeman say it looked like suicide."

"You're kidding!" Brennan couldn't keep the shock from his voice.

"Let me tell it, Millie," the first woman exclaimed. "Weston saw the letter! And the rifle! He's in there with the police, right now. I wasn't allowed in."

Millie sniffed at her friend's additional information, and both women turned to face the police officers who were walking toward the crowd.

Brennan turned and headed for the motorcycle. His heart was pumping furiously, and his brain jumped. Was this it, then? he asked himself. Was it finally over? Had George Jesse really been behind the letters and the shootings? Was he married to Jane Scarlett?

"Hey, you!"

Brennan turned to the policeman who had called out. "Sorry, officer, just getting directions." Quickly he re-placed his helmet and jumped on the bike, more anxious than ever to get to Catherine and share this new information.

With a screech of tires, two more police vehicles came up the street. Before he could start the motorcycle, the policeman who'd yelled at him had crossed the street. "Aren't you Brennan Richards?"

Brennan took off the helmet and turned around. "Yeah? So?"

"Hang on, buddy. We want to talk to you."

Brennan held up his hands in mock surrender. "No problem," he said, silently cursing. It probably was a problem to be caught in front of his ex-business manager's home.

THE WIND BLEW GENTLY from the south, pushing Catherine's heavy hair off her neck and cooling the perspiration that had gathered there. The red-and-white polka-dot scarf tied around her neck snapped in the breeze, and the crisp sound picked up her spirits as she got out of the Mercedes.

She was three thousand feet up in the foothills above San Dimas. Across the clearing from where she'd parked, Catherine spotted Mickey. He was surrounded by actors and the staff from Niagra beer, while four technicians were busy filling huge silk balloons, which lay on their sides.

"Hey, boss lady," Mickey yelled. "Ready to go up, up and away?"

"Not too far away, I hope," Catherine yelled back. "Is everyone here?"

"You're who we were waiting for." Mickey briskly walked toward her. Suddenly he stuck out his hand and grasped her arm. "As soon as we get back down, I need to show you something."

Recoiling in shock because the standoffish Mickey had touched her, Catherine met the cameraman's eyes. They were serious and full of nervous energy. "Of course. I'm sorry I couldn't see you before, but—"

"Yeah," he interrupted, dropping his hand. "I'm sorry, too. Are you okay?"

"I'm fine." Catherine felt her pulse race as a premonition of danger grew into full-blown fear. She wanted to reach for Mickey, but he had moved out of her range. He had dropped his eyes and busily dug in the leather film bag that hung from his shoulder. "I want to look at those pictures you told me about. Are they—"

"Hi!" a woman interrupted, walking over from the hot-air balloons. "Are you Catherine Grand?"

Catherine nodded as Mickey introduced her to the public relations liaison from Niagra beer, Sue Cronin, and to the two balloonists who were going to pilot the craft they were using for the pictures.

"Can you run through the itinerary one more time for us, Catherine?" Sue asked.

The group listened attentively as Catherine outlined the route. The large part of her job was organizing publicity stunts and events. This required her to be there in person on the dry runs, and usually on the big days, too, when some minor glitch always threatened to ruin things.

"Okay," Catherine began, "everyone knows what we want now. This is a practice flight for the promotional drop on Saturday over the Rose Bowl. Mickey and I will follow you, Sue, and shoot the photos to send out to the press so they'll have them on the day we do this."

"We got clearance from the F.A.A. to stay between a thousand and fifteen hundred feet. But we can't drop any samples until Saturday, right?" Sue asked. She busily scribbled in a lined steno pad she had pulled from her purse.

"Right," Catherine confirmed. Niagra beer had hired the card section at the U.S.C. game to do a promo for them during halftime. And the balloons were going to fly over and drop rubber key chains shaped like beer bottles onto the crowd.

Catherine answered a few questions, made a mental note to check that the Pasadena police department had been notified about the key-chain drop. When it was finally time to load up the gondolas and go into the air, Catherine cast a wary eye toward a billowing silk balloon twenty yards away. The noise of the burner was loud, and the whoosh of air from the oxygen tanks seemed eerie in the quiet setting.

"We're ready to board," one of the technicians yelled.

"Let's load you two up." Sue motioned for Catherine to join Mickey in the second balloon. Its yellow-and-white striped silks were swollen and blowing in the air. The tether holding the basket to the ground was taut.

Catherine let Mickey go first, then she climbed in, juggling Mickey's camera equipment. The red cotton jumpsuit was the perfect outfit, though she realized too late that she should have brought a sweater. The sun was hot, but the breeze stiff.

Their pilot, a slim Oriental man, smiled broadly. He wore heavy leather work gloves and goggles.

He gave Catherine a thumbs-up sign as they watched the other balloon rise slowly into the air. Its huge blue silks, painted with the silver-and-white Niagra Brew logo, shimmered in the late-afternoon sun.

"Hold this." Mickey handed her his light meter and a case of film, oblivious to her loaded arms. He turned away and steadied his aim.

Within seconds their balloon was also rising in the air. Until that minute, Catherine had not thought much about the operation of hot-air balloons, or about the safety of riding in one. But now, as her stomach seemed to float halfway between her knees and her feet, she watched the pilot in fascination.

He adjusted the level of the propane heater constantly, and the balloon rose and bobbed slowly as the warmed oxygen expanded inside the huge enclosure. Quickly, quietly, they were fifty feet up, then three hundred. As the pilot adjusted the burner and they began to drift westward, Catherine relaxed and looked around.

Below her the hillsides were brown and dry, parched by the California drought of the past few years, and the sky was gray-streaked and sooty as the smog banded above the Los Angeles basin, but to Catherine the view was magnificent. She flashed a victory sign to the crew in the other balloon. The soft whir and snap of Mickey's camera echoed as he moved around the five-by-three-foot gondola.

Below her a two-lane road wound up through the mountains like a faded ribbon. A motorcyclist waved furiously, and she lifted her hand and absently waved back, then turned to look at the sky and allowed her mind to go blank. Mickey's mysterious behavior and even more mysterious request receded from the center of her attention, as did the past week's incredible happenings.

With the exception of one. Meeting Brennan Richards had been a shock, a headache, a struggle and now, Catherine realized across the distance that separated her from the ground, a thrill. He was a star of a man, uniquely male and more attractive than anyone she had ever met.

The fact that he was also more demanding, arrogant and more stubborn than a farm boy's cowlick didn't detract from his charisma. She had slept with him, and she was emotionally involved with him and more than a little in love with him, Catherine admitted. But the haunting question was, could she trust him?

"Check it out!"

Mickey's voice interrupted her thoughts, and Catherine looked off to the south. Santa Anita Park was clearly in view, the bleachers a hodgepodge of colorful clothes and hats, the horses miniature flashes of sleekness. The balloon pilot pointed toward the foothills, where the afternoon shadows were beginning to creep down toward the freeway.

The sun was blinding, and Catherine shielded her eyes and watched the Niagra beer balloon. The airspeed was hard to estimate, but the gauge in her balloon said ten knots. They were making good time toward the Rose Bowl. They would be there in plenty of time to practice one landing, then go back up for the return flight to San Dimas.

Catherine allowed herself to enjoy the view. She glanced at Mickey, but he hadn't moved his face from the camera viewfinder. The pilot kept his hands busy, and they continued in a fairly straight line, a good thousand feet above the ground. It crossed her mind to ask Mickey what was so important, but she squelched it. If the cagey Mickey wanted to open up about something, the last thing she needed to supply was an audience.

Her mind focused briefly on a hunch that Mickey might know something about Jane Scarlett and the attack at Pretenders, but she remained silent. Asking the photographer if he knew the identity of a would-be murderer was not the best way to conduct a peaceful publicity session. And since peace was the biggest thing missing from her life now, she leaned back and enjoyed it.

Minutes later the high concrete walls of the circular stadium that sat atop Pasadena like a crown came into view. The sprawling parking lots nearby were empty, save for the cars clustered at the golf course and country club that bordered the stadium.

"Hold on," the pilot ordered, "we're going to go up a little before we come down."

Catherine grabbed the ropes and felt the stiff breeze in her face. It was dizzying but bracing, and she suddenly wished that Brennan was here to share this experience with her.

Mickey shoved his camera into the leather case at his feet and held on to the ropes next to her, careful to make no physical contact. He seemed pale to Catherine, and his skinny arms showed each vein.

The Niagra beer balloon was dropping fast, directly in the middle of the Rose Bowl playing field. ''Here we go!'' their pilot yelled, then adjusted the burners. Instantly their balloon began its descent. The grass rushed toward them, then stopped as the pilot made an adjustment for speed. Catherine noted the group of vehicles on the track near the east goalpost and identified those belonging to the Niagra beer ground crew. A motorcycle was also parked by the cars, and she saw the driver sitting on the parked vehicle, helmet on, watching the balloons.

Her glance roamed to the far end of the stadium where she saw a car parked in the shadowy area behind the bleachers. It looked boxy and European, but she couldn't make out the figure standing beside it from this distance.

''They're down,'' Mickey said grimly, then looked around. ''Do you mind if I get off first?''

''No.'' Catherine was surprised at how pale Mickey was. Maybe he was afraid of heights, she thought. They watched, hovering a couple of hundred feet above the field, as the ground crew grabbed the ropes and brought in the Niagra craft safely. They tethered it and lifted the crew out, then signaled for Catherine's pilot to bring their balloon all the way down.

Slowly the balloon descended, twenty feet, then ten, then only two feet lay between them and the grassy field. The pilot threw down a woven rope ladder. "This is just to hold on to. We'll help you down. It's safer not to bring the balloon all the way to the ground. Watch me."

Gracefully he draped his legs over the side, then jumped, steadying himself against the side of the gondola. Mickey scrambled across the tiny space and clumsily threw a leg over the side. Suddenly he stopped and turned to Catherine. "Catherine, you need to know something. About Sydney Carr's—"

Before he could finish the sentence, a snarling crack from a rifle rang out.

Mickey screamed and fell off the side of the gondola, crashing onto the pilot of the balloon and the man holding the tether ropes. The balloon tipped precariously, then seemed to bounce in the air and flew upward, pitching Catherine onto her hands and knees.

A second gunshot split the quiet air. Several voices below cried out in fear.

"Help me!" Catherine screamed. She tried to stand, but the balloon shot crazily upward, then jerked to a stop when one of the men on the ground madly grabbed the rope.

Clawing at the wicker sides of the gondola, Catherine finally managed to stand. A gleam of reflected sun on metal coming from the direction of the solitary car distracted her, then a third shot rang out. With a shock of terror Catherine heard the bullet whiz by her. The man holding the rope dropped it and fell to the ground, covering his head to protect himself.

The balloon jerked once more, then rapidly ascended. Catherine clutched the ropes and screamed. Numbly, she saw the motorcycle take off around the track and disappear through the exit. A last peek over the side showed the men below getting smaller and smaller as the blue sky seemed to suck her upward into the unforgiving sun.

Chapter Sixteen

Brennan squeezed the accelerator and shifted the motorcycle into high gear. When the bike hit the straightaway he chanced a look up and saw Catherine's head appear over the side of the balloon. The yellow striped silks were still rising rapidly. The tether lines dangled, and the gondola swayed slightly with the off-balanced load.

He slowed, squinting into the fading sun. A glance upward confirmed the balloon was directly above. Thankfully it was drifting in a fairly straight line above the narrow street curving beside the Rose Bowl. He doubted that Catherine had any experience operating such a balloon, but surely the other crew would take the second craft up and coach her down, Brennan reasoned. What worried him most was that she was moving at a low altitude, less than three hundred feet, he estimated.

At that height, the huge power lines on the hills beyond the residential Pasadena neighborhood were an immediate threat. Not allowing himself to dwell on the danger to Catherine, Brennan put his head down and drove, checking her location every few seconds.

"Please," he said, "don't let her be shot." If she was bleeding and in shock— "Bloody damn!" he yelled at the empty road in front of him. How could this happen? How could he be on the verge of losing the first woman in his life who meant more than the past, who meant the future?

Minutes ago, he had watched from across the field, sure that the mystery was solved and the danger over. The cops at George Jesse's house had given him a letter to read and had then grilled him about why he had come to the house. Finally they had let him go at three o'clock. He'd been smugly convinced that the mysterious events and the threats had been eliminated. Brennan had been relieved, excited even, at the prospect of resuming a normal life.

But the gunman at the stadium proved him all wrong.

Grimly Brennan snapped off his thoughts and rode carefully, knowing he had to stay with Catherine if he was going to have any chance of helping her.

Struggling to signal to the motorcycle rider below, Catherine grasped her hair and pushed it from her face. She fought to regulate her breathing, telling herself to be calm and to figure out how to get down. All the questions screaming inside her about the identity of the gunman receded as she ordered her mind into a state more capable of dealing with a far more urgent question. How was she going to save her own life?

Saving her life was more important than ever, she realized with a jolt. Catherine cast another look over the side, sure that the figure below was Brennan. His black hair glistened in the late rays of sun, and the determined hunch of his shoulders told her that he was going to help.

But how? Catherine braced herself and pulled up the tether lines, hoping that would restore the balloon to a more even course. With that chore done, she hunched over the burner, trying to recall the exact moves the pilot had made. It was useless, she realized, staring at the two gauges. She had been absorbed with the view, her thoughts and Mickey.

Mickey. Catherine felt a twist of betrayal. Had Mickey meant to warn her when the gunshots scattered them? Was he working with Jane Scarlett? George Jesse's mention of Jane's boyfriend slammed into her mind, and she swallowed hard. It must be Mickey, she realized with a final drop in spirits. And it was Mickey who always knew her schedule. Mickey who had access to office supplies and customer information. Mickey who had attended Johnnie Lord's concert. Grand Illusions had been sabotaged from within. And she had blindly assisted!

A draft of cold air splashed against Catherine, returning her to the present. The balloon was listing wildly to one side. Frantically she looked around. A hillside, thickly wooded and steep, loomed ahead. She had to figure out some way to steer the balloon and get some elevation, or she would crash.

Grimly Catherine grasped the propane burner jet and turned it slightly to the right. The flame sputtered, then burned brighter. Slowly, but consistently, the balloon began to rise. A strong, cool current of air from the west washed over her, and the treetops receded another hundred feet. For several moments Catherine allowed herself to relax, thankful that the on and off knobs were easy to turn. When it was time to go down, she would know which way to turn them.

Thinking of landing made her clutch the sides of the gondola and search the ground for a flat, open area. She was still drifting over the road, but was clearly moving to the north while the paved surface was curving to the south. Scrub pine and underbrush on the hillsides was giving way to mature trees. Within minutes, Catherine realized, she would be over the thick forests, with no clearings and no road on which Brennan could follow.

Suddenly the balloon jerked sideways, then plunged down fifty feet, then fifty more. Catherine screamed and was pitched into the side of the basket. Nausea and dizziness overwhelmed her. Fighting against the urge to close her eyes and hide on the floor, Catherine grabbed at the heavy cable that lashed the balloon to the gondola and pulled herself to her feet. The balloon seemed to be hovering at a stable height now, but the treetops were very close.

Her heart beat frantically as she realized she could no longer see the road or Brennan. The balloon was drifting fast toward Mount Wilson. Catherine's arm shook with the effort, but she hung on. She knew that the closer she got to the higher elevation the more blustery the wind would be. Her condition would be even more precarious. She had to bring the balloon down. And she had to bring it down now!

Fighting to keep her hands steady, Catherine reached for the burner knobs. Out of the corner of her eye, she caught sight of a glint of reflected light and jerked her head toward it. What she saw made her moan with terror. Directly in her path loomed a line of power poles, their huge, metallic arms opening toward her like angels of death.

Unable to bear imagining what kind of death that would be, Catherine grabbed for the burner and jerked the knob. The balloon began to descend, listing precariously to the left as the cool air off the mountain slammed into the sides of the sensitive silk. But the balloon drifted closer to the mountain and away from the power poles, at least for the moment.

Numbly Catherine ventured another look down. The dusty outline of a fire trail cut through the trees. She turned the knob again, and the balloon fell more quickly. The trick must be to hover just above the ground, she reasoned, flicking the knob back and forth gingerly with the uninjured fingers of her right hand. Her technique seemed to work. The gondola skidded and shuddered, bouncing against the prickly treetops.

The thought struck her that she might be able to bail out of the ninety-foot-tall balloon and into the trees, but at the speed the air was carrying her, it would be suicidal. She remembered reading that jumping from a car going as slow as twenty miles an hour could kill a person, despite all the television cop show examples to the contrary.

Besides, Catherine told herself, she was still a hundred feet or more off the ground, and the thought of shimmying down a tree from that height seemed dangerous.

No, her best bet was to keep babying the burner controls and trying to set the balloon down on the fire trail. Catherine took a deep breath, allowing a moment's feeling of control to refresh her. As she did, the yellow-blue flame sparked bright, then died.

Immediately the gondola swung in a wide arc. Catherine screamed and fell to her knees. The craft careened into a towering pine, and the jarring crash threw her backward. The crack of the basket against the trunk hurled Catherine across the gondola again. For an instant she stared into a sky full of yellow silk, then lost consciousness as the balloon, the basket and her body came crashing to earth.

BRENNAN GUNNED the motorcycle up the incline, but it was too steep and the engine died. Furiously he jumped off and threw the bike to the side. He had lost sight of the balloon over the ridge of the hill, but was praying Catherine would continue to drift in a northerly direction. By following the fire path, he hoped to intercept her somewhere soon, and to be there to help coax the silk-shrouded death trap out of the sky.

He began to run up the rutted and scarred path. He sent stones and bits of rock skittering in a thousand directions with his heavy leather boots. His heel caught in a hole, and Brennan went sprawling onto the five-foot-wide pathway, but he pushed himself up and continued on. The hills were quiet and cooling fast. No breeze stirred, and sweat ran down his forehead. He tried not to imagine what would happen to Catherine if the wind died completely.

His gut wrenched as he remembered the startled and frightened look on her face as the balloon had taken off suddenly. "Hang on, Cath," he muttered, realizing he was talking as much to himself as to her.

After ten minutes of exhausting straight-up climbing he reached the crest of the hill. Shading his eyes against the glare, Brennan searched the sky for the yellow silk balloon. He spotted it, bouncing and jerking like a marionette's puppet three hundred yards to his right. The basket skimmed the trees, throwing an enormous shadow as it scudded low across the treetops. Brennan ran faster, shading his eyes to pick up a sign of Catherine.

The trees were thick, but he darted into them, trusting his sense of direction to lead him to Catherine. Twenty seconds later he heard her scream and watched in horror as the wicker basket, trailing shredded lengths of billowing silk, crashed into the treetops.

"CATHERINE? CATHERINE? Wake up!"

The words were sharp-edged and stern, and Catherine tried to move away from the speaker. But the arms cradling her were tender, and she was held fast. Her eyes flickered open to find Brennan's face inches from hers, his blue eyes anguished, his mouth a slash of fear.

Weakly she raised her left hand toward his cheek. "Brennan."

He kissed her fingers and pulled her closer. "God, Catherine, I thought you were a goner for sure."

"What happened? I remember tipping and falling..." She shivered, unable to say more.

"Shh. You came down. You were inelegant as the devil, but you came down. That huge group of burned-out yearlings cushioned you." He waved toward the embankment. Catherine's gondola rested on it. Adrenaline flooded him. "Are you okay, Cath? Does anything feel broken?" He looked at her intently. "You weren't hit by the bullets?"

At his words, the chilling memory returned. "No." Catherine resisted the comfort of Brennan's embrace and sat up. She tied the scarf at her throat. "Did you see who was shooting, Brennan? Was it George? Or Jane?"

"No. I didn't see who was shooting at you. But it wasn't Jane or George."

"Don't be too sure. George came to see me. He had a picture..." Catherine's voice trailed off. She was miles away from help, traumatized and at the mercy of the Irishman with the bad temper and strong arms. If she was wrong about him, she could have just fallen, like the fat, from the pan into the fire. But the look of concern, even love, on Brennan Richards's face convinced Catherine once and for all that the picture, like so many other things this past week, had been a carefully orchestrated hoax.

"What is it, Cath? What did George show you?"

"A picture of you. Holding a rifle."

His head snapped back as if he had been slugged. "Me with a gun? Never. I've never owned a bloody rifle, nor would I."

"I know. I think the photo was concocted by Mickey. He was going to give it to me Friday, but then the bomber stepped in." Quickly she filled Brennan in on her suspicions about the photographer. "I think this proves something we've been missing all along, Brennan. There are two factions at war. Two sides trying to stop the Johnnie Lord concert."

Somewhere in her mind several pieces of the puzzle snapped into place all at once. "So tell me why you're sure it wasn't George Jesse or Jane."

"Jane's dead. So is George." Brennan's voice grew hard as he reached into the pocket of his leather jacket. "I went to see George when I left the hospital. Ellen and Liam couldn't go yet, so I thought I would do some more snooping. The cops were there when I got there. They'd come to tell George that Jane was killed in a car accident this morning. They think by a bomb."

Her stomach rolled and she clutched Brennan's leg with her hand. "My God. The car on the freeway this morning. It was probably Jane's car. And there was another bomb?"

"Yeah. But when the coppers showed up they found George dead from a self-inflicted shot to the head. He left a suicide note and this note for me." Brennan yanked out a grayish white envelope and opened it. "Do you want to read it or should I do the honors?"

"Go ahead," she answered wearily, leaning against him.

Dear Brennan,
Now you'll know the truth about the last few days and about ten years ago, too.

It's not a pretty picture, and it's all about revenge. Jane and I wanted some when you upended our careers, so we planned to ruin your L.A. gig. Mitch saw Jane right after the accident. She shot him in panic, Brennan, and never expected him to die. She was in a mental institution for several years after that, too, trying to get well.

I never wanted anyone to die, Brennan. Especially Ellen's husband. When I found Jane had started harassing you again and picking on Catherine Grand, too, just to get to you a second way, I knew she was losing her grip again. But when she took a shot at Johnnie Lord, all out of some twisted hate she still had for you, I knew it was over.

I think she killed herself because she couldn't take the guilt anymore. I can't either, Brennan. Forgive me. Forgive us.

Catherine and Brennan stared at one another for a second. Brennan dropped his gaze and carefully folded the letter and shoved it in his jacket.

"But I don't understand—"

"Don't you?" Brennan countered.

"No. George Jesse just implicated Jane Scarlett as Johnnie Lord's attempted killer, but—" her voice faltered "—it doesn't ring true."

"That's because it's a lie. Just like your look-alikes, Catherine. It seems like a suicide note, but the stadium shooter proved it for the fake it was."

"You mean someone killed George and faked this note?"

"I think so." Brennan got to his feet and held out his hand. "It's not safe for us out here, Catherine. If I could find you, so could he."

She slipped her hand in his and stood. "Where to?"

Brennan headed downward, toward the motorcycle. "We'll ride over and get the van and then go to Santa Monica. Casa Ugly. Let's see what Sydney has to say now."

CATHERINE HUGGED her knees to her chest, ignoring Brennan's directive to use a seat belt. After what she had been through today, admonishments over traffic accidents seemed absurd.

The florist's van stopped with a squeal of tires in front of Sydney Carr's house. "Did you think Liam looked bad?" Brennan asked without turning toward her.

"Yes. But I'm sure Ellen will watch him." They had dropped the couple off after making their way off the hillside and back to the stadium. The Rose Bowl was crawling with police, and Brennan and Catherine had found out why the other balloon hadn't followed to help her. One of the bullets had torn a huge gash in the side and ruptured the butane heater.

After giving their statements, they'd picked up Liam and Ellen, had take-out dinners and had only stayed in Malibu long enough to shower and bandage Catherine's newest abrasions.

Catherine looked at her watch. She needed to speak with Ellen alone and air a few new hunches. They just might end all the speculation once and for all. But she would probably have to wait until morning. It was nearly eleven, dark and forbiddingly foggy along the waterfront. Within the hour, the steep, twisting road would prove undrivable.

"Thanks for offering to come with me," Brennan said.

"This is no time to be out by yourself, especially the way you drive."

"I get us where we're going, don't I?"

Catherine ignored his logic. "It's also certainly no time to be paying a call on Sydney Carr and his Bride of Frankenstein."

"My, my, how you talk about your employer," Brennan said. "Don't worry, what I have to say to Sydney won't take long."

"Why don't you give me a preview?" Catherine replied. "I hope you're not bringing us to a man who has tried to kill us several times and who has killed two other people."

"Nah. Sydney's no triggerman. He never had the guts. But I'm betting he knew about this. He and George did several deals in the old days, and there's no reason to think he wouldn't have known about Jane Scarlett's part in

Mitch's death ten years ago. Or anyone else's part,'' he added in an ominous tone.

"So this is still about the past?'' Catherine asked softly.

Brennan turned toward her as the hulking outline of Carr's house showed in the headlights. "Everything is about the future now, Catherine. Our future. We're going to get Sydney to let you out of your contract. Once that's done, I say we'll stop being targets.'' His hand came down possessively on her thigh. "Then we'll do what you've wanted to do all along and let the cops untangle the last clues.''

"Don't worry about my business, Brennan. I think there may be some bigger issues here.''

He stopped the van and took her by the shoulders. "Tell me what you're thinking, Miss Grand. I know you're gnawing on something.''

The front porch light flicked on. Catherine nodded toward it. "Not now. Come on, you want to beard the lion in his den. Let's do it.''

"A kiss first.''

"Brennan—''

Brennan's mouth covered Catherine's before she could protest further. After several moments he released her. "Okay. Now I'm ready.''

Gently he helped her from the car and they made their way to the front door. They rang the bell three times. Sydney Carr himself opened the door.

The owner of Carousel was dressed in a red silk bathrobe and thongs. A heavy gold chain glinted around his neck. "Miss Grand! Rather late for a business meeting, isn't it?''

"We need to come in, Sydney.'' Brennan's splayed fingers pushed on the smooth wood.

Sydney glanced at Brennan's hand and smiled thinly. "Sure, Brennan. What's mine is yours. Hasn't that always been the way it is?'' The record company owner stepped back and allowed them to pass.

Catherine followed Brennan down the hall and into the dimly lit living room. The French doors leading to the ocean were all closed, but the drapes were open to reveal a wall of fog. It was blue black and iridescent, and it rolled and curled off the surface of the cold Pacific.

It gave the huge area a strangely claustrophobic aura, and Catherine found herself taking measured gulps of air. A single light in a corner was lit. Siobhan Carr, sans makeup, lay on a green velvet chaise wrapped in a white terry robe, smoking.

Catherine glanced at Brennan, who stood in the center of the room staring at Siobhan.

"We have guests, my dear," Sydney intoned from behind them. "Do put on a better mood and ring for Geraldine to bring some coffee and brandy."

Siobhan took a deep drag from the cigarette, then stood up slowly. She smiled at Brennan sadly, ignored Catherine and left the room.

"Well, sit down. Sit down and tell me to what I owe this pleasure, Brennan. Did you change your mind about making your comeback at the Knight Records bash?" Sydney collapsed on a huge white sectional couch.

Brennan crossed his arms. "No. I didn't. So I guess the bucks you gave George to get me to do just that was money ill-spent."

Catherine inhaled sharply and sat down. "Let me start at the beginning, Mr. Carr. We have reason to believe that you, or someone working for you, hired George Jesse and Jane Scarlett to disrupt my company and shoot Johnnie Lord."

The silence in the room was thick enough to touch. Sydney rubbed the bridge of his nose, then took a fat cigar out of his robe pocket. His eyes flicked toward the exit Siobhan had taken. "Why would I do that, Miss Grand?"

"Because you're a lousy, two-bit—"

"Brennan!" Catherine beckoned him to sit next to her, but he glared at her and only leaned. Catherine continued, "At first, I suspected you were doing it out of animosity for Brennan, Mr. Carr. But now I think it's something else."

"Something else?" Sydney prompted, again letting his glance drift to the door. "You mean like publicity? I shot at your actor and had George Jesse plant a bomb in your office for publicity?"

Catherine cringed at his sarcasm but nodded.

"You're wrong, Miss Grand. I had no reason to sabotage your plans to stage Johnnie Lord as a Brennan Richards look-alike."

"Well, somebody bloody did." Brennan crossed the room and sat inches from Catherine. "And it hasn't stopped yet." Briefly he recounted the events leading to George Jesse's and Jane Scarlett's murders.

Sydney seemed visibly shaken at the story that George Jesse was dead. "Well, so what do the police say?" he asked.

"They thought it was over," Catherine began, "but then I was attacked during a publicity stunt at the Rose Bowl. That occurred *after* George and Jane were dead. So we're back to square one. Trying to find out who is stalking us."

"And why," Brennan added bitterly. "I just don't understand the why."

Siobhan Carr walked into the room. She was carrying a brass tray loaded with coffee and a fresh bottle of brandy. She seemed very nervous and gave Sydney a questioning look.

"Ah, here you are, Siobhan. Well, why don't you pass out drinks for our guests?"

"And maybe answer a few questions," Brennan suggested.

"What's going on?" Siobhan asked, wide-eyed.

"Did you hire one of my employees to sabotage the Johnnie Lord concert?" Catherine asked, folding her fingers around the splint on her injured hand.

The silence in the room was tense. Siobhan sat on the footrest of the chaise and smiled distractedly at Sydney. "Are you asking me if I tried to kill Johnnie Lord?"

"No one's accusing you, Siobhan—" Sydney began.

"Don't be a fool, Sydney. She is doing just that," Siobhan shot back. She looked directly at Catherine. "I hired one of your employees to do something, but not that."

"Mickey Stolie?"

Siobhan deflated a little at Catherine's accurate guess. "Yes. Mickey wanted to be a rock video producer, and I offered to help."

"To help if he wrecked Catherine's business?" Brennan snarled. "Nice trade, Siobhan."

She colored at the animosity in Brennan's voice. "It was a fair trade in this business, Brennan. The kind of trade you've made in principal many times, even if you don't like to admit it." Siobhan looked at Catherine again. "But we didn't shoot at Johnnie Lord. And we didn't send you a bomb. My plan was for you to go out of business and renege on Sydney's contract."

"But why?" Catherine demanded. "First you try to buy me off, then you resort to this? Why didn't you want the Brennan Richards look-alike concert to go on?"

Sydney stood suddenly. "My wife doesn't need to explain anything more, Miss Grand. I've paid off Mickey Stolie, who I think you'll find has disappeared to another state by now. I'll also make complete reparations to you for any lost business. We'll just keep this among ourselves, for, say, a $5,000 bonus?''

"You can't buy your way out of everything, Syd." Brennan was agitated and could barely contain his anger. "I'm taking this to the police. They'll see it a bit differently, I'd say. And they'll find out the real reason Siobhan wanted this concert stopped. I think the reason has to do with Mitch's death."

Siobhan looked ill, and Sydney grasped her arm. His voice was full of menace. "Don't fool yourself, Brennan." Sydney pulled his wife closer, waving his cigar in the air. "Jane Scarlett and George Jesse are dead. The news reports tonight said the police were quite sure Jane planted the bombs, and was also killed by one. There are no loose ends for the police to look into, and if you push it, the whole nasty story will spread across every television set in America. I can put up with the heat, but I don't think you or your sister and her children can!"

"I was shot at today," Catherine said. "I'm sure they will consider that a loose end."

"I never—" Siobhan started.

"Shut up, Siobhan! Now," Sydney ordered. He narrowed his eyes at Catherine. "No one was injured, Miss Grand. Please, let this go now. Siobhan handled things badly, but she won't interfere in your life anymore. I'll cover the cost of any loss suffered by the balloonists, and as I said before, when the concert is over, we can forget all this ill will. Brennan can go home, you can go on to new clients. I'll be glad to refer them, and the past will be just that, the past. Forgotten."

"You're crazy if you think I'll let you get away with this." Catherine's voice shook. "And crazier still if you think I'll go ahead with the concert."

Sydney shrugged. "It's your choice, Miss Grand. But I think Brennan knows that the only time in my life I passed up a lawsuit was when I took pity on someone. His sister Ellen was a sweet and innocent girl, and I was young. You, Miss Grand, are anything but innocent, and I am no longer young."

Brennan made an impulsive move toward Carr, his fists clenched, but Catherine stood in front of him. "And the Johnnie Lord concert goes on?"

"Yes. Now, my wife and I need to take care of some things. So if you'll excuse us?" Brennan and Catherine watched Sydney lead Siobhan out of the room. The blonde looked as if she was in a trance.

"I can't believe him," Catherine whispered.

"Believe him, Cath." Brennan stared out at the bank of fog. He took Catherine's hand and led her out into the cold, unfriendly night.

Chapter Seventeen

"Well, at least it's all out in the open now. You were right about there being two sets of foes. Jane and George were the A team. The B team consisted of Siobhan and Mickey. What do you want to do now?" Brennan asked, as they slowly made their way down the fog-shrouded road from the Carr estate.

"I don't know." Catherine's mind buzzed with fatigue, but she was so keyed up over what had just happened it seemed like someone had poured itching powder down her back. "I still think there's more. Sydney knows something about Mitch's death. Something still isn't right."

"I got that impression, too. Siobhan was nervous as a cat. The question is, about what?"

Catherine shook her head and stared out the windshield. She could see nothing outside, but a thought occurred to her and she mulled it over. After several minutes of Brennan swearing at the weather, they finally found their way to the Pacific Coast Highway.

"Brennan, let me think out loud for a minute."

"Great. Go ahead."

"Okay. Now if we accept that Jane Scarlett, with or without George Jesse's help, shot at us on the beach, sent both of us bombs, and tried to kill Johnnie Lord, where does that lead?''

"To the fact that the girl was a real twisted sister."

"Brennan, I mean it. What's odd about that string of events? Add in that my business was sabotaged."

"Whoa." Brennan hit the brakes and waited for a police car to go by. "Okay, what's odd? It's all odd! Malicious. Destructive."

"I think we're missing something. Siobhan went to a lot of trouble to get us to not have the concert. And so did Jane and George. Or did they?"

"I don't follow." Brennan chewed on his lip.

"I just have the feeling that while Siobhan really didn't want the concert to go on, Jane was acting more to encourage publicity than to stop me. Why would she do that?"

"Siobhan hated me," Brennan began, "and she couldn't stand the thought of Sydney resurrecting me, even through a look-alike."

"I don't think this happened because Siobhan hates you," Catherine said quietly. "I think she was scared of something. And Sydney knows what it is and thinks he can handle it." Catherine felt a surge of excitement as she spoke, and her intuition told her that she was on to something.

Brennan sped up as the fog ahead of them lightened. "But why was Siobhan interested in screwing things up for you and Sydney?"

"I don't know. But look at the anonymous letters, the bombs, Johnnie getting shot—" The minute she said those words a thought struck Catherine with the strength of a blow. "Oh," she whispered.

"What?" Brennan slapped his hand against her knee and squeezed. "What is it, Catherine?"

"We need to talk to Ellen, Brennan." Catherine turned to him. "I think she might have the answer."

ELLEN PUSHED her heavy black hair off her forehead and reached for the mug of tea Catherine offered her. "You look like hell, if you don't mind me saying such a thing, my dear."

"I don't mind. And I'm sure you're right." Catherine smiled and sat down across from the petite woman.

"Sorry we had to wake you, sis, but it's very important." Brennan looked at his sister and gently brushed a tendril of hair off her cheek. "Did you talk to the kids today, by the way?"

"Three times. Rose sends her love. Neal says to tell you he wants to go to all the Vikings home games this year." Ellen smiled at Catherine. "Forgive this family talk, my dear."

"No, no. Forgive my being here at all." Catherine looked at Brennan and felt a stab of what felt uncomfortably like jealousy. Brennan had such a full family life.

"Well, let's get down to it, Ellen. Catherine wants to ask you some questions that might be tough, and if they upset you, I want you to let us know and we'll back off."

Catherine gave him a sharp look.

Ellen slapped his thickly muscled arm. "Don't be babying me, Brennan Sean Richards. Ask away, girl. What do you need to know?"

"It's about your child. The one you gave up."

Ellen twitched but her grip remained firm. "Yes. A boy. I gave him to a couple in Liverpool who had tried for years to have a child. Liam handled the adoption. I think it was one of his first cases."

"How long ago was that, Ellen?"

The older woman hesitated for a few seconds. "Twenty-seven, twenty-eight years ago. But I don't understand, Catherine. What could this have to do with what's been going on with you and Brennan?"

Probably everything. Catherine blanched at her thought and squeezed Ellen's hand tighter. Several nagging pieces of dialogue, spoken by several people, drifted across her eyes as if written there. "It may be nothing, Ellen. But has the child ever tried to contact you?"

Ellen pulled her hand from Catherine's and smoothed her hair. "I didn't—" she began, then took a sip of tea. Finally she looked at Brennan. "I never told you, but Mitch said we shouldn't be surprised if the boy looked us up. When I asked him why he'd make a remark like that, he refused to explain. Said he would tell me later."

"When was that?" Brennan pressed.

A tear fell from Ellen's eye and she hastily wiped it away. "It was the night he was killed. We'd had a hurried luncheon, Siobhan Carr was coming to talk to us, and Mitch wanted to get away before she showed up. I never mentioned it before because—" she looked stricken and touched Catherine's hand again "—because it never meant anything."

Catherine had stiffened at the mention of Siobhan Carr's name. Why was that woman always on the periphery? She hovered just above the circumstances, both past and present, that threatened them all. "Did Siobhan have lunch with you that day before the concert?"

"No. She never showed up."

"Why do you ask, Catherine?" Brennan demanded.

"Are you saying—" Ellen broke in.

"I'm not saying anything, Ellen," Catherine replied gently. "I just think it's an angle we should check on. Do you think Liam could find out the name of the family who adopted the child?"

"I'd bet on it." Brennan got up from the table. "I'll go wake him."

"You'll do no such thing, young man." Ellen pointed to the chair. "Surely this can wait until the morning."

Catherine met Brennan's glance and nodded. "Yes. Let him sleep, Brennan." She stood. "In fact, we all need to get some sleep. Since I took all my clothes home, I wonder if one of you could lend me a T-shirt or something."

"I'll get one. You two finish your tea." Ellen bustled out of the kitchen, leaving Catherine and Brennan alone.

"You can bunk with me," he said and smiled.

"No, thanks," Catherine responded. Suddenly she felt more alone than she ever had in her life. More alone and disconnected than she had after her marriage broke up, more solitary than when she'd learned she wasn't who she had grown up thinking she was.

When Ellen returned with a shirt, Catherine said goodnight quickly and went to bed, unwilling to expose or share another shred of herself with anyone.

THE NEXT MORNING Ellen, Brennan and Catherine waited patiently for Liam to come to breakfast. The three of them watched nervously while he thumbed through the paper and finished his coffee. His color was better, and he ate well.

"Listen to this!" Liam demanded excitedly as he scanned the entertainment section of the Los Angeles *Times*. "Sydney Carr and Knight Records announced last night that their gala birthday celebration will go on as scheduled!"

Catherine and Brennan looked at one another, then looked away. "We know, Liam. Now if you're finished—" Brennan said.

"You know?" Liam interrupted. "What are you talking about, Brennan? Can't this imbecile see that it's foolish to go on with this?"

"It's a long story," Ellen said softly. She poured him another mug of tea. "Now, Liam, Catherine wants to ask you something."

"Yes?"

Catherine cleared her throat, suddenly unwilling to hear the answer to her simple question. "Can you find out the name of the family that adopted Ellen's son?"

The middle-aged attorney paled and sent a shocked look in Ellen's direction. "What in the world?"

"Just answer the question, dear," Ellen said, patting his hand.

Liam glared at Brennan, who was sitting stony-faced, then turned to Catherine. "Young woman, you've brought considerable strife into this family. Now before I answer any of your questions, I—"

"For heaven's sake, Liam. Don't lecture the woman! Answer her question so we can explain!" Brennan ordered.

Liam looked around the table then put down the paper, taking time to fold and crease it. "I may be able to. There's no law sealing the information, and I know the solicitor we dealt with still practices in London. But it will take a while for him to check. After all, it was years ago!"

"It's important for all of us that you try. Please call now." Ellen pressed his hand. "It's something we should have done years ago, Liam."

The attorney, hearing the anguished urgency in his lover's voice, stood and squeezed her hand. He gave Catherine a dark look, then turned and left the room.

Brennan clenched the edge of the table. "Anyone care for coffee?"

Catherine nodded. For the next two hours, aware of the muffled conversation in the bedroom down the hall, Catherine and Ellen and Brennan scurried around, trying to keep busy and keep out of each other's way. To Catherine, the time passed painfully. In her heart, she was already sure of the name Liam would find. The name would surely break the hearts of all present.

At ten minutes to one Liam joined them in the living room.

"Well, out with it, man," Ellen pressed.

"Did you find out?" Brennan echoed.

Liam nodded curtly, then turned to Catherine Grand. "I finally located the solicitor. He was having lunch at his daughter's house. He didn't even need to check his files. It seems he handled the wills for the family. The father of the child died ten years ago of heart trouble, and the mother in 1983 of pneumonia. The boy's been in the United States for ten years, he told me. In California."

Catherine sucked in a lungful of air. "Their name was Lord."

"Right," Liam answered sharply, "John and Edith Lord. Their boy is Johnnie. Johnnie Lord."

"Not the boy that was shot!" Ellen exclaimed.

"Yes," Catherine answered tightly. "The very same one."

Chapter Eighteen

Catherine unlocked her front door and turned to Brennan. The exhausting crisscrossing of their lives was finally at a close, and she felt miserable at the thought he was going to turn away and be gone. "Won't you come in?"

"No. I'm going back. Liam booked tickets to take Ellen to Minnesota this afternoon. She wants to meet with Johnnie, but Liam convinced her that a letter should be her first overture to the boy. Especially in light of all that's happened."

Catherine felt her stomach clench, and her eyes burned with unshed tears. "Brennan, I don't know what to say. I never would have gotten involved if I'd known."

He stared at her stone-faced. "It's too late now, Catherine. What's done is done. I'm going to try and talk to Johnnie before I go back. I want to see what his intentions are."

"His intentions? I don't understand."

"The news that Brennan Richards has an illegitimate nephew running around, one who looks and sings just like him, will make a splash. Surely you must realize that? I want to know what he's got in mind, so I can prepare Ellen's children." His voice tightened and he looked away.

"I'll go with you."

"No!" His blue eyes blazed. "You've done enough, Catherine."

She turned from his accusing tone and pushed the door open. "Well that's it then. When are you going back to Minnesota?"·

"Soon."

It was unbelievable to her, but she saw that it was over. Brennan Richards's brief foray into her life had been exciting and wonderful and maddening and dangerous, but now all that was left was resentment. Inadvertently or not, she had exposed his family to shock and turmoil.

"Goodbye, Brennan." Catherine held out her hand.

Brusquely he grabbed her and crushed her to him. Catherine could feel his heart pounding, and she fought to not beg him to stay. She was choked with emotion, and couldn't speak. But maybe that was better, she realized. For what could she say?

"Goodbye, Cath. Take care." With those words, Brennan turned away and hurried down the walkway.

He never once turned back.

SATURDAY NIGHT WAS COOL and clear, a perfect California evening. Catherine parked the Mercedes at the fairground, smoothed her white skirt and looked around. People were teeming in and out of the gates, dressed in cone-shaped headdresses and laced-up jousting outfits. Jugglers, face painters and minstrels roamed the crowd. Vendors dressed in tunics and tights and bell-laden hats mingled with blue-jeaned tourists.

The smell of meat pies and cotton candy wafted on the breeze as Catherine scanned the parking lot for Sydney Carr's Rolls. She spotted it behind the administration building.

Gamely she started walking toward the set. It was seven-thirty. Carr's guests were to meet for cocktails in a huge tent on the back lot. Johnnie Lord's entertainment was to begin promptly at nine.

Catherine cringed at the thought of the young man. She had spent the week leaving messages for him, but not one had been returned. Sydney Carr had also not returned her calls. He'd sent two checks, both for $25,000. One she cashed to cover expenses, the other she returned. She had slept for days, eaten huge meals, put her business back together and supervised the workers who were repairing her office, but she had not heard from Sydney, Johnnie, Ellen or Liam. Or Brennan. That name sent a knife of pain through her, and she pushed him out of her mind. He and Ellen and Liam had obviously gone back to Minnesota and their lives.

A lot of publicity about Brennan and his life had filled the television and newspapers because of the deaths of George Jesse and Jane Scarlett, but no word had been murmured in the press about Johnnie Lord and his parentage.

Catherine walked through the gate and picked up her press credentials. She didn't know what to make of it, but she had a feeling Johnnie Lord might be waiting until tonight to make his announcement. How Johnnie had reacted to Ellen's contact, she couldn't imagine. But something told her his heart would not be sympathetic to her story.

"Catherine. I need to speak with you."

Surprised at hearing her name, Catherine looked around. Siobhan Carr, dressed in green sequins and chiffon, was standing in the shadows. She beckoned to Catherine. "Please, I must talk to you. It's urgent."

Catherine walked over to her. "What's this about, Siobhan? Where's Sydney?"

"He's with the board of directors. Come with me." The blonde's nails dug into Catherine's arm as she pulled her along.

Siobhan opened the door to a small trailer that served as a dressing room and stepped inside. Catherine followed. She gasped when the door closed behind her.

"HELLO, MISS GRAND. How do I look? Like the real thing?"

Johnnie Lord, in full Brennan Richards costume, sat in front of a lighted makeup mirror. A black satin eye patch such as the one Brennan had worn ten years earlier was tied rakishly across his eye.

"Why haven't you returned my calls?" Catherine asked. "I've tried to reach you all week." Warily she watched as Siobhan, looking as trancelike as she had at their last meeting, came and stood beside Johnnie.

"Sorry, Miss Grand. I never got your messages. You see, I've been staying with the Carrs, and sometimes their housekeeper forgets to tell us who has phoned. Besides, I've been practicing, practicing, practicing. Just like you suggested. Sydney thinks I'm good enough to try a video, doesn't he, Siobhan?"

Catherine's eyes met Siobhan's reflection in the mirror, and the blond woman nodded her agreement. Outside the trailer, the sounds of popping firecrackers and screaming children escalated. Siobhan reached into her purse, pulled out a red lipstick and began to freshen her makeup with stiff, robotlike motions.

Forcing herself to look away, Catherine took a step toward Johnnie. "Well, Johnnie. There are some things I want to talk to you about, but they'll wait until after the concert."

"Okay. But the reason I sent Siobhan out to get you can't wait." Johnnie grinned into the mirror, reached a hand to the glass and touched his image. "I want you to handle some publicity. Will you take on a new happening for me?"

"What kind of happening?" she asked with an edge in her voice.

"A press conference," Siobhan interrupted. "He's going to hold a press conference and announce he's Brennan Richards's nephew."

Johnnie glared at Siobhan but turned away from the mirror and held up his arms in triumph. "Great idea, huh, Miss Grand? You get the press and the networks and the magazines there, and I'll do the rest. We'll be front page everywhere!"

Even though she'd been expecting it, Johnnie's plan hit Catherine like a falling rock. "Why do this, Johnnie? Don't you think you and your mother—"

"Don't use that word with me!" Johnnie's voice rose fiercely, then he smiled to cover his emotions. "I'm not playing up the fact that Ellen Chapin's my mother in my announcement, Miss Grand. No need for that. What I want to highlight is my relationship, and my incredible similarity, to my uncle, Brennan Richards." His eyebrows rose. "This should get us a much bigger market share than the shooting did, don't you think?"

His words made the skin along Catherine's spine crawl. She swallowed the hard lump that constricted her throat, sure once and for all that her darkest suspicion was true. "You had Jane shoot you, didn't you?"

Johnnie threw his head back and laughed wildly. Catherine met Siobhan's vacant glance in the mirror.

"I told you I didn't do it," Siobhan said like a sleepwalker, her hand holding the lipstick frozen in the air. "You should have believed me."

Johnnie's voice broke in. "That's very, very good, Miss Grand. It's easy to see why my uncle was so smitten with you. You're bright."

Catherine took two steps back. She wanted to flee the claustrophobic room, but something warned her against turning her back on these two. "And you are very cool to take a bullet in order to get some publicity, Johnnie. Did you also send bombs for the same reason?"

The young man's laughter stopped abruptly. "That's really enough questions, Miss Grand. I'll let you know the date of the press conference. You can go now."

"No, she can't." Siobhan's voice had dropped to a deadly serious tone, as deadly as the pistol she had drawn from her bag and that was now aimed directly at Johnnie's head.

"Siobhan!" Catherine hissed. "Put that away."

"Did you hear Miss Grand, Siobhan? She's a very smart lady. We both know that," Johnnie added with less bravado than before. "Put that away or I'll call the police and tell them some things that even your rich husband's money and power won't be able to make right."

Siobhan cocked the pistol. "Don't threaten me. You've blackmailed me for years with threats like that. You even dared to hit me in my husband's house when I told you to get out. You're smug, Johnnie. You think I have to cooperate with you forever. But I don't have to anymore. And I don't need Sydney to settle things between us."

"You're the one who brought all this on, Siobhan," Johnnie yelled. "You're the one who came to me ten years ago in Liverpool with the story about how I could cash in on the big time. I can't help it if Brennan dumped you, and if you had to murder Mitch Chapin to cover your tracks when he found you sabotaging the stage set!"

Siobhan blanched at the mention of Mitch, her hand visibly shaking. "I didn't want to kill Mitch. But he threatened me. He said he would go to Brennan.'' The memory seemed to galvanize her, and she held out her arm with steely control. ''I got Jane Scarlett to help me sabotage the set, just to ruin the concert, not to hurt anyone. So don't try to duck your responsibility in this, Johnnie. You're the one who got Jane Scarlett to do your dirty work. She nearly killed Brennan trying to help you become a star!''

''Oh, and you care about Jane?'' Johnnie's voice was wild, and he took a menacing step toward Siobhan. ''Is that why you sent George Jesse the picture of me posing as Brennan? To get Jane off the hook? Or to put her on the hook with the one guy who really suffered in this mess?''

The sordid revelations were too much for Catherine. ''Your father,'' she moaned. ''My God, Johnnie, George Jesse was your father! You didn't kill him?''

Johnnie spun on his heel and faced Catherine, his face white and the blue eyes dark with pain. ''No, I didn't! But when I found him dead, thanks to the broken heart Siobhan provided, I typed a suicide letter for him.'' The young man's face contorted. ''The letter worked, too!'' He turned in a rage toward Siobhan. ''No one had to know anything about this, Siobhan. And no one would have if you'd just kept quiet.''

When Johnnie whirled and advanced on Siobhan, the pistol went off, the shot biting into the side of the trailer just past Johnnie's head. Catherine screamed and Johnnie lunged for the pistol as it went off again. A bullet struck the mirror. Glass flew in all directions.

Catherine hit the floor, jarring her splinted hand horribly and feeling the bite of glass in her knees. She covered her head as the pistol fired a third time. Catherine heard Siobhan groan in pain then fall to the floor.

Outside more firecrackers rattled the hot night. The sounds were similar to the frantic sounds of death that came from the trailer. Suddenly the door rattled, then flew open. "Catherine! Are you all right, girl?"

She moved her arms from over her head, stumbling to her feet and into Brennan's arms. "Where did you come from?" she cried, then hugged him, burying her shaking body in his arms.

"Shh, Cath. It's fine. Don't cry, darling. I promise, you're going to be fine," Brennan murmured. But when his gaze fell on the young man who clutched the gun, he saw that he had just made a promise he couldn't keep.

FIFTEEN MINUTES LATER, Catherine and Brennan sat back to back, tied securely at the feet and hands, in the deserted dressing room. Through the trailer vent, Catherine heard the show's announcer calling the crowd to attention and introducing the president of Knight Records, Sydney Carr.

"How you doing, Cath?" Brennan's voice was garbled by the makeshift gag Johnnie had tied in his mouth, but he knew they had to come up with a plan.

"Okay," Catherine whispered around the rag stuck in her mouth. "When does the bomb go off?"

"I couldn't see how Johnnie set it. Probably an hour."

"Right. After his show." Her eyes fell on the lifeless body of Siobhan Carr. Johnnie had covered her before he left. Catherine cringed.

"Don't look," Brennan ordered.

She nodded, then tried unsuccessfully to pull at the knots in the heavy rope that bound her hands. Catherine felt Brennan's fingers and squeezed her own against them, hoping to comfort them both.

"Can you work yourself free?" he asked.

She scraped her fingernails against the rope to no avail, but caught the flat steel splint on her pinky against the knots. "I don't know. Maybe." For several seconds she blocked out the jolting, throbbing pain in her finger as she used the splint to pry against the knot.

"Cath?"

"I think it's coming, Brennan," she answered hoarsely. Beads of perspiration stood out on her forehead, and her shoulder muscles felt as if they'd been invaded by killer bees, but she could feel the knot begin to loosen.

Then the splint fell. It made a hollow ping on the linoleum floor, and Catherine mumbled a string of the worst words she knew.

"Cath. Let's try to get to the door," Brennan finally said, aware that she was near the breaking point. It seemed to him that an hour had passed already, but however much time they had before the bomb on the dressing table behind them went off, it was time to move.

"How?" Catherine croaked.

He began to rock. Catherine groaned. He realized that they were not only tied into chairs, but that the chairs were tied together. Brennan sat still, trying to think.

"We need to get to the door," Catherine mumbled.

"You're right. Together."

"What?"

"You're facing the door. We'll go your direction." Brennan began to rock and tried to spring with his leg muscles. The steel folding chair bounced and moved an inch along the slick floor. "Bounce. Like a ball."

It took her several tries to equal his rhythm, but Catherine got the hang of it. The two of them managed to move about two inches every minute toward the door. The applause outside got louder, and Catherine thought she could hear Johnnie singing "Michelle" in Brennan's voice.

"Hurry, Cath, we've not got much time!" Brennan urged.

Catherine realized she had stopped bouncing. She allowed her brain and her bones to settle for a moment, then resumed. Five minutes later, convinced that she was suffering permanent spine damage, Catherine was next to the door.

Neither of them could reach the lock, however. After several efforts, they'd nearly toppled over. Catherine hurt in every region of her body. Brennan was panting with the effort of trying to break his bonds.

Then, like a miracle, someone rapped on the door. "Siobhan? Are you in there?"

Catherine and Brennan tried to shout through the gags, but a huge display of fireworks went off above them, drowning out their cries. Catherine realized at that moment that the concert must be over. Which meant that the bomb would go off.

Suddenly she thought of her mother and father, her sister's adoring friendship, her brother's hug. Then she thought of Brennan, the man she knew she loved. Whatever he had come back for didn't matter. She'd let him leave her one time without a fight. She was damn well not going to let death intercede. She managed to scream the one word guaranteed to get action.

"Fire!"

Seconds later the door burst open. Mickey Stolie stood there, shock and guilt washing over his features. "Catherine!"

"Hurry. Untie us," she managed to say. Mickey leaned down and took out her gag, then Brennan's.

"There's a bomb across the room," Brennan explained. "Get us out! And get Siobhan," Brennan ordered.

Mickey took out a pocketknife of impressive proportions and cut the cords. Brennan sprang to his feet, then stumbled and fell. Catherine could barely move, so the two men dragged her out, then Mickey raced in and brought out Siobhan. Costumed people were milling around, the sky was ablaze, but no one seemed to think they looked odd.

Catherine realized that everyone thought they were in costume. "Shut the door to the trailer, Mickey. And go get the police. We've got to keep people away." Brennan laid Siobhan's body in the back of a pickup truck parked near the fence.

"Catherine, I'm so sorry," Mickey offered. "I've got so much to explain."

"Go, man! Explain later!" Brennan's words sent Mickey off. He turned to Catherine and hugged her. "Are you going to make it, Miss Grand?"

"I think so. But Johnnie—"

"Let's go get him. Can you find your way to the back of the stage?"

She remembered the turret that had nearly killed her when it fell onto the stage. The exit door was built right in. They could wait there for Johnnie.

Steadying herself, Catherine tugged on his arm. "Follow me."

They made their way through the crowd of gaily painted and dressed patrons. Many were in costume.

By the time they circled around behind the stage, waves of applause from the grandstands facing the set were breaking across the summer night. Catherine and Brennan stepped into the exit space behind the moat just as Johnnie Lord's voice, so like Brennan's, came to Catherine's ears.

"Thank you all for coming tonight. I'll be back again, because Brennan Richards lives!" he shouted.

"The little sod." Brennan tensed.

The applause grew louder, and Brennan and Catherine waited. When the lights went off, the door opened and an unsuspecting Johnnie Lord stepped through. Brennan fell on him and tied him with the same rope with which John- nie had sequestered them.

"Glad to return the favor, mate," Brennan said through clenched teeth.

Johnnie Lord fixed a murderous stare on Catherine.

"If looks could kill, I'd be dead," Catherine said. An explosion in the direction of the trailers cracked through the gaiety, and screams of panic and alarm replaced the ap- plause.

Brennan pushed Johnnie up against the wall. "I'd say your reviews aren't going to be good, Johnnie." Moments later the police arrived, and then Catherine's night of illu- sion was finally over.

When the police hustled Johnnie off, she pulled Brennan aside before following them. "Why'd you come back?"

He laughed his sexy, soul-melting laugh and hugged her against him. "For a second date?" he teased.

"Brennan..."

Suddenly his mood changed. Gently he let her go, touch- ing her face with his hand. His earring glittered in the ash- scented night. "I was a fool, Catherine Grand. I had noth- ing to go home to with you here. Ellen gave me a week to realize it myself, then filled me in on her views last night. I got back here as fast as I could."

"I love you, Brennan," was all Catherine could manage in response. But it was enough.

Chapter Nineteen

The reporter from *People* magazine smiled and leaned toward Catherine with a conspiratorial look. "I'm so glad we could finally do this interview, Miss Grand. Your story has all of America and half of Europe talking."

"Really?" Catherine picked up her frosty glass and glanced around the room. No sign of Brennan. And he'd promised. She put the glass down gently, realizing he must have chickened out.

"Oh, absolutely. You two are the hottest thing going!"

For several minutes Catherine allowed herself to be quizzed. She listened to several direct and several indirect questions about Johnnie Lord, but refused comment on all of them. Ellen and Liam were providing the funds for his legal and psychiatric care, but the world had no legitimate claim to that information.

She did offer her opinion on the upcoming trial of Mickey Stolie. "I'll be there to testify on his behalf," Catherine said firmly. "He's a friend."

"I'm amazed you feel that way," the reporter cooed, wide-eyed. "After what he did."

"Especially after what he did," Catherine shot back. "He saved my life."

The reporter pressed on, asking gossipy details about Sydney Carr and George Jesse, hinting at a rumor that Jane Scarlett had once worked for Catherine's company. Again Catherine fended off those questions. It was easy. Until the woman got to her last one.

"Well, thanks so much for your time, Miss Grand. Let me just ask you one more thing."

Catherine gulped down her drink, still scanning the lunch crowd for Brennan's familiar dark head. "Sure. Anything."

"Is it true you and Brennan Richards are going to be married at Christmas?"

Catherine nearly choked on her drink. She felt the reporter waiting for a response, but took her time, allowing her composure to return. Yikes, Brennan had just asked her last night! They'd only told her mom and dad this morning. News certainly traveled fast!

"Excuse me, Miss Grand. I need a word with you, please."

Catherine and the reporter both craned their necks to see the man who'd spoken. A tall priest in full clerical garb stood with his hands folded around a Bible. He wore dark glasses and a black beaded crucifix.

"Of course." Catherine rose and smiled apologetically at the reporter. "You'll excuse me, won't you? But I'm going to have to leave now."

"Oh, of course. Of course. I'll just call you later to get an official response to my question. So I can finish my article. I'm on deadline, you know."

"Yes, yes, of course." Catherine nodded and fought to keep her balance as the priest pulled her along the hallway leading out of the restaurant. She bit the inside of her lip to keep from laughing. The reporter would certainly be frustrated when she tried to call Catherine at work.

"Did you tell her?" the priest whispered as he held the door to the patio open.

Catherine scampered through the opening and into the cool October air. "No. Never got the chance."

"So she doesn't know you've sold the business to your mother and dad?"

Catherine grinned. It felt so good to hear the words "mother and dad" and not feel the jerk of anxiety she had felt only a month ago. It was funny, she realized, how a real threat of loss could put an imaginary one in the right perspective. "No. But I think she'll find out. After all, she's on deadline."

The two of them giggled. Then the man snapped off his heavily starched collar and tossed it aside, drawing Catherine into his arms for a long, deep kiss.

Finally Catherine came up for air. "Nice disguise, rock star."

"Ex-rock star."

"Right." Catherine nibbled on Brennan's earring, then settled into his arms. "Once a balladeer, always a balladeer. You did say that to me once."

"I did?" His blue eyes twinkled. "Your point, Miss Grand?"

"Sing 'Michelle' for me, Brennan."

"Right here?"

She looked at the flowers and the sunshine and the deserted metal tables around the fountain. "Right here."

"How about upstairs, in my room?"

"Your room? But we won't sing."

Brennan ran his finger along her collarbone, then kissed it and touched her lightly on the mouth. "Oh, yes, we will. I promise you that. In perfect harmony."

Warmth flooded her skin. "Braggart," she teased.

Brennan winked and did a bodybuilder's pose. "Rock star."

"The genuine article," she replied. "Come on, rock star. It's showtime."

PENNY JORDAN

Sins and infidelities...
Dreams and obsessions...
Shattering secrets
unfold in...

THE HIDDEN YEARS

SAGE — stunning, sensual and vibrant, she spent a lifetime distancing herself from a past too painful to confront... the mother who seemed to hold her at bay, the father who resented her and the heartache of unfulfilled love. To the world, Sage was independent and invulnerable— but it was a mask she cultivated to hide a desperation she herself couldn't quite understand... until an unforeseen turn of events drew her into the discovery of the hidden years, finally allowing Sage to open her heart to a passion denied for so long.

The Hidden Years—a compelling novel of truth and passion that will unlock the heart and soul of every woman.

AVAILABLE IN OCTOBER!

Watch for your opportunity to complete your Penny Jordan set.
POWER PLAY and SILVER will also be available in October.

Take 4 bestselling love stories FREE

Plus get a FREE surprise gift!

Special Limited-time Offer

Mail to Harlequin Reader Service®

In the U.S.	In Canada
3010 Walden Avenue	P.O. Box 609
P.O. Box 1867	Fort Erie, Ontario
Buffalo, N.Y. 14269-1867	L2A 5X3

YES! Please send me 4 free Harlequin Intrigue® novels and my free surprise gift. Then send me 4 brand-new novels every month, and bill me at the low price of $2.49* each—a savings of 30¢ apiece off cover prices. There are no shipping, handling or other hidden costs. I understand that accepting the books and gift places me under no obligation ever to buy any books. I can always return a shipment and cancel at any time. Even if I never buy another book from Harlequin, the 4 free books and the surprise gift are mine to keep forever.

*Offer slightly different in Canada—$2.49 per book plus 49¢ per shipment for delivery. Canadian residents add applicable federal and provincial sales tax. Sales tax applicable in N.Y.

180 BPA ADL5   380 BPA ADMK

_____

Name   (PLEASE PRINT)

_____

Address   Apt. No.

_____

City   State/Prov.   Zip/Postal Code

This offer is limited to one order per household and not valid to present Harlequin Intrigue® subscribers. Terms and prices are subject to change.

INT-91   © 1990 Harlequin Enterprises Limited

HARLEQUIN®
OFFICIAL SWEEPSTAKES RULES

NO PURCHASE NECESSARY

1. To enter, complete an Official Entry Form or 3" x 5" index card by hand-printing, in plain block letters, your complete name, address, phone number and age, and mailing it to: Harlequin Fashion A Whole New You Sweepstakes, P.O. Box 9056, Buffalo, NY 14269-9056.

   No responsibility is assumed for lost, late or misdirected mail. Entries must be sent separately with first class postage affixed, and be received no later than December 31, 1991 for eligibility.

2. Winners will be selected by D.L. Blair, Inc., an independent judging organization whose decisions are final, in random drawings to be held on January 30, 1992 in Blair, NE at 10:00 a.m. from among all eligible entries received.

3. The prizes to be awarded and their approximate retail values are as follows: Grand Prize — A brand-new Mercury Sable LS plus a trip for two (2) to Paris, including round-trip air transportation, six (6) nights hotel accommodation, a $1,400 meal/spending money stipend and $2,000 cash toward a new fashion wardrobe (approximate value: $28,000) or $15,000 cash; two (2) Second Prizes — A trip to Paris, including round-trip air transportation, six (6) nights hotel accommodation, a $1,400 meal/spending money stipend and $2,000 cash toward a new fashion wardrobe (approximate value: $11,000) or $5,000 cash; three (3) Third Prizes — $2,000 cash toward a new fashion wardrobe. All prizes are valued in U.S. currency. Travel award air transportation is from the commercial airport nearest winner's home. Travel is subject to space and accommodation availability, and must be completed by June 30, 1993. Sweepstakes offer is open to residents of the U.S. and Canada who are 21 years of age or older as of December 31, 1991, except residents of Puerto Rico, employees and immediate family members of Torstar Corp., its affiliates, subsidiaries, and all agencies, entities and persons connected with the use, marketing, or conduct of this sweepstakes. All federal, state, provincial, municipal and local laws apply. Offer void wherever prohibited by law. Taxes and/or duties, applicable registration and licensing fees, are the sole responsibility of the winners. Any litigation within the province of Quebec respecting the conduct and awarding of a prize may be submitted to the Régie des loteries et courses du Québec. All prizes will be awarded; winners will be notified by mail. No substitution of prizes is permitted.

4. Potential winners must sign and return any required Affidavit of Eligibility/Release of Liability within 30 days of notification. In the event of noncompliance within this time period, the prize may be awarded to an alternate winner. Any prize or prize notification returned as undeliverable may result in the awarding of that prize to an alternate winner. By acceptance of their prize, winners consent to use of their names, photographs or their likenesses for purposes of advertising, trade and promotion on behalf of Torstar Corp. without further compensation. Canadian winners must correctly answer a time-limited arithmetical question in order to be awarded a prize.

5. For a list of winners (available after 3/31/92), send a separate stamped, self-addressed envelope to: Harlequin Fashion A Whole New You Sweepstakes, P.O. Box 4694, Blair, NE 68009.

PREMIUM OFFER TERMS

To receive your gift, complete the Offer Certificate according to directions. Be certain to enclose the required number of "Fashion A Whole New You" proofs of product purchase (which are found on the last page of every specially marked "Fashion A Whole New You" Harlequin or Silhouette romance novel). Requests must be received no later than December 31, 1991. Limit: four (4) gifts per name, family, group, organization or address. Items depicted are for illustrative purposes only and may not be exactly as shown. Please allow 6 to 8 weeks for receipt of order. Offer good while quantities of gifts last. In the event an ordered gift is no longer available, you will receive a free, previously unpublished Harlequin or Silhouette book for every proof of purchase you have submitted with your request, plus a refund of the postage and handling charge you have included. Offer good in the U.S. and Canada only.

HQFW·SWPR

HARLEQUIN® OFFICIAL SWEEPSTAKES ENTRY FORM

4-FWHIS-3

Complete and return this Entry Form immediately – the more entries you submit, the better your chances of winning!

- Entries must be received by **December 31, 1991.**
- A Random draw will take place on **January 30, 1992.**
- No purchase necessary.

Yes, I want to win a FASHION A WHOLE NEW YOU Classic and Romantic prize from Harlequin:

Name _____ Telephone _____ Age _____

Address _____

City _____ State _____ Zip _____

Return Entries to: **Harlequin FASHION A WHOLE NEW YOU,**
P.O. Box 9056, Buffalo, NY 14269-9056   © 1991 Harlequin Enterprises Limited

PREMIUM OFFER

To receive your free gift, send us the required number of proofs-of-purchase from any specially marked FASHION A WHOLE NEW YOU Harlequin or Silhouette Book with the Offer Certificate properly completed, plus a check or money order (do not send cash) to cover postage and handling payable to Harlequin FASHION A WHOLE NEW YOU Offer. We will send you the specified gift.

OFFER CERTIFICATE

Item	A. ROMANTIC COLLECTOR'S DOLL	B. CLASSIC PICTURE FRAME
	(Suggested Retail Price $60.00)	(Suggested Retail Price $25.00)
# of proofs-of-purchase	18	12
Postage and Handling	$3.50	$2.95
Check one	☐	☐

Name _____

Address _____

City _____ State _____ Zip _____

Mail this certificate, designated number of proofs-of-purchase and check or money order for postage and handling to: **Harlequin FASHION A WHOLE NEW YOU Gift Offer,** P.O. Box 9057, Buffalo, NY 14269-9057. Requests must be received by December 31, 1991.

ONE PROOF-OF-PURCHASE

4-FWHIP-3

To collect your fabulous free gift you must include the necessary number of proofs-of-purchase with a properly completed Offer Certificate.

© 1991 Harlequin Enterprises Limited

See previous page for details.